BOWIE

Speed Demons MC

Jules Ford

ISBN:

Copyright 2023 Jules Ford,

This is a work of fiction. Names, characters, business, places, and incidents are either the product of the author's imagination or used in a fictitious manner. Any resemblance to actual living persons, living, or dead, or actual events is purely coincidental.

ALL RIGHTS RESERVED

This book contains material protected under International and Federal Copyright Laws and Treaties. Any unauthorized reprint or use of this material is prohibited. No part of this book may be reproduced or transmitted in any form or by any means, electronic or mechanical, including photocopying, recording, or by any informal storage and retrieval system without express written permission from the author/ publisher.

Cover by JoeLee Creative

Formatting by Md Foysal Ahmed

Editing and proofreading by Ellie Race

With thanks.

Dedication

Elizabeth N Harris ~ One of the best people I know.

Thank you for everything.

You know what you did.

Other Books by Jules

Speed Demons MC

Bowie

Cash

Atlas

Snow

Breaker ~ Coming Soon

Soulless Assassins MC

Tyrant's Redemption (Co-author Raven Dark)

"Mess with a Demon
And we'll raise Hell."
~ Bandit 1968.

Table of Contents

Chapter One 1

Chapter Two 9

Chapter Three 17

Chapter Four 28

Chapter Five 40

Chapter Six 51

Chapter Seven 59

Chapter Eight 69

Chapter Nine 80

Chapter Ten 90

Chapter Eleven 97

Chapter Twelve 101

Chapter Thirteen 108

Chapter Fourteen 115

Chapter Fifteen 119

Chapter Sixteen 129

Chapter Seventeen 139

Chapter Eighteen 145

Chapter Nineteen 153

Chapter Twenty 161

Chapter Twenty-One 168

Chapter Twenty-Two... 175

Chapter Twenty-Three	181
Chapter Twenty-Four	190
Chapter Twenty-Five	193
Chapter Twenty-Six	202
Chapter Twenty-Seven	210
Chapter Twenty-Eight	216
Chapter Twenty-Nine	224
Chapter Thirty	232
Chapter Thirty-One	237
Chapter Thirty-Two	245
Chapter Thirty-Three	249
Chapter Thirty-Four	254
Chapter Thirty-Five	258
Chapter Thirty-Six	262
Chapter Thirty-Seven	265
Chapter Thirty-Eight	268
Chapter Thirty-Nine	272
Chapter Forty	275
Chapter Forty-One	281
Chapter Forty-Two	284
Chapter Forty-Three	287
Chapter Forty-Four	300
Epilogue	305

Chapter One

Layla

Footsteps startled me awake.

My eyes flew open before settling on a moonlit grey wall. I blinked, confused. My bedroom was painted a soft matt white. The man who mixed the paint up for me at Home Depot called the shade, *Snowdrop*.

Definitely not grey.

My ears pricked up at the click of a door sounding through the room, and my heart lurched. Goosebumps trailed down my arms as the cool night breeze settled on my skin, and confusion turned to awareness as memories of that day prickled through me.

Cara, my best friend, called me that morning. Her fiancé had agreed to fix a date for their wedding, and naturally, she wanted to celebrate.

Earlier, we went to the Irish pub in town called the *Lucky Shamrock*. We had such a blast that when they closed, we didn't want the night to end. Cara suggested we go for a nightcap at the local MC's bar, which stayed open late.

My eyes locked on his as soon as we walked in.

Gage 'Bowie' Stone was a thousand bad decisions and a million heartbreaks all rolled together to make one gorgeous biker. That phrase, 'all the girls want him, all the boys want to be him,' was created with Bowie in mind.

The first time I saw him was eleven years ago, on my first day of high school. Bowie walked past me in the hall, and my heart flipped over.

I'd never seen anyone like him before. He was an eighteen-year-old quintessential bad boy. I was a painfully shy fourteen-year-old girl, and for him, I didn't exist.

But he existed for me.

Every time I saw his arm slung across another girl's shoulder, an ache gripped my insides.

I think, deep down, I knew I didn't stand a chance, but my naïve young heart still held out hope. Why did he make me feel so much if he wasn't meant to be mine?

My stomach churned every time he flashed his sexy grin because he seemed to flash it at every girl except me.

So, earlier that night, when I walked through that door into the MC's bar, and he finally smiled at me, it was everything.

Bowie looked better with age. He was a beautiful boy at eighteen, but now, he was an even more beautiful man. Six foot two, golden brown eyes. His thick, black hair, all sexy and mussed up, was cut shorter than before. My eyes kept flicking toward him as I imagined running my hands through it.

He wore blue jeans that stretched across his muscled thighs and ass and a white tee that highlighted his hard chest. His black leather jacket had his club patch sewn on the back; it strained across his broad shoulders and showed off his muscular build.

I couldn't take my eyes off him, and when he turned and caught me staring, my cheeks turned pink.

My heart raced as he approached me at the bar, then I shivered when his fingertips gently settled on my back.

"Hey, I'm Bowie," he rumbled, leaning into me. His stare swept from my face to my toes, then slowly back up again. He threw me another sexy grin, and my heart fluttered with excitement.

I sent up a prayer, thanking God for finally sending him to me.

I went to shake his hand, but he held my fingers instead while his thumb stroked over mine like it was always meant to.

Close up, Bowie's eyes were a light shade of brown, but they swirled liquid gold whenever he talked about his blood family and, by extension, his MC brothers. He was the most dazzling man I'd ever known, and he made me feel that way, too, because he gave me his undivided attention.

When his eyes held mine, everyone else seemed to disappear. He was everything that I knew he'd be and more.

Later, we left the bar and walked hand in hand to his house. My heart swelled when he stopped in the middle of the street, tugged me into him, then kissed me until I was breathless.

We got to his house, and Bowie took me to his bed. He held a shaking hand to my heart while it raced. "Do you feel it, too?" he asked.

I whispered that I did because the pull between us was so tangible that I felt it down to my bones.

Our bodies connected together like two pieces of the same puzzle. My skin tingled under his touch as he built me up and up, and I cried out as he moved inside me while his hand remained on my heart.

Bowie smiled against my lips when he made me come, then pushed his face into the side of my throat when I came again. His hard body pinned me down, and he let out a tortured groan while his hips bucked hard against mine.

In the afterglow, Bowie did something that touched my soul. He pushed up on both hands and gently kissed me, first on the forehead, then on the tip of my nose.

In that instant, my schoolgirl crush blossomed into something palpable, something real, and I just knew he'd finally seen me.

My eyes caught a movement from outside. It jerked me away from the earlier memories, back to the here and now. I sat, pulling the sheets up to cover my nakedness. My attention was immediately drawn to Bowie through glass doors. The orange glow from his cigarette danced in the darkness.

My heart fluttered as I watched how the moonlight highlighted the muscles in his bare back that rippled every time he moved. I smiled when I noticed the small half-moon indents left from my nails.

My eyes continued their perusal down to his firm ass, which was encased in fitted denim once again. My skin heated, and my nipples puckered. A base reaction to my beautiful man.

He must have felt my eyes on him because I saw his body stiffen, and he slowly turned to me. The instant our gazes met, my insides quivered with a thousand fluttering butterfly wings that whispered his name.

A smile played over my lips, relishing the desire that tugged my stomach. I needed to go to him, flatten my front against his back, wrap my arms around his hard waist, and give him my heat. I was in his thrall.

My fingers trembled as I pulled the sheet back. I was about to swing my legs over the side of the bed when the door clicked again.

My head snapped up, and our gazes locked.

I didn't know how gold could be so chilling, but at that moment, his eyes were so frozen over that I shivered, then my heart sank.

Bowie stood four feet away, close enough that I could almost reach out and touch the wall he'd built around himself while on the other side of that glass door. The butterfly wings that whispered inside my stomach turned into a violent clench that made me want to double

Bowie

over. Something ugly slithered through me. I knew what was going to happen.

I stood, pulled my shoulders back, jutted my chin in the air, and waited, determined to hold my head high while he trampled all over my heart.

Bowie couldn't even look at me, but eventually, his cold stare settled on a spot behind my shoulder.

A nerve ticked in his jaw. "Doll. Got an early start in the morning. You need to get gone."

My breath caught at the ache in my chest.

I bent down to retrieve my clothes, keeping my head ducked to hide the burning shame I knew my face would betray. My fingers trembled as I pulled on my panties, jeans, and tee.

"You cool?" he asked, tone flat.

I cleared my throat, trying to alleviate the lump that had formed. "I'm fine," I said, cringing at the croak in my voice.

Bowie blew a huge sigh of relief from his beautiful, cruel mouth, and it crushed me. "Want me to call you a cab?"

"No. Thanks." *Keep it together, Layla, keep it together.*

He let out an exasperated breath. "You can't walk, Laura. You live miles away."

I felt the punch to my core. Unshed tears burned my throat. I took a deep breath, forcing them back down, telling myself he wasn't worth it.

See, whenever the MC rode through Main Street, necks craned. The club members couldn't buy groceries or even sit quietly and drink coffee without women approaching them. It was plain as day that Bowie saw me as one of them. A biker groupie.

I wasn't, not even close. The only time I'd had sex was the night I conceived my daughter.

What hurt me most was the realization that the pull between us was all in my head because he hadn't cared to get to know me at all. The cold hard truth was, he thought so little of me that he didn't even let my name fester. The looks, the sweet kisses, and how he held my heart in his hand were all lies.

He'd played me.

Anger rose up. My fists clenched at my sides, and for the first time in a long time, I snapped back.

"Layla," I hissed. "My name is Layla." Tears filled my eyes, I tried to blink them away, but one traitorous drop rolled down my cheek.

Unease flashed across Bowie's face. "Fuck," he gritted under his breath.

I began to stutter. "I—I thought that w—we—"

"—What did you think, babe?" Bowie gestured between us. "That this was more?" He glared at me disparagingly while I angrily swiped at my face. "And now you're turnin' on the waterworks, just fuckin' typical."

I looked down, expecting to see blood ooze from my chest, but instead of red, it was just my black halter and skinny jeans. Desperation to get out of there made my heart pound. I scooped up my purse and headed for the door.

"Wait, I'll call you a cab," he called out as I stomped over to the doors.

I ignored him and grasped the handle. The door slid open, and I stepped out into the cool night. "Don't bother." All I needed was to get my ass out of that room so that I could scratch away the itch that was crawling under my skin.

Hambleton was full of stuck-up rich people who looked down on me because I was a single mom.

Small town. Small minds.

Bowie had just shown me that he was no better than them. If anything, he was worse because he'd made me believe he was more.

Bowie

I always took their shit for the sake of my daughter. If I didn't fight back, at least they left her alone, but right then, the compulsion to retaliate was overwhelming. What made *him* think that he was better than me? He looked at me like a whore, but I'd seen him plow through the girls in town, even at the tender age of eighteen, whereas I'd had sex *once*.

Frustration curled in my chest, and before I could talk myself out of it, my feet ground to a halt. My head snapped up. I sucked in a deep breath and called out, "Gage 'Bowie' Stone."

His irritated groan indicated he'd heard, even though I was facing away. I slowly turned, and finally, he looked me in the eye.

"Twenty-nine years old," I continued. "Two brothers, Xander, a year older, and Kit, a year younger. You've also got a sister, Freya."

Shock flashed across his features.

"You rebuild classic cars and bikes at the MC's auto shop. Sometimes you work on the door over at the *Demon's Haven*. You said you enjoy it because you get to use your boxing skills."

Bowie folded his arms across his chest, lifting one eyebrow.

"The first time I saw you was in high school. You never noticed me, and that's okay; I was younger than you. But we talked tonight, and I thought you were different from the others." I smiled sadly.

Bowie's stare hardened.

"My name's *Layla*," I repeated. "And just so we're clear, I really don't need a cab; I don't need anything from you. I'm good." Cocking my head to one side, my eyes swept over him dismissively. "If you see me around, Bowie, do me a favor and keep walking." Turning away, I took a deep breath, trying to calm my racing heart. I started toward the street, but after a few steps, I stopped again. I didn't turn around. I didn't need to; I knew I had his attention.

"It's true what they say." I clipped out. "Never meet the cool people. They'll always be a letdown."

He let out a low, deep growl.

Without a glance back, I walked down the street and then the four miles home alone. Because even though some folk would say I didn't have much in life, there was one thing I did have that nobody, including Gage 'Bowie' Stone, could take away.

My dignity.

Chapter Two

Bowie

Layla's parting shot kept floating through my head, even though three days had passed since I'd stood in the dark and watched her walk away. I'd be doing something as mundane as working on a car in the MC's auto shop when without warning, her hurt eyes would flash through my head.

Even now, I was sitting in the middle of a church meeting, minding club business, and there it was.

Never meet the cool people. They'll always be a letdown.

I blew out a breath, trying to expel the irritation burning inside me. No one and done, had ever got under my hide like this.

Prez's rasp of a voice cut through my churning thoughts.

"Freya's looking into it."

I looked up at him, dazed. "Huh?"

"Two more girls were spiked with Rohypnol," he continued.

My shoulders tensed. Over the last few years, young women from Hambleton and the connecting towns had been turning up at the local ER, drugged to the eyeballs.

They'd been sexually assaulted but were so out of it they couldn't identify their attacker. The sheriff's office was worse than useless, so the club had started its own investigation.

My sister, Freya, was in med school. In the Summer, she volunteered over at Baines County Memorial.

Prez, or Dad, as he was also known to me, Freya, and my brothers, had her asking questions from her end. My sister could've been FBI; she put the cops in this town to shame. But the truth was, regardless of that, we'd hit a dead end.

"Still think the Sinners are involved, Prez?" Abe asked.

Dad nodded. "Yup. The Burning Sinners control all narcotics across three counties. They'd sell their mothers for a bigger slice of the pie." He turned to Atlas. "That scumbag still not talkin'?"

Saturday, we'd been working the door at our bar, the *Demon's Haven*, and caught some asshole tryin' to smuggle roofies in.

The Sergeant at Arms shook his head. "Nah. He's just a dumb rich kid who didn't think shit through. Doubt the idiot would've had the balls to go through with it."

"Bullshit," Abe chimed in. "If you've no intentions of assaultin' a woman, don't buy drugs that say different."

"Agreed," Prez said. "Can we hand him over to Grady?"

Atlas smirked. "Nope, Bowie and me worked him over good. Pigs'll ask too many questions. But I'm willin' to bet this week's paycheck that he won't do that shit again."

Snickers rose through the air.

My mind returned to Layla. What would she say if she saw the state of the asshole's face, the one we locked in the *Cell*? Would her doe eyes widen like they did the moment I slid deep inside her tight little cunt? I remembered how slick she was for me, and my cock jumped.

She was about five-four, slimmer than my usual type but still soft. Her long chestnut brown hair nearly touched the top of her tight little ass.

Her puffy pink lips were created to suck dick, but I was so desperate to get inside her pussy that I never got to test that theory.

These days. I wasn't interested in much more than my custom Softail and big fat bank balance. I used to get a buzz from fuckin', but women had been throwing themselves at me since I was fifteen, so it was wearing thin.

Friday, I went for a ride on my bike, then deposited my nice fat paycheck at the bank. After I knocked back a few beers at the clubhouse, Colt, Reno, and me made our way down to the *Demon's Haven.*

Boredom started to take me over, and I needed some shuteye, so after downing a few beers, I was ready to drag my ass home to bed.

Then she walked in.

I must have sensed her 'cause I glanced up at the moment she came through the *Demons* door and did a double-take.

There was something familiar about her; I couldn't put my finger on it. But regardless, I shrugged it off, then made my play. She was sweet as a sun-ripened strawberry. It was glaringly obvious that she wasn't experienced in biker, and I dug that. Then later, when I stripped her down and felt how inexperienced she really was, I dug her a whole lot more.

After I came so hard that my head rattled in my skull, her doe eyes drew me in.

For the first time in a long time, I felt at peace.

The boredom that had afflicted me for months was gone because she chased it away. Contentment swirled in my chest as I watched her sleep. Then fear rushed through me as familiar panic set in.

I needed air. I needed to breathe.

I got up, pulled on my jeans and boots, then went outside. After a smoke and a come to Jesus talk with myself, I went back in and laid it all out, clear as day.

Fuck knows why I called her Laura.

It was a dick move, and I regretted it as soon as it came outta my mouth. But instead of doing the decent thing and apologizing, I kept right on with the annihilation and watched her pretty face burn with humiliation.

"Fuck," I muttered out loud, squirming in my seat.

"You got somethin' to add, Bowie?" Prez asked.

I looked up and blinked, not knowing what the hell was happening. "Huh?"

Prez's eyes turned to slits. "I asked if there was any other business before I close down Church. What do ya wanna add, son?"

Dad had been known to pop a vein if one of us zoned out during church, so my brain scrambled for something to say.

I cleared my throat. "Gotta shipment of spares comin' in tomorrow. Need the prospects at the shop."

Prez cocked an eyebrow. "You can have 'em till noon. Got a fuck load 'a kegs gettin' delivered to the bar in the p.m. I need some muscle."

"Gotcha," I nodded.

"You finished that Chevy yet?" Iceman, our Road Captain, rumbled from further down the table.

I leaned forward so I could see around Atlas. I had to lean in pretty damned far seein' as our SOA was six foot five and probably around two-hundred n' sixty pounds.

"Got an original bumper comin' in tomorrow," I told him. "It'll be good to go by the end of the day."

Ice let out a low whistle. "That's one sweet ride," he said under his breath before waggling his eyebrows. "Heard you had a sweet ride Friday night, too, Bowie boy. That pretty little mama who lives down by the creek."

Bowie

My gut clenched.

Dad sat up. "What's that?"

Ice let out a hoot. "You know. That little girl who's got all them pearl clutching asshole's panties in a twist."

"Who the fuck are you talkin' about?" Dad asked.

"That girl who got herself in the family way."

Abe let out a chuckle. "Ice, hate to tell ya this, but women can't knock 'emselves up. Need a man to get the job done."

"That ain't the work of a man, Abe," Ice argued. "No man would put a sweet gal in that predicament, then not do the right thing by her. Especially in this judgy fucking town. Them's the actions of a fucknut."

"Can somebody please tell me who in God's name we're talkin' about?" Dad demanded.

Hendrix, our VP, spoke up, "Remember that gal who helped me, boss? You know that time I forgot my wallet? She covered my bill at the coffee shop before that hippy chick took it over."

Dad rubbed his chin. "The one you said counted the change outta her wallet cos she didn't have a bill?"

"Yup."

"Lisa!" Atlas boomed.

I let out an exasperated breath, slowly shaking my head. "Her name's Layla."

Pop gave me a weird look. "Layla Hardin? Steve Hardin's baby girl?"

"Dunno 'bout that, but yeah, that's her name." I shrugged.

Dad leaned forward, mouth twistin' with anger. He pointed a gnarly finger at me. "Bowie. Please. Tell me you didn't do her, then scrape her off."

I grimaced at the fury in his voice.

Pop's hand lifted to rub his forehead. "Jesus, Son."

"Hold ya fuckin' horses," Abe butted in. "Steve Hardin? Wasn't that your bud? He passed, what, twenty years ago, give or take?"

"Yup," Dad drawled as his angry stare focused on me, even though he was replyin' to Abe. "The same Steve Hardin whose girl, Layla," his voice got louder, "is my fuckin' goddaughter."

Surprised grunts floated through the room.

"The same goddaughter that I tried to check on for years after her dad died in a car wreck," Pop yelled, eyes like flints. "The same goddaughter whose nutjob mother threatened to call the cops if I went near her kid!"

My heart fell into my gut as I wondered if my talent for mechanics stretched to building a 'Back to the Future' replica. 'Cause right then, I had a hankering for goin' back three days previous and not treating Layla Hardin like a goddamned whore.

Funny thing though, my hankerin' didn't extend to goin' back three days and not fucking Layla in the first place.

No siree.

"Not cool. Bowie," Hendrix drawled drily. "That girl was hurtin' for green and still covered my ass. Why the fuck are you shittin' on women who should be protected by the club?"

I squirmed under the VP's angry glare.

"Where's she live?" Dad demanded.

Ice shrugged one shoulder. "Down near the creek is all I know."

Dad's stare veered straight to our tech guy, and Colt's fingers began to tap on the iPad. "Gimme a minute, Prez."

"Steve grew up in a house down by the creek," Dad mused. "His ma probably left it to Layla, seein' as she hated the girl's mom."

"Good for us that Barrington's too fuckin' miserly to invest in decent security," Colt muttered as he continued to tap. "Got it," he announced. "Layla Jane Hardin, twenty-five, mother to Sunshine Hardin." He glanced up at Dad. "You were right, Prez. She inherited her grandmother's place, Willow Cottage."

Colt turned back to the iPad and tapped again. "Son of a bitch," he grated out.

"What?"

"Barrington's bleeding her dry. She's struggling with a loan he gave her." Disgust flashed across his features. "She paid her installment one day late a few months back. Barrington whacked on so many charges that the balance is higher now than when she first borrowed."

A dark cloud blanketed the room. More curses echoed through the air.

"Take my cut, Friday. Settle it," Drix rasped.

My head flew around to Dad's right-hand man. "What the fuck you doin' that for?" I barked. "Thinkin' of trying ya luck?"

"Maybe. The girl's a pretty lil' thing." Hendrix smirked.

Tiny needles of jealousy pricked at my chest.

Fucker.

Colt grinned as he watched us. "Done, Veep." He turned back to the screen, tapped again, then grimaced. "Prez."

"What?"

"Barrington took the bulk of her money this morning. He hasn't even left her five bucks. She's got payments due out Thursday."

Dad's lip curled in disgust. "How the fuck have I missed this?"

"How the fuck did I miss you had a goddaughter?" I mumbled under my breath. This was bad. I'd unknowingly fucked and chucked a girl who, technically, I should've protected. My ass clenched at the thought of the punishment that could bring.

"Steve used to bring her over all the time to play with you boys," Dad mused. "You were only eight or nine when he died."

I racked my brains. "I don't remember."

"I know that, ya goddamned dog's dick," Dad glowered. "'Cause maybe, if you did, you wouldn't've fucked over a Demon's princess."

I brought my hand up to rub the back of my neck. Usually, I ensured the bitches I hooked up with knew it was a casual thing. Thing was, I knew from the second Layla walked into our bar that she was different from the rest.

Since our night together, I'd been askin' myself why I dipped out of my usual stable. Only answer that came to me was that I must've been bored stupid with the same old, same old.

Now, I was fucked, 'cause my dick was tellin' me that sun-ripened strawberries tasted a whole lot better than used-up old steak.

Dad let out a grunt. "We'll ride over to her place. I'll introduce myself. We'll see what she needs."

"Wait, Prez," Abe said. "If a convoy of bikers rides up to her door, the poor girl'll have a conniption. Freya's back from Med school Thursday. Let her go over. She can see how the land lies."

Dad frowned.

"In the meantime, we'll sort that loan," Abe continued. "I'll get the Prospects to do a couple of drive-bys. She'll be okay."

"Okay," Dad agreed. "Freya'll do it, but in the meantime, brothers, if you see Layla in town, be nice. If you see her struggling, you help. And if you see anyone givin' her shit, you sort it." Pop pointed at me again. "And as for you, fucknut. You've got an apology to make."

Excitement traveled all the way down to my dick. Now I had a reason to see her again.

A huge grin spread across my face, and I jerked a nod.

Well, alrighty then.

Chapter Three

Layla

I groaned as I hauled the water-filled bucket to the top step of the beautiful oak staircase. My back ached so badly that I needed to sit, just for a minute.

The problem was, if I rested, Mrs. Barrington would snipe at me about lazy staff and threaten to look for another housekeeper. Cleaning the Barrington place was my primary source of income, so jeopardizing my position wasn't an option.

I got to the top of the stairs and placed the bucket on the upstairs hallway floor. Reaching into my back pocket for my cell, I checked the time. There were two hours to kill before I had to get my girl from preschool. Perfect. I still had time to hit the grocery store.

I jumped slightly as an angry voice sniped behind me. "I don't pay you to mess around on your cellphone, Layla."

"Sorry, Mrs. Barrington." I stiffened, turning to face my employer. "I was just checking to see if I had time to clean the bathrooms before school finishes for the day." I slipped my phone back into my pocket.

Mrs. Barrington pursed her lips. "If you didn't spend all your time playing on your cell, you'd get the job done a lot quicker. Don't you agree?"

A retort bubbled up, but I pushed it back down. It wasn't worth the crap it would cause.

I'd learned an important lesson while working at the Barrington mansion. It was no use trying to defend myself because Mrs. Barrington was always right.

She didn't work. I guess she didn't have to. Her husband owned the bank where I opened my account, making them one of the richest families in town. I knew this because Sydney, their daughter, boasted about it constantly.

Mrs. Barrington was a tall thin pale-faced woman with dark blonde hair. God only knew why she had a permanently pissed-off expression on her face. I didn't know if the Botox was freezing it that way or if she was just plain miserable.

Sydney was my age. We were best friends in middle school, then things changed as soon as we went into high school. She began to hang out with the cheerleaders and the jocks, and me, the shy girl, got left behind.

Determined not to give Mrs. Barrington any cause for complaint, I leaned down, grasped the bucket handle, and hauled it up. The cheap plastic snapped in my hand, causing the bucket to drop to the floor with a loud thud. Water splashed up over the sides and onto the gleaming wood of the steps.

I looked up and sighed. Why was the joke always on me?

Mrs. Barrington let out an impatient huff as she rolled her eyes. "You'd better hurry and get that mess cleaned up. I want every bathroom cleaned before you go. Don't for one minute think I'm paying overtime because of *your* clumsiness."

I stared at the dripping water. "Yes, Mrs. Barrington."

The cold glare she threw over her shoulder took me straight back to three nights before, but instead of

Bowie

Bowie's light brown eyes, hers were dark blue. My stomach clenched.

"I want that wood shining again by the time you leave," she ordered as she reached the bottom of the staircase, her voice sharp as a knife.

I swallowed the tears rising in my throat and bowed my head. "Of course, Mrs. Barrington," I whispered.

"It's been declined," the girl at the checkout drawled.

Panic rose in my throat, and I shook my head. There were over a hundred dollars in my account when I checked last night. What the hell had happened to all my money?

"It can't be," I mumbled, wringing my hands. "There's money in the account. Please. Will you try again?"

Whispers rose before a low giggle sounded from someone in the queue behind me. I steeled myself and put my debit card back into the reader. My fingers keyed in my PIN and the enter button.

I held my breath. "Please, God. Please, God. Please, God," I chanted under my breath.

A dull beep sounded from the card reader. "Sorry," the cashier griped, not looking sorry at all. "Looks like you'll have to put it all back."

My throat tightened. If I could have made myself invisible at that moment, I would have. "B—But I need milk." My eyes darted to the queue of people behind me. "Can I please speak to Mr. Allen?"

The cashier picked up a telephone handset by the side of the cash register and jabbed her finger on a blue button, letting out a huff. Nausea swirled in my gut as she snipped, "Emergency. Mr. Allen to register one. Mr.

Allen to register one." Her voice crackled loudly through the speakers, no doubt heard by the entire store.

My face burned as the queue of people started to grumble.

A teenage girl standing directly at the back of me whispered behind her hand to her friend, who was standing with her. "Oh, my God. What a mess." She quietly laughed.

Moisture sprang to my eyes even though I pretended I hadn't heard.

"What's the holdup?" the man behind the girls demanded in a hard tone. I turned to the people waiting and shrugged apologetically.

The woman behind him let out an annoyed sigh. She checked her watch, sighed again, and then glared at me.

"I'm sorry," I murmured, cheeks on fire. "There's a problem with my card."

"Yeah, right," the teenage girl snorted.

My eyes lowered.

"Emergency. Mr. Allen to register one," crackled loudly again around the store.

My eyes darted around. People looked to see what was going on. As the girls behind me quietly laughed, I flinched and prayed for the ground to swallow me whole.

"What's the problem over here?" a loud voice boomed.

My eyes swung around to see the owner of *Allen's One Stop Shop* making his way over.

Richard Allen was in his early fifties, short, bald, and ill-tempered. I'd heard that he and my dad were friends in high school, but you wouldn't think so by how he looked at me at that moment. His mouth went tight when he saw me.

"Mr. Allen. I have money in my account, but my card won't work." I explained in a low voice.

He folded his arms across his podgy chest and looked at me pointedly.

"Please, Mr. Allen," I quietly begged. "Could I take my groceries and come back and pay tomorrow?"

His lip curled at me. "No," he barked. "If you can't pay, you have to put it all back."

A sob rose in my throat. I nodded unseeingly. I had nothing in my fridge except for some old, hard cheese and a drop of milk. How was I going to feed Sunny?

As I turned blindly for the exit, I thought I heard someone call my name. Ignoring it, I ran for the door. I needed to get out of there.

The five seconds it took me to get outside seemed like an hour. The warm air hit me. My feet slowed, and then I scurried to an alley at the side of the building, away from the prying eyes and mocking faces. I just needed a minute to collect myself. I couldn't let Sunny see me like this. But then I remembered that I had no food for her, and another sob escaped me. What was I going to do?

As I stepped into the alley, a woman's voice called my name again.

Oh God, why can't these people leave me alone?

"Layla," she called again.

My back hit the wall. "Go away," I muttered under my breath. A tear rolled down my cheek as my hands flew to my face, and I broke down.

Sobs racked through me for a good minute before the voice said, "Layla," as soft fingers grasped mine.

I looked up through my tears to see a pair of hazel eyes looking at me sympathetically. Anna Bouchard, who owned the town's only beauty salon, smiled kindly down at me.

I burst into tears again.

Surprisingly strong arms wrapped around my shoulders as I sobbed and hiccoughed on her elegant shoulder. "It's okay, sweetheart," Miss Anna's soft Southern accent crooned in my ear. "I've gotcha."

Two weeks ago, I'd got talking to Miss Bouchard outside the coffee place. She'd opened the beauty salon a few months back when she'd moved up from Georgia.

I pulled back and swiped at my face. "I'm sorry, Anna," I said as I took a couple of deep breaths. "Just give me a couple of minutes, please."

Anna tossed her beautiful red hair over her shoulder. "Sweetheart, tell me what happened."

Tears welled up again.

"I know we don't know each other very well, honey," Anna continued as her fingers stroked mine, "but you can trust me. Now, tell me, what's going on?"

My head lowered. "I can't," I whispered as moisture filled my eyes again.

Anna's beautiful hazel eyes softened as she pointed to the floor. "Look."

My gaze veered down to three bags, and my heart filled with gratitude as I saw they held the groceries I'd just had to leave behind.

"Oh my, God," I breathed.

"I'm sorry that happened to you, honey," Anna said in a tight voice as she gestured toward the store. "There's nothin' worse than folk who say they're Christian but don't act Godly."

"It's okay," I explained. "My card wouldn't work. You can't blame Mr. Allen for that."

Anna let out a quiet harrumph. "You've lived in this town all your life Layla. That mean old coot knows you're good for it."

"I guess," I agreed, giving her a watery smile.

"Honey. How did that happen?" she asked. "I've seen you runnin' around going from job to job. You work every hour God sends."

My shoulders lifted in a shrug. "I do, but I only get paid minimum wage, and I can't seem to make it stretch."

She looked shocked. "Minimum wage?"

I nodded absentmindedly, remembering the time. Pulling my phone from my pocket, my belly filled with dread. "Sunny!" I exclaimed. "I'm gonna be late."

Anna's eyes flew to her watch then she grabbed hold of the leather purse that hung on her shoulder, "Here," she said as she unzipped it and handed me a small packet of wipes. "You clean that pretty face up, and I'll go over to the school and get your girl. Tell 'em you got held up."

Gratitude washed over me. "Are you sure?" I asked.

"Sure, I'm sure," she smiled as she started to walk. When she got to the top of the alley, she turned back to me. "Be a sweetheart and phone the school office. Let them know I'm on my way. I'll be back in two shakes of a lamb's tail."

"Thank you," I called back, giving her a low wave.

After making the call and taking time to wipe the tears from my face, I picked up the groceries, then walked up the side of the store and out into the parking lot.

Happiness replaced sorrow at the sight that met me. Anna was walking toward me hand in hand with my girl, who was skipping beside her, face beaming.

"Hey, Sunny Sunshine," I yelled.

Anna bent down to say something in my daughter's ear, pointing at me.

Sunshine saw me and screeched, "Mama!" as she hurtled toward me.

I crouched and held my arms out, and my baby flew into them.

"Mama!" Sunny repeated. "Miss Anna gots me from school."

"So, I see," I laughed, lifting her onto my hip.

My girl nodded excitedly before throwing her arms up in the air. "She's gonna drive us home."

Anna strode toward us with a huge smile. "I hope you don't mind, but those groceries need puttin' away. Then I thought I'd treat us all to pizza." Her smile and her face turned serious. "There's a few things I want to talk to you about."

"Pizza!" Sunny shouted. "I loves pizza."

"Thank you, Anna," I said, "but I have to go to the bank and pay back your money."

Anna shook her head. "No, honey. You've had a day. Forget about the money right now. We'll work something out." She tweaked Sunny's nose. "Anyway, I promised this little lady pizza."

Sunny chattered excitedly as we loaded the groceries into the back of Anna's silver Range Rover. I strapped her in the back seat as she talked about her day.

Ten minutes later, we were home. After the pizza got delivered, we sat at the kitchen table while I watched Sunny tuck into her food.

A ribbon of guilt coiled through my chest as I watched my girl smile from ear to ear. I could rarely afford treats like this. Money was so tight that I could barely afford the basics.

Anna looked closely at us while she sipped on some iced tea. She waited for me to pour Sunny some water and sat back in her chair. "Layla. It's good that you're working hard to provide for your daughter, but you must struggle if you're working for minimum wage."

My gut churned. She was right. I was struggling; today had proven that. "It's not easy. My work will never make me rich, but I'm caught between a rock and a hard place." I gazed down at Sunny, who was munching her food with sauce all around her mouth. "Nobody will give me a job with decent pay."

Anna leaned forward and rested her arms on the table. "What would you say if I offered you a position at the salon?"

My heart sank a little. "I'd say thank you, but I'm not a stylist. I don't think I could be much use to you." Tears formed in my throat again. I would have loved to work for her. I knew she'd be a great boss.

"My receptionist left last week. Her husband got a new job in Denver," Anna explained. "I need someone who doesn't need much training. Someone who can also manage the ordering and stock. Are you interested?"

A spark of hope bloomed in my chest. "I used to make appointments and manage the office for Mr. Stafford."

"The lawyer? Why did you leave?"

I bit my lip. How could I tell her I got fired? This offer was the best thing to happen to me for years. But as I looked at the woman who had been so kind and generous that day, I knew I had to tell her everything and let the cards fall wherever they were meant to.

"He let me go when I got pregnant with Sunny," I explained.

Anna inhaled a sharp breath. "He fired you because you were having a baby?"

I replied with a jerk of my head.

"Jesus, Layla, he can't do that. He should know better."

I knew this, but I was jobless and pregnant at the time. I didn't have the money or the know-how to do anything about it. Pregnancy made me throw up morning, noon, and night. I didn't have the strength that I would have needed to fight. Especially as I would have been going against a man who knew the law inside out.

Anna looked down at Sunny, who was still engrossed in her pizza. "You'd be working five days a week. I'll need you some Saturdays, but you'd get a day off in the week."

Hope began to build in my chest. "I'll need to look into childcare," I thought out loud.

"No, you wouldn't. Sunny would be fine at the salon. I've been thinking of setting up a kid's corner with toys, books, and crayons, so she won't get bored."

A flicker of warmth lit my stomach. "That's genius. I know from experience that there's nothing worse than wrangling bored kids while trying to get stuff done."

Ann looked at me thoughtfully. "You could take Sunny to school in the morning, then come straight to the salon. If you only took a half-hour lunch break, you could take some time out in the afternoon, then collect her and bring her back to the shop until we close around five."

Excitement made my heart race, and a curl of gratitude swirled in my stomach. In one fell swoop, Anna Bouchard restored my faith in human kindness.

Then she said something that made my eyes go huge.

"I pay fifteen dollars per hour."

Wait. What?

Fifteen dollars an hour was more than double what I earned cleaning. And I'd be working more hours.

Previously, I'd been limited to working while Sunny was at school. It would take some pressure off if Anna was serious about letting her hang out at the salon.

Numbers began to float around my brain. I made some calculations. When I added everything up, I almost fainted.

"T—Th—That's over five hundred and fifty dollars a week," I stuttered.

Anna threw me a wink.

My throat squeezed so tight I struggled to breathe. Five hundred and fifty dollars a week would mean that even after taxes, I could save for a car. I could do the work around the cottage that was getting desperate. I could even take Sunny on a little vacation to the beach.

Tears sprang to my eyes for the second time that day, but they weren't caused by worry and embarrassment. That time they were tears of relief.

Mine and Sunny's lives had been an uphill struggle for five years. If it wasn't for Nanna leaving me the cottage, I had no doubt we'd be homeless.

As I looked down at my girl, I blew out a huge breath and, in that one action, heaved out five years' worth of drudgery, pain, and sadness.

My gaze swung back to Miss Anna. My eyes shone joyfully, and my smile spread so wide that my jaw ached.

Ann Bouchard was my guardian angel.

I beamed and said the four words I knew would change my and Sunny's lives forever.

"When can I start?"

Chapter Four

Bowie

The clubhouse was silent as I made my way through the bar.

Wednesday mornings were always quiet. Most of the brothers were either working in the auto shop, our bar, or were out on a job as part of the club's construction crew.

From the inside, you'd never know the place used to be an old warehouse.

When the club bought the building twenty years ago, the brothers handmade the oak bar that ran along the back of the room. The walls had been covered with wooden panels varnished the same color as the bar.

A couple of dozen tables dotted the room. About a year ago, we'd brought in some huge black sofas. The games area comprising of pool tables, dart boards, and a couple of vintage video game machines, was sectioned off in one corner.

As I reached the hallway that led to the offices and the stairs—which in turn led to the basement—my gaze fell onto the wall covered in old photos and rows of cuts.

One, in particular, caught my eye.

I reached up, touching the soft, black leather, and like always, I smiled as I took in the patch. A motorcycle that had a single wing on each side. Our name, *Speed Demons MC*, curved over the top, and our state, Wyoming, across the bottom. Nineteen-sixty-eight was stamped inside the design.

It was in September of that year when my grandpa founded the club with his best friend, Bob Henderson.

The two men were born on the same day and were inseparable throughout school. When they both turned twenty, they enlisted together and were drafted into the same infantry unit. Ten years later, they arrived home with honorable discharges after being shot while fighting side by side during a battle in Saigon.

They were both thirty years old.

My grandpa, Don 'Bandit' Stone, was a true outlaw. He took from the rich, which, funnily enough, caused the downfall of his friendship with Bob, seeing as Bob's dad was not only wealthy but also the Mayor of Hambleton.

Due to my grandaddy's hankering for crime, Bob left the club before following in his father's footsteps to become mayor, a title he also passed down to his son, the current Mayor of Hambleton, Robert Henderson the Third.

My father, John 'Dagger' Stone, was also a man who embraced his father's legacy. He took his place as president of the Speed Demons when Don passed away twelve years before.

Dad steered the club on the straight 'n' narrow. We said adios to our one-percenter diamond patch when he became prez. The club opened successful businesses, which to this day, kept the member's pocket's full of scratch.

Were we squeaky clean? Not entirely. But our illegal activities only extended to running crime out of our town, underground fighting, and the odd beatdown, which, lo and fuckin' behold, was why I was headed down to the Cell.

The steps to the basement echoed as I walked down the narrow walkway. Directly ahead, there was a grey metal door. As I pressed my thumb to a keypad on the wall to the right, it gave a high-pitched beep while the locks disengaged. I pushed the door open and made my way inside.

Colt had recently installed a top-of-the-range thumbprint sensor on the club's underground room. We used it partly to hide our firearms and partly as a place to deal with people who fucked with us.

All that technological mumbo jumbo flew way over my head. I was a mechanic and a boxer. The nearest I got to technology was when I plugged a diagnostic machine into a car.

As I hustled my ass through to another corridor, I was met with two more steel doors. The one to my left was where we stored all our firepower and cash. The one to the right was where we beat the snot out of the assholes who mistakenly thought the club could be messed with after we gave up our little diamond-shaped patch.

Fuckin' idiots.

As I held my up thumb again to get access to the room, the door beeped as it simultaneously clicked open. I walked into the darkened room and could make out Atlas bent at the waist, talkin' to a guy who was cuffed to a chair.

Gavin Cooper was the sick fuck we'd caught red-handed trying to take drugs into our bar.

He'd been down here since Saturday night. Atlas and me questioned him on where he'd scored the pills. He'd given us a description of the dealer pretty much from the get-go, but still, a lesson had to be taught.

Gavin was so engrossed in what Atlas was sayin' he didn't hear me enter the room. I leaned back against the far wall, happy to watch the show.

"Let me explain what a Sergeant at Arm's duties are, Gavin, my boy. Yeah?" Atlas rumbled in his deep baritone.

The SAA had the look of someone you didn't wanna piss off. He was six-foot-five and built like a brick shithouse. His huge, muscled arms had a solid block of black ink tatted onto both wrists, which went up to just below his elbows. His biceps were covered in grey and black images. One of his solid pecs had a single crow's wing etched into it.

As usual, he wore jeans, boots, a white wife beater, and his cut. He always dressed the same way. Didn't matter if it was the freezing cold of winter or the blistering heat of summer.

Atlas's dark brown hair was buzzed, his beard neat. It always amazed me how his dark brown eyes could dance with humor one minute and glint with the promise of death the next. Right then, those eyes were glaring the latter toward the bastard who had the stupid idea to bring drugs into our bar.

I almost rubbed my hands together with fuckin' glee because Atlas was very good at his job.

Gavin was stripped to his shorts. The cut above his left eye, courtesy of me, Saturday, was beginning to heal. The bruising around his right eye, courtesy of Atlas the day before, was still an angry dark purple.

I couldn't stop grinnin' as the SAA put the fear of God into the prisoner. I always enjoyed watching Atlas work, and in addition, we had a little wager on this one.

"My main duty is to protect this club," Atlas continued as he folded his meaty arms in front of his chest. "Our patrons are among the people I'm trusted to look out for. Get me?"

Gavin furiously nodded his head.

"So, what d'ya think I'm gonna do if I ever see your face in this town again?"

The guy visibly gulped and then stuttered, "Y—Y—You'll kill me?"

"Bingo," Atlas shouted.

Gavin flinched back into his seat.

The SAA bent down so his face was level with Gavin's before putting one hand on each arm of the chair and letting out an earsplitting roar in the other man's face.

Gavin screamed, and then his entire body began to shake.

Atlas scrunched his nose before leaning into Gavin and sniffing loudly. "The fuck's that smell?"

The smaller man closed his eyes as a yellow stain began to spread slowly over his white shorts.

Atlas glanced up at me and grinned. Then his face morphed back into a beast as he got further into Gavin's face and boomed. "Have you fuckin' pissed ya'self?"

Gavin looked down at his wet shorts and let out a hiccough.

A chuckle rose through my chest. I tamped it down so that Cooper didn't hear. No way did I wanna ease the tension for the twisted little bastard.

"Right, Gav. It's your lucky day," Atlas continued. "We're gonna send you back to the rock you crawled out from. But before that happens, I need you to remind me of the first promise you made Uncle Atlas this mornin'."

After a few seconds, Gavin paled and stammered, "I—I won't ever buy drugs again."

"That's a good little boy," Atlas grunted. "Tell me promise number two."

"I—I won't go to the cops," Gavin cried.

"No, you fuckin' won't, Gav. Tell me why you won't go opening your trap?"

Gavin's bottom lip wobbled. "Because I'll get arrested for possessing narcotics."

"Yup," Atlas nodded. "And what else?"

Gavin tried to swallow. "And because you'll rip off my head and shit down my neck."

"Good man, you passed the test." Atlas reached into the inside of his cut and whipped out a knife. Quick as a flash held it up to the other man's throat.

Gavin let out a high-pitched squeal.

Atlas pressed the blade against Gav's neck, his face a mask of anger. "Listen to me, you goddamned, no good, rapey piece of shit. If I ever see you again, I swear to God. I'll slice your scrawny little throat. Do you fuckin' get me?"

"I'm sorry. I'm sorry," Gavin sobbed. "I'll never do it again."

Atlas put his knife back inside his cut and reached into his jeans pocket. He pulled out a little silver key, and within seconds, Gavin was uncuffed.

He cried out as Atlas grabbed him by the back of his mousy brown hair and hauled him to his feet. Gav stumbled but then managed to right himself quickly.

"This is your one and only chance, Gav, don't fuck up again," I called out.

He jumped a foot high at the sound of my voice cutting through the room. His eyes swung to me and widened comically.

I raised my hand, then pulled my index finger across the front of my neck in a slicing action.

Gavin gaped, then a frightened squeak sounded from the back of his throat.

I pushed down another laugh.

"You got one minute to get dressed," Atlas ordered.

Gav immediately scurried over to the table where his clothes were folded, just as a loud knock sounded from the door.

Atlas looked up. There were cameras on the other side of the door so that whoever was inside could have eyes outside.

"Ahh, look, Tinky fuckin' Winky, and Dipsy, at last," Atlas said. His eyes skirted back to Gavin. "Just in time to drive your pissy ass home."

The prisoner gulped nervously while fastening his pants.

I made my way to the metal door, opened it, and ushered our two prospects inside. "Remember," I told 'em "One driving, the other in the back with our guest."

"Got it," Boner replied. He walked across the room and gripped Gavin's shoulder.

Sparky gave me a chin lift before he and Boner pushed Gavin toward the open door.

"Remember what we said, Cooper," Atlas warned as we followed the men into the hall. "If you see us on the street, you better fuckin' run the other way. Prospects, make sure you drop him off exactly where I said."

Sparky looked back at us from the stairs, nodding once. "On it, boss."

The SAA made his way back into the room.

I closed the door, following him to a pile of chairs stacked against a wall. I watched as he grabbed two and placed them next to the table.

Atlas parked his ass in one while pointing to the other with a knowing smirk.

The instant I sat, he held his hand out, palm up. "You gonna pay the fuckin' piper?"

I shot him a glare, stood, and grabbed at the chain, keeping my wallet secure in my back pocket.

"Told you I'd make him piss himself," he said, voice amused.

I pulled a fifty from my wallet and held it out. "Took you fuckin' long enough," I grumbled.

Atlas' face split into a huge smile. "You know I like a good strong finish." He chuckled as he snatched the bill and smacked a kiss on it.

I returned my wallet to my back pocket before sitting back down. "Did ya get anything else outta him?"

"Only what he told us when we nabbed him. That he got 'em off some guy down behind Birch Street."

"Well, that narrows it down to a fuckin' thousand," I mused.

Atlas nodded his agreement. "We just gotta keep puttin' the pressure on, Bowie. The fucker'll slip up soon enough, and when he does, we'll be there, waitin'."

Atlas made sense, but it didn't ease my mind. We'd hoped for a while the attacker would've gotten overconfident and slipped up, but we were wrong. If anything, he was gettin' more proficient.

Hambleton was a far cry from the city. Crime was low, and everybody knew each other, which made the townsfolk pretty trusting. The girls who grew up here could be naïve, which was the reason the sick fuck could play 'em.

Either that, or it was someone they knew, and it didn't flag as suspicious if he went near their drinks.

"Freya still home tomorrow?" Atlas asked. I watched as he picked up a pack of smokes from the table.

"Yeah, should be here by noon."

He lit a smoke and took a deep drag. "You don't look very fuckin' happy about it, Bowie."

Atlas was right; I wasn't happy at all. "You know I think the world of my sister, but I worry about her while this shit's goin' on. You know how she loves partying."

"Ya sure you don't want her home 'cause Prez will tell her to bring your girl around the club?"

Unease prickled my skin. "Fuck off. Layla's not my girl."

Atlas barked out a laugh. "So that wasn't you who I saw yesterday, sittin' in your truck mooning at her like she was shittin' rainbows?"

Goddamn, fuckin' busted.

After days of allowing the memories of fucking Layla that night to take over my whole goddamned existence, I may or may not have calculated that she'd be at the school around three-thirty to collect her kid.

I knew that if I tried to talk, she'd tell me to eat shit and die, but tell that to my self-flagellating brain, 'cause I went on mission fuckin' impossible, regardless. My reasonin' was that if I caught up to her when she was with her kid, she'd at the very least not tell me to go fuck myself up the ass with a giant dildo.

I'd jumped in my truck and drove through town, all while tryin' to convince myself that it didn't matter if I'd already missed her. Then, as I moseyed past *Allen's One Stop Shop*, I looked up, and there she was.

Jeans, Zeppelin tee, chestnut hair in one'a those bun things with all the bits fallin' down all sexy, like I'd just reamed her from behind.

I parked up, unable to tear my eyes away from the sight of her and her kid. The love between 'em burned so brightly that I had to close my eyes.

I knew firsthand how that light could make a man feel 'cause I'd felt it in my blood that night I took her home.

Layla was real and honest. She didn't play the fucked-up games like the others.

She gave herself over to me, no hesitation, no bullshit. Then I went and fucked everythin' up.

I sat in my truck staring at what could've been if I hadn't been so fuckin' terrified. Regret burned my throat. It was like I needed her glow if I was ever gonna be warm again.

"Yo. Earth to Bowie," Atlas boomed.

I nearly jumped outta my seat, "Jesus," I muttered.

"Nothing wrong with actually likin' a woman for more than what's between her legs, brother," he said, face thoughtful.

Anxiety gripped my chest. "I know that, Atlas."

"What happened with that chick, Samantha messed up you up, but it's time to put that shit in your rearview and move the fuck on."

"I was over that years ago, Christ's sake. I have moved on," I snapped.

"Yeah?" Atlas said knowingly. "So why you don't let women get close?"

My chest tightened instinctively. "'Cause the type of bitches I get in my bed aren't exactly the type I can introduce to my fuckin' ma."

He cocked his head. "And yet you went looking for sweet. Wonder why that is?"

I rubbed the back of my neck.

"You can't kid a fuckin' kidder, Bowie. Don't you think I've noticed you turnin' down your regulars?"

"No, I—"

"—Don't you look in my face and fuckin' lie. You have."

I stared down at my boots.

"How long did you go without any before Friday night?" Atlas demanded.

My eyes veered back to him.

"Tell me?" He paused. "Three, four months?"

Our SAA saw everythin' that went down in the club.

I wasn't surprised he noticed that I hadn't been on form for a good long fuckin' while.

I heaved out a breath, then braced. "Eight."

The SAA let out a long whistle. "So, let me get this shit straight, 'cause I swear, brother, I'm tryin' my utmost to wrap my head around the fucked up world of Bowie Stone. You hadn't sniffed out a bitch for eight long months, then lo-and-behold, one night, Layla Hardin struts her ass into our bar, and suddenly your dick takes notice?"

I nodded.

"Then, you take her to your house, which incidentally ain't the norm, seein' as your usual MO is to bang 'em in your shithole room at the club." Atlas stubbed out his cigarette in the ashtray on the table beside us. "Tell me, brother. When you did the deed, was it different? Was she different?"

My eyes looked everywhere except at him.

"Right, I'll take that as a hell yeah," he mocked under his breath. "Okay, now, I'm gonna ask you somethin' else, and I want God's honest truth, get me?"

I jerked my head again.

"Did you feel somethin' other than the wad shooting outta your dick?" he smacked a closed fist against his chest. "Somethin' in here?"

My eyes closed slowly.

"Bowie?"

"Yeah," I admitted.

"So why the fuck did you treat her like shit you'd trodden in?"

My throat closed up.

The guilt and self-recriminations that had been eating at me for days swirled through my chest. A name swirled through my noggin, *Samantha.* I ignored it and pushed it aside.

My breath heaved out. I looked at Atlas, and I revealed my shame. "I got spooked, alright?"

A huge smile split Atlas' face. "Yup," he drawled. "You got scared 'cause you're still hung up over somethin' that happened fuckin' years ago." He leaned forward. "I rest my fuckin' case."

A stab of pain jabbed my chest. Atlas knew me as well as anyone. "Thing is, brother," I said. "I know it's time now. I've been mulling it over for months. I'm ready."

"Then go get your fuckin' girl, Bowie," he demanded.

I winced. "Too late, I fucked it."

"No shit, but I also know that when you want somethin', no fucker'll stop you," Atlas retorted, rising from his chair and approaching the doors.

I stood and followed.

Atlas glanced at me over his shoulder. "I've seen you with the ladies, Bo. You could charm the birds outta the goddamned trees."

"Don't think she's the type to fall for that shit, Brother," I replied.

The SAA swung the door open, stopped in the doorway, then turned back to me. "Then you get serious, Bowie. You gotta do the one thing that'll get you back in her good books."

"What's that?" I asked, heart sinkin' into my stomach.

Atlas patted my cheek, then relayed the words that almost made me groan out loud.

"You get on your knees and fuckin' beg."

Chapter Five

Layla

I was about to put the key in the lock when my ringtone cut through the air. Glancing at the screen, I smiled and hit the green button. "Hey, Cara, give me a minute to get inside the house."

Sunny began to jump up and down, her face filling with excitement. "Auntie Cara," she screeched. "Please, Mama, can I talk to her?"

As I put the cell phone on loudspeaker, my best friend laughed softly down the phone. "Is that my Sunny Sunshine?"

Sunny let out one of her adorable giggles as I pushed the key in the lock, turned it, opened the door, and tugged her gently inside. "Auntie Cara, guess what?" she shouted excitedly.

"Umm. Did you get all your spellings right?" Cara asked as we walked through the hallway and into the kitchen.

"Well, yeah. But this is something to do with Mama," Sunny yelled as she hopped up and down.

"Hmm, okay, I give up," Cara said matter-of-factly. "What's momma done?"

"She's got a new job with Miss Anna. She's gonna be in charge of all the stuff, and I get to go there after school and play, and Miss Anna said if I'm good, she's gonna paint my nails when school's out." Sunny didn't stop for a breath.

There was a moment of silence as Cara took everything in. "Well, I guess you better put your mom on the phone, Sunny Sunshine. I've got questions." Her voice was filled with curiosity.

I smiled at my daughter. "Go and get one of your board games. We'll play before dinner."

"Yay!" Sunny yelled, then raced from the room.

I sat at the table and took the phone off the speaker. "Hey," I breathed.

"I go out of town with my fiancé for a few days; get back, and you've scored a new job?" Cara questioned.

I sat back, grinning sheepishly. "It's a long story."

"Then you better start talking, Layla. I've got school reports to write."

Cara Landry and I met when we were both eighteen, on the day her family moved to Hambleton from New York.

Her dad, Seth, had just taken the position of Principle of Hambleton High, while Cara's mom, Deborah, took over the Science Department.

Cara, who graduated college a few years before, also took a teaching position at the school about a year back. She taught art, though honestly, I didn't doubt that she could make it as a painter and sculptor in her own right. She was that talented.

My eyes went to the portrait of Sunny that I'd hung on the kitchen wall. Cara painted it last year for my birthday. "How was Denver?" I asked.

She sighed. "It was great. Though I wish Robbie hadn't insisted we take a break during the semester."

Cara was engaged to Robert Henderson, the Fourth. Robbie's dad was the Mayor of Hambleton, and he made sure everyone knew it.

I wasn't a fan. He was arrogant, cold, and rude. God only knew why, but Cara seemed hellbent on marrying him the next month.

As far as I was concerned, she was making a huge mistake.

Robbie had tried to cause issues between Cara and me before. It was weird, but he seemed jealous of our friendship.

Cara had supported me through the birth of my daughter and the subsequent treatment the assholes of Hambleton threw at me. So, I was determined to support her through thick and thin, regardless of what asshole she married.

"Anyway, enough about me," she said. "Tell me what's been going on."

Over the next five minutes, I talked to Cara about the incident at the grocery store. I told her how Miss Anna had paid for my food, then about the job offer.

"Why did the bank refuse the payment?" Cara demanded angrily.

I let out a deep breath. "Mr. Barrington took the money for a late charge."

"Layla. You've paid those charges already. He can't keep fleecing you every month."

I closed my eyes at her angry tone. "I know. I went to the bank this morning and spoke to him. He put the money back."

"Keep an eye on it, Layla, or better still, change your bank."

"I will," I muttered. "But while I have this loan, keeping everything with one bank is easier. Once it's paid, I'll switch."

"Okay," she said. Then her voice took on a teasing tone. "Have you seen Bowie again?"

My heart dropped.

I hadn't seen Bowie Stone since *that* night, but he took up so much of my headspace. It was like he was constantly around. My thoughts flew back to Friday and the hard look on his face when he told me to get out of his house, and I cringed. Hopefully, my guardian angel would do me a solid and let some time pass before I had to face Bowie again. Twenty years, or thereabouts, should do it.

"No, I haven't," I replied. "And if I never see him again, it will be too soon."

"I don't understand what happened," Cara mused. "Bowie seemed really into it. I swear, Layla, he couldn't take his eyes off you. Even when you went to the restroom, he kept his eyes on the door and hovered until you came out."

Sadness swirled in my chest. "I know. I thought he liked me too, but we were both wrong. He just used me."

"I used to know him pretty well, Layla, but I've never seen him like that with a girl. Not ever."

Cara went out with Bowie's older brother, Xander—or Cash as everyone called him—for years. She'd got along really well with his parents, his brothers Bowie and Kit, and his sister.

Three years ago, she came home from college and went to see him at the club. She found him in bed with another girl.

Cara was so distraught she didn't get out of bed for three weeks.

After finding her passed out on her living room floor, drunk and heartbroken, I was so worried that I went to her parents for help.

Eventually, they agreed that she needed some time away, so Seth found her a six-month placement at a school in Kansas.

After she left, Xan got into a fight with Cara's now fiancé, Robbie, and beat him so severely that he was convicted of assault and sent to the State Penitentiary for five years. Rumour had it that he was due for parole soon.

Bowie

"When I knew Bowie, he didn't often talk to women," Cara continued. "He only had one girlfriend I heard of just before I met Xander. Women always hung around him, but he was never really *with* anyone."

A lump formed in my throat. The thought of Bowie surrounded by the girls who partied at the club made me feel sick. It was no wonder he didn't want me. Cara had told me stories about what went on at those shindigs. She never mentioned that Bowie was involved, but I wasn't stupid.

I cleared my throat. "It's okay, Cara. I'm good. It taught me a lesson, and if one good thing came out of it, at least I'm not pining after him anymore," I lied.

"Good," she said, her voice low. "Those brothers are players, Kit included. They should all come with a health warning saying. *'Do not touch. This man will decimate your heart'."*

A sigh escaped me. "Have you had any more letters from Cash?"

"Yeah, but I don't know why he bothers. He knows I'm getting married to Robbie."

My heart squeezed at the pain in her voice. "Are you sure about this wedding, Cara?" I asked gently.

She let out a huge sigh. "I don't know. I'm noticing things about Rob that sets my teeth on edge." She paused as if she was trying to decide whether she should continue. "We went out to dinner in Denver, and he was so rude to the waitress that I went back the next day to apologize for him."

My stomach twisted. "Oh, Cara. I'm sorry. What are you going to do?"

"Think long and hard, I guess." She went quiet for a few seconds. "Anyway, I better go. I've got reports to write and paintings to grade."

A loud thump sounded from the door.

"Yeah," I agreed, "you coming over Sunday?"

"Of course, see you then."

We said our goodbyes and ended the call as more banging started.

"Alright, alright, I'm coming," I mumbled as I walked through the hallway.

I got to the door and peered through the peephole. My eyes went wide when I saw the beautiful woman standing on the other side. My heart began to thud. What the hell was she doing at my house? A thought hit me. Disappointment made my chest tight. I wondered if Bowie had sent his sister to warn me away from him.

"Layla," she called out. "My name's Freya Stone. My dad, John, asked me to come talk to you. Is that okay?"

I froze. *Her dad?*

Right then, Sunny came racing down the hall. "Mommy, there's a lady outside," she yelled.

Shit. She must've heard.

"Layla?" Freya called through the door.

I blew out the breath that I'd been holding. "Baby. Go to your room for a minute while I talk to the lady."

Sunny's little face fell, but she did as she was told and dragged her feet to her bedroom.

I turned the handle and cracked the door open a few inches. "Hi." I smiled nervously. "Can I help you?"

Freya Stone reminded me of Olivia Culpo. She was two or three inches taller than my five foot four, with long dark brown hair, exotic bronze eyes, and lips that women would point to in a brochure and say, 'I'll have those ones, please.'

Freya was smart. She'd graduated top of her Ivy League school when she was only twenty before setting tongues wagging when she turned down an offer from Harvard, opting instead for the University of Colorado's School of Medicine.

"Can I come in for a minute?" Freya asked. "My dad asked me to come by and talk to you."

"I can't imagine what he'd want." I smiled to take the sting out of my words.

She gestured to the porch. "We can talk outside if it will make you more comfortable."

Curiosity curled inside my chest. "Okay," I relented. "Can you give me a minute?" What the heck had John Stone sent his daughter to talk to me about?

I headed into the house and rounded up Sunny, her doll, and some coloring books and crayons. I put glasses and a pitcher of tea on a tray and headed back outside.

Freya held the door open as I walked through, and then she crouched on her haunches as Sunny walked out behind me. "Hey, pretty girl. I'm Freya. What's your name?"

"Sunshine Hope Hardin," Sunny said in her sweet voice.

Freya pointed to the doll my girl was clutching. "And who's this?"

"Barbie Hardin," Sunny replied, holding Barbie up by the hair.

"Do you think Barbie Hardin would like to play in the grass over there?" Freya asked, pointing to my lawn.

Sunny looked at Freya like she was crazy. "Barbie's not real, she's just a doll, but if you want to talk to Mama, I can make a daisy chain."

Freya let out a laugh, tilting her face back to Sunny. "You're a very smart girl." She smiled. "Would you mind me talking to your mom for a little while?"

Sunny shrugged. "Okay."

"Thank you, baby," I called out as my girl skipped over the lawn toward a patch of flowers.

I sat on one of the three wicker chairs I kept on the porch in summer, gesturing for Freya to join me. While she got comfortable, I poured three glasses of tea, then handed one to her.

Freya took a sip, and her eyes flicked over to Sunny. "Okay," she began. "First thing I want to get out of the way is—my brother's an idiot."

Unease made my stomach clench as my cheeks heated.

"I'm sorry," she went on, "I'm not here to embarrass you."

"You don't even know me?" I questioned. "And Bowie's your brother."

She lifted one delicate shoulder in a shrug. "Yeah, but that doesn't mean I can't see when he's being an asshole."

I sipped my drink, hoping it would cool my burning face before Freya said something that nearly knocked me off my chair.

"If it's any consolation, I think he regrets it."

My eyes bugged out. "What?"

"I'm well aware he played the fool with you, but he's not altogether stupid."

I bit back the retort that bubbled up my throat. Freya wasn't there that night, she didn't see, but it also wasn't her fault that her brother hurt me.

I took another sip of my tea and tried to change the subject. "Why did your dad send you here?"

Freya studied my face. "My pop told me that your dad died when you were young, and your mom didn't handle it well."

My eyebrows drew together. "How does he know that?"

She crossed her legs. "Our dads were good friends. Did you know my dad's your godfather?"

I froze, mind whirring. "What?"

"Yeah. When your dad died, mine tried to see you and make sure you were okay, but your mother made it difficult for him."

Her words didn't really shock me. I grew up witnessing my mom's paranoid rants. When my dad died, she went into a deep depression throughout my childhood. She took solace in the bottle, which meant that I grew up with a mentally ill, alcoholic mother.

But it still hurt, even angered me. My childhood was chaotic. I would have given anything to have someone I could go to or rely on.

"Your mom threatened to call the cops if Pop went near you," Freya went on. "The Demons back then—well, they weren't exactly squeaky clean. The sheriff was just waiting for an excuse to sniff around. Dad didn't have much choice."

I stared at Freya intently. Growing up, I knew that the Speed Demons were involved in bad stuff, but I also saw them do charity runs every year for the children's ward at Baines Memorial. I remember noticing their deep familial connection to each other and wishing that I had that too.

I didn't dwell on my childhood. If anything, I wanted to forget it. But I was angry that I could've been a part of that. It was hard not to feel cheated.

I'd seen John in town over the years, but he never spoke to me, even after I moved into my cottage. "I left home when I was eighteen. Why has it taken him this long to contact me?" I asked.

"Dad lost track of you. Then getting the club clean took up all his time. It was only when someone mentioned your name to him the other day that he realized who you were."

Heat flushed my cheeks again. Oh, God. I could only imagine why I was being talked about.

"He wants to get to know you and Sunshine," Freya said softly. "I'm aware that we don't really know each other, but when it comes down to it, you're both our family."

Warmth spread through my chest.

When Bowie told me about his siblings on Friday night, I wished I could give that to Sunny one day. She deserved to have a tribe, people who would adore her and guide her as she grew. I wanted to meet John and the others, but the thought of being around Bowie made my belly turn over. It was all so overwhelming.

"I don't know what to say," I breathed.

Freya tapped a finger on her lip. "The club's having a family barbeque on Sunday. Why don't you bring Sunshine along?"

Ice filled my veins. "I don't know."

"C'mon," she coaxed. "There will be other kids there for Sunny to play with. We've got a huge pool, and the guys will put the bounce house up."

"A bounce house?" a little voice said.

My head turned. Sunny was standing on the top step of the porch, arm laden with daisy chains. Her eyes went huge. "Mama, please, please, please," she cried. "I wanna go on the bounce house."

Great. How was I supposed to say no now? "Baby, I'm sorry, but I start my new job the day after."

Sunny put her hand to her forehead like a little drama queen. "Mama, the bounce house is my bestest thing in the world," she cried.

My eyes darted between Freya and my daughter.

"Please, mama. I'll be good," Sunny pleaded just as Freya said, "You don't have to stay late."

My shoulders sagged. "Why do I get the feeling that you get your own way more often than not?" I muttered.

Freya's grin morphed into a dazzling smile. "I'm not only the youngest but also the only girl. It's a perk."

A warm little hand slipped into mine. Sunny was gazing up at me with big eyes. "Please, Mama," she begged.

My whole body deflated. How the hell could I say no to that face? It only took a few seconds for me to relent. "Okay."

Sunny let out a delighted squeal and threw her arms around my thighs. Then she skipped over to Freya and did the same. The other woman patted Sunny gently on the back, and her eyes turned to me. "Make sure you wear a bikini," she said, waggling her eyebrows.

Dread whirled in my chest. "Freya," I warned.

"Bowie's going to lose his tiny little mind." She laughed.

I raised my eyes to the heavens. Did I really just agree to spend an entire afternoon at a biker compound and in the company of the man who kicked me out of his house after he'd had sex with me.

"It'll be alright, Layla, you'll see." Freya sang.

I huffed out a breath. "I really hope so."

Chapter Six

Bowie

"Can't believe I'm not partyin' on a Saturday night," my younger brother Kit
grumbled. "Shoot me the fuck now."
I deadpanned. "Don't goddamned tempt me."
Honestly, patrollin' wasn't my favorite thing, either. But with all the drink spikin' going on in town, the club voted to send a couple of guys out every weekend to check out the bars which had been affected.

We didn't bother going to the Demon's Haven. Nobody would dare start shit there.

There were only two other bars in Hambleton. Business owners had to jump through hoops to get permission to open any kind of drinkin' establishment here.

The mayor put the kibosh on a lot of business proposals. The official word was that the town committee wanted Hambleton to retain its small-town atmosphere. But anyone with half a brain knew that if you wanted to open a business here, you needed to give Mayor Henderson a big financial kickback.

The Demons had to pay big bucks to open our bar, but we got that back tenfold in the first year, so we didn't care so much. Puttin' a bullet in Mayor Henderson's head had been brought to the table, but as Dad said, we were meant to be getting clean.

Me and Kit glanced at each other as we swaggered up to the door of our first destination, the *Lucky Shamrock*.

Kit gave me a bored glance as he grasped the handle and pulled. The door swung open, and a blast of cold air from the AC hit our faces, along with the chatter and laughter of the patrons.

It was set up a bit like the place in 'Cheers.' A square bar sat to one side of the room with stools pulled up to it. There were more chairs and tables dotted around and a large square dance floor, which was already packed even though it wasn't yet ten.

A Dua Lipa song that I'd heard Freya blasting in the clubhouse thudded through the air as we weaved through the packed room and up to the bar.

Three bartenders rushed around serving drinks. One of the men caught my eye, grinned, then made his way over.

"Good to see ya, Bowie," he said with a chin lift.

I bumped his fist. "You too, Cal."

Callum O'Shea was the bar owner's son. He took over running the place when his dad retired.

The O'Sheas were good friends of the club. Callum often brought his crew to the *Haven* after he closed the *Shamrock* down for the night, seein' as our bar stayed open later.

"Seen any shit goin' down?" I asked.

Callum glanced around the room. "Not now. Kicked Henderson Junior and his minion out a little while ago, but apart from that, not a peep."

Kit pushed out a heavy breath. "What'd that asshole do now?"

"Just bein' his usual belligerent, entitled self." Callum shrugged. "Had too much to drink and got it in his head that he was God's gift to the ladies."

Kit's face hardened. "Dick!" he rasped.

It was safe to say Kit hated Robbie Henderson with fuckin' bells on. To be fair, we all did. Henderson was the sole reason my brother Xander got locked away on a five-year stretch.

A woman shouting from across the room made my ears prick up. The crowd behind us began to talk louder, then I caught a flash of movement out the corner of my eye. My neck craned to see a chick quickly making her way toward the lady's restroom.

"Somethin's wrong over there," Kit muttered.

"Fuck," Callum bit out as he hauled himself over the bar and jumped down next to me on the customer side. I turned back to see what was happening and noticed Kit was already making his way over to the crowd of worried-looking women.

"Looks like we got trouble," I rasped as we hurried toward the commotion.

My brother was talking to a young blonde. She was gesturing furiously with her hands toward the ladies' room.

Adrenaline rushed through me so forcefully I could feel it pounding in my ears. Something was really off here. My gut stabbed, but I tamped the nerves down, tryin' to keep my mind calm and focused.

As we reached Kit, he turned to us. "Her friend, Leah, is passed out in there. She was feeling dizzy, so she went to the bathroom." He jerked his head to the blonde woman. "Lucy and her girls just went in to check on her, but she's locked inside a stall."

My blood immediately cooled, and I fell into step behind Callum as he raced to the bathroom. "Kit," I called over my shoulder. "Call an ambulance. Now"

"And tell those two behind the bar to clear everyone out," Callum added.

Kit dipped his chin, then headed off. The blonde woman trailed him, wringing her hands.

The lady's bathroom was long and rectangular. It had five stalls along the right. A massive mirror covered the opposite wall, with hand basins running underneath.

Three young women were talking in a huddle while a redhead stood on a toilet seat in one of the stalls. She was looking over the top of the right-hand partition in the next cubicle and shouting over.

"Leah," she begged. "Please wake up. Leah. *Leah.*"

The huddle of women all turned to us at once.

"Our friend's passed out in there, but we can't get to her. The door's locked," one of them cried.

"We'll get her out," Callum said reassuringly.

I gestured for the woman in the stall to move out and then raced in. I climbed on the toilet seat and peered over the partition.

Another redheaded was slumped down, and her head and shoulders were hunched against the wall.

"Leah," I called out. "Sweetheart, can you hear me?"

Silence.

My head swiveled to my friend. "She's in bad shape, Cal."

Leah's head was angled down, so I couldn't see her face, but I could hear her breathing choppily as if she was short of air.

"Get her out. Now, Bowie," Callum ordered.

With no effort, I hoisted myself up and over the top of the stall. Boxing gave me a strong core and good upper body strength. It was easy for me to swing my legs and torso over the top, all while avoiding the unconscious woman's body.

I dropped onto the floor, quickly reached over to pull the metal bolt across the door, and then pushed the door open.

Callum appeared. He pulled Leah off the seat, then carried her out.

I heaved a sigh of relief.

Bowie

As I raced from the stall, I saw that Callum had lifted the woman into his arms. He was carrying her with her face to his chest. His left arm was around her back, and his right was holding her legs from behind the knees.

"Get the door," he demanded. One of Leah's friends raced ahead and heaved it open. We followed him as he carried the unconscious woman out of the restroom and back into the bar.

The place was quiet now. I turned to see the last of the patrons being pushed out the door by the two servers. "Come back tomorrow," the female bartender shouted to the back of the crowd of guys who were just departing.

Kit, who'd been leaning on the bar talking quietly to Lucy, looked up at me with angry eyes. "Leah only had one drink tonight, Bo," he griped. "She was meant to drive a few girls home later."

"She doesn't really drink," one of the women from the bathroom added. "Leah's my cousin. Both her parents have mobility issues, so she keeps a clear head in case they need help during the night."

I made an exasperated noise. Fuck. It looked like she'd been spiked, and right under Callum's nose, too. Leah had all the symptoms, dizziness, blackouts, and shallow breathing.

A sliver of guilt curled its way through my chest. Rohypnol took about twenty minutes to take effect. Assuming that's what she was spiked with, we didn't get here in time to stop it from happening.

"How long is the ambulance gonna be?" Callum demanded as he looked down at Leah.

"They said about ten minutes, Cal," Kit replied. "Won't be long now."

"This is the third time this has happened here in the last six months," Callum rasped quietly. "Whoever's doing this is a real sick fuck."

"Don't have to tell me, Cal. We've been after the skeevy prick for years." My eyes narrowed. "You gonna tell your pa?"

"Don't have a fuckin' choice, Bo. Third time's a charm. Gonna have to get a couple of boys at the door doing searches. It's gonna cost."

"Sorry, brother," I replied. "Wish we could do more."

Callum shrugged. "You're doin' all you can, Bo, but I worry about who me da's gonna call in."

"Fuck," I muttered.

Callum's dad, Lorcan O'Shea, was descended from an old New York street gang of Irish immigrants called the Dead Rabbits. He wasn't a mobster, not even close, but he was connected.

The last thing the Demons needed was for the Irish Mob to descend on the town. The Sherriff's office couldn't organize an orgy in a brothel. It would become a fuckin' shitshow. Those men were ruthless.

"I'll have a word with him," Callum added. "Dunno what good it'll do, but if I tell him that you guys are watchin' out, it should help."

I nodded to Leah. "Want me to take her?"

"Nah, I got it."

As he spoke, I picked up sirens wailing in the distance.

"They're here, Bo," Kit called over. He did a double take outta the window and looked back toward me. "Oh, shit," he said quietly.

Two paramedics walked into the bar. One of them looked around, caught sight of me, and smiled seductively.

Sydney Barrington was a girl I used to fuck, right up until I didn't. She'd called me non-stop for about a month after I ghosted her.

I always made sure that the bitches I ran with knew the score from day one. If they weren't good with it, I walked away. God only knows why Sydney thought she was different.

Irritation stabbed me as she walked toward me, hips swayin'.

"Fuck me," I muttered under my breath.

"Hey, Bowie," she said, her eyes eating me up.

I folded my arms across my chest.

Sydney was a typical spoiled rich girl. I knew it all along but wasn't around her enough to care. She wasn't someone I'd ever consider long-term.

"Long time no see," she said breathily.

"Yeah."

"How have you been?" she asked as she bit her lip.

I shook my head in disbelief. "Syd, have you not noticed a girl over there who's in bad shape? Shouldn't you be seein' to her?"

I looked over to where the other paramedic checked over Leah, who was flat on the floor. He was listening to her chest through a stethoscope.

"Oh, she'll be okay." Sydney shrugged. "Stuart's got her."

"Nice to see your heart's as big as ever."

The other paramedic stood, face like thunder. "Get over here, Barrington."

Thank fuck.

"See you later, Bowie," Syd said with a wink. "You've got my number."

Kit looked at me and made a face. I made one back.

The paramedic stood up to talk to Sydney, pointed to Leah, and then outside and shook his head. Syd looked back at me, swingin' her hips as she walked out.

"She gonna be okay?" I asked the paramedic.

"Her vitals are good," he replied. "Gonna take her to the ER and get her checked over."

My shoulders sagged in relief. "Freya Stone's on duty in the ER tonight. Tell her that Bowie said to check her blood for drugs."

"I'll try," he said as he craned his neck to see what Syd was doin' outside. "I saw Freya earlier tonight. She was busy seeing to another girl, same problem. It's happening more frequently, but this is the first night where there's been two."

I jolted slightly. "Two?"

A loud rattle came from the door. Sydney returned, pushing a stretcher in front of her. She and Billy lifted Leah gently, then strapped her on securely.

"Later, Bowie." Sydney winked as she left. A minute later, the sirens wailed again as the ambulance sped off.

The girls that were with Leah followed them outside, chatting worriedly.

Callum saw them into a couple of cabs, then came inside and locked the door. "Da's gonna fuckin' flip." He grimaced.

"Yeah," I replied. "Mine's not exactly gonna be jumpin' for joy either."

Kit looked at me. "What you gonna tell him?" he asked.

I pulled out my phone, went to my call list, and clicked on my dad's name. I waited until he picked up. "Bowie," he said. What's goin' on?"

"Dad," I said, staring at my boots. "We gotta problem."

Chapter Seven

Layla

Even though Saturday night I'd prayed for rain and wind, Sunday morning dawned warm and sunny.

I woke up at six thirty being shaken by my daughter, who was so excited for the club barbeque that she'd already been awake for an hour.

I dragged myself out of bed, made breakfast for Sunny, then sat bleary-eyed at the kitchen table, staring into a big mug of coffee.

Nine A.M. and three cups of coffee later, Sunny was sashaying between her bedroom and the kitchen like a mini supermodel, and I was helping her pick out her outfit.

One pink frilly adorable bikini and a matching playsuit later, she was happy. But I was stressing the hell out.

"What are you wearing?" I demanded down the phone to Cara.

"My new red two-piece, shorts, and a tee. I have a new black two-piece. Wanna borrow it?"

I felt like punching the air. "Yes, please."

The problem with being a single mom with no money was that every spare dollar went on clothes for Sunny, not me. Because of that, my wardrobe was extremely limited.

"I'll come earlier." Cara laughed. "That way, you can put it on under your clothes before we leave."

My brow furrowed. "Are you sure you want to come with us?"

There were a few seconds of silence before Cara spoke. "Yeah, John said I'm always welcome at the clubhouse, and I've missed the guys and Freya."

"She seems nice, right?" I questioned.

"Freya's really great. You'll get on with her, and Sunny will love the barbeque. Their family days are the best." Cara cleared her throat. "All that time I was with Xan, I didn't know about your connection to the Stone family. It's so weird that it never came up."

"Right," I agreed. "But if I didn't know about it, how were you meant to?"

"I never mentioned your name to anyone at the time," she mused. "Never really thought to."

"It's okay. You and Xan hardly came up for air anyway, so you probably didn't get the opportunity."

Awkward silence screamed down the phone.

Foot meet mouth.

I could have cried for my friend. She always insisted that she'd moved on from Xander, but I wasn't sure. While he was in prison, it was a case of out of sight, out of mind, but he wouldn't be locked up forever.

"Sorry, Cara," I murmured.

"Stop, it's fine," she said a little too brightly. "Water under the bridge. I'm getting married next month. Xander's in the past."

"You sure you're okay?"

"Of course. Anyway, I've got to go see my mom and dad before I pick you up. I'll get to you about one-ish. Okay?"

"Cool, see you later."

After we hung up, I wandered back to my room and stared critically inside the wardrobe.

Bowie

Luckily, I was around about the same size as I was at eighteen. Likely because the food I bought was put on the table to make sure that Sunny never went hungry. I got what was left over, but not for much longer.

My stomach leaped excitedly.

I started my new job the next day. More money meant no more going hungry, new clothes, and, more importantly, I wouldn't have to put up with Mrs. Barrington's snippy remarks.

My eyes rested on a pair of cut-off denim shorts and an old Pink Floyd band tee I hadn't worn in years.

I pulled them out of the wardrobe and held them up against my body as I scrutinized myself in the mirror and wondered. What exactly did a girl wear to a biker barbeque?

A few hours later, Cara, Sunny, and I pulled up outside the Speed Demon's clubhouse. Cara and I got out of the front and slammed our doors closed. I turned and waved to the young guy who opened the gate and let us inside the compound.

"It hasn't changed a bit." Cara sighed.

I looked at the massive old warehouse.

It was the length of half a football pitch and fifteen meters high, spanning two floors. The sun reflected off the whitewashed brick walls so brightly that I had to shield my eyes.

I turned to the back of Cara's jeep, opened the back door, unstrapped the kid's seat, and pulled Sunny out. She wriggled her little legs until I set her down on her feet.

"Wow!" she gasped as she gazed up at the building.

At that moment, one of the big wooden double doors flew open, and Freya ran outside.

"Hi!" she exclaimed, then her eyes darted to the woman beside me, and her hand flew to her mouth.

Cara gave a low wave and a huge dazzling smile. "Hi," she breathed.

Freya flew at my friend. Within seconds, the two women were hugging and laughing. "I've missed you so much," Freya cried.

"Missed you too," Cara whispered.

Freya dropped her arms, shot me a smile, and crouched down to Sunny. "Hey. How's my favorite five-year-old?" she inquired.

Sunny jumped and down on the spot. "Where's the bouncy house, please?" she asked excitedly.

Freya laughed and nodded her head towards the clubhouse. "This way. Come on." She linked arms with Cara and me as we made our way to the doors leading inside.

The thought of seeing Bowie made my throat tighten. I tried to resist the urge to play with the hem of my shorts as nerves began to rise. My eyes darted around inconspicuously, trying to hide that I was looking out for him.

The problem was, if I wanted to get to know my godfather and give Sunny any semblance of a family, I had to suck it up and remember that having John and Freya in our lives didn't mean I had to be around Bowie.

The inside of the warehouse was dark, not a dingy dark, but a cozy dark. A bar ran the entire length of one wall. The room was empty apart from two men wearing Speed Demon MC cuts, watching soccer on the giant TV mounted on a wall.

"This way," Freya said. She led us to the far end of the room and through a door. We entered a massive industrial kitchen and were met by two women prepping food. They looked up from what they were doing and smiled big.

I liked them immediately.

A beautiful older lady with long grey hair stepped toward us and grinned over my shoulder at Cara. "Nice to see you home at last," she said.

I looked on astonished as Cara swiped at her eyes and walked straight into the lady's open arms. My chest got tight. My heart squeezed at my friend's heartache.

With Xander came a club full of family who she loved. When she ended things with him, she had to cut everyone else off, too. It was the only way she could get a clean break.

Then, when Cara started seeing Robbie, she stayed away. It was awkward because it was his word that put her ex away.

"I'm sorry," my friend whispered into the lady's shoulder.

"Nothin' to be sorry for," the lady soothed as she pulled away and looked into Cara's face. "You're home now. That's all that matters."

Her eyes swung to me, then down to Sunny, who clutched my legs shyly. "Well, who have we got here?" the lady asked. She smiled down at my girl, then held her hand out to me. "I'm Iris, Abe's ol' lady."

I gave her a puzzled look. She wasn't old. She didn't look a day over fifty. "Old lady?" I questioned as I gave her hand a shake.

Iris let out a hoot. "It's what these bikers call their significant others. It's a term of endearment."

Another lady stepped forward. "You'll get used to it. Nice to meet you. I'm Rosie, Atlas' sister."

"Atlas?"

"The club's Sergeant at Arms. Big guy, tattoos," she explained. "You'll know who he is when you see him."

"Amen," sang Iris. She crouched down to greet Sunny, who was clinging to me now. "Well, look at this pretty little thing." She winked. "And what's your name?"

My girl hid behind my legs. "Sunny Hope Hardin," she mumbled sweetly.

Iris blinked. "Sunny day Hardin?" she teased.

"No, Sunny *Hope* Hardin."

"Well, Sunny Hope, why don't I take you outside to meet Rosie's kids? She's got a daughter, Maddie, who's around your age."

"Really?" Sunny said hopefully before turning her wide eyes on me. "Mama. Can I, please?"

I nodded. "Be careful of the pool. No swimming until I come out."

Iris let out a snort. "Don't worry about that; we've got a Prospect babysitting the hellions."

Iris took Sunny's hand and walked through a set of French doors.

I followed them to the threshold, then looked outside and gasped.

The enormous built-in pool, the funfair-sized bounce house, and the lawn games were Sunny's paradise.

I noticed a few kids sitting down on the grass, being supervised by a young guy wearing a cut. Iris approached him with my girl.

"Will she be okay?" I fretted as I watched Iris it Sunny next to another little girl, then began to make her way back.

"Sparky's got them," Freya said. "He'll probably pass out from exhaustion by sundown, but he's good with kids."

Iris stepped back into the kitchen. I swallowed a gulp as she leveled me with a curious stare. "So, you're the one who's got Bowie chasing his tail, huh?"

My stomach did a backflip, then another. My hand pressed down on it.

I thought back to that night and his dismissive, angry look. No way would that man be chasing anything because of me. She must have got me confused with someone else.

Bowie

I looked to Cara, who lifted one shoulder in a shrug, then to Freya, who was shaking her head and smirking.

"I—I think you're mistaken," I stammered.

"You're Layla, right?"

I gave her a confused nod.

"They said you were pretty, but they didn't say you were gorgeous," she muttered to herself. "No wonder he's mooching around like his tackle fell off."

Freya and Rosie looked at each other and began to laugh. Cara raised her hand to her mouth and snickered.

I blushed scarlet. "I-I-don't thi-" I began to say, then my voice trailed off as heavy footsteps sounded from the bar.

A deep voice rumbled. "Cara!"

My head swiveled round to see a man appear in the doorway.

"John," Cara said, eyes shining.

He walked over and gave her a tight bear hug. "Good to see you, darlin'," he rasped into her hair.

I hadn't seen John Stone around in a while but recognized him immediately. He was over six feet, muscled with salt and pepper hair and the same golden-brown eyes as Bowie. All four of his offspring had the look of their dad.

People said I also had my father's grey eyes and reddish-brown hair.

My chest twinged with a yearning to hug my dad like that. I looked down, blinking furiously at the tears that burned my eyes.

John released Cara and looked straight at me. Shock flashed across his face as his eyes flicked over my features. "Jesus, Layla. If your dad could see you," he rasped.

The twinge in my chest turned into a searing ache. I cleared my throat to push away the tears clogging my throat. "Hi," I mumbled with a weak smile.

John's footsteps clomped on the tiled floor as he approached me. "Happy to have you here, darlin'," he said quietly. "I'm sorry it wasn't sooner."

I looked up into his earnest brown eyes. "Thank you," I replied.

John took me in for another minute, then pulled me into his arms. "We'll sit down later and have a good chat," he mumbled into my hair. "Okay?"

I murmured my agreement.

He reluctantly let me go, then turned to Iris. "Need some help takin' the food out?"

"Yeah." She nodded. "Send 'em through. We're ready."

John went to the door and put two fingers in his mouth. An ear-splitting whistle ruptured the air. Within seconds, big, burly men in Speed Demon cuts filed into the kitchen from outside, picked up covered dishes and trays, and carried them outside.

"C'mon ladies," Iris said as she nodded toward the garden. "We've done our bit. It's time to relax and let the men do some work."

The other woman and I walked outside together and then went over to a cluster of picnic benches at the side of the clubhouse. A gazebo had been set up right next to the seating area, with men milling around outside, wearing an array of shorts, jeans, and wifebeaters.

Rosie's eyes wandered over to a group of guys wearing shorts; some of their chests were bare. She let out a loud sigh. "I love family day," she said, holding her sunglasses down her nose to see better.

"Eeww," Freya replied as her face twisted in disgust.

"Frey, you may look at these fine men as family, but I don't," Rosie retorted. "Now, leave me alone to look at the scenery, please."

Freya huffed.

Cara laughed.

Rosie pushed her sunglasses back up and began to ogle discretely.

I turned toward the play area to make sure Sunny was okay. She was as happy as a pig in mud as she ran around the grass, squealing with a boy chasing her around.

"She's as pretty as her momma," a rich voice sounded beside me. I turned quickly and was met with a good-looking guy around my age who looked a little like John. I did a double-take.

Kit Stone.

He was tall, dark, and handsome, with a lopsided grin that made the girls of Hambleton swoon. I'd heard his road name was Breaker because of the sheer number of women whose hearts he'd shattered.

Kit directed that famous one-sided grin directly at me. I couldn't help but smile at his flirtatious smirk. He had a relaxed vibe about him that I liked, but strangely, he didn't make my pulse race, not like his brother.

Kit looked over my shoulder. Without warning, he threw his arm around my shoulder and pulled me hard into his bare chest.

I froze in panic.

"Just go with it," he grunted in my ear.

I squirmed a little. "What?"

"Trust me."

He turned us both to the side and then announced in a loud voice, "I think I've found what I'm gonna snack on today,"

Everyone in the vicinity turned toward us.

My face must have burned bright red. If I could've grabbed my Sunny and ran home, you wouldn't have seen us for dust.

I stared around helplessly. Freya quirked a perfect eyebrow at Kit, then she fixated on something over my shoulder and beamed.

Cara's eyes flicked to Kit, me, and behind my shoulder. A wide grin spread across her face, then she brought a hand to her mouth to hide her smile.

Suddenly, someone growled, and a deep, angry voice demanded, "Get your fuckin' hands off her, asshole," from behind me.

I stilled. My heart began to beat so hard and fast it bounced off my ribs. The hairs on my arms stood up as the air crackled around me.

My mind began to reel. No, no, no, no.

Kit craned his neck. "Don't start your shit with me," he barked.

I closed my eyes and prayed to God to give me the power of invisibility. But the big man wasn't listening to me that day, like usual.

A tendril of fire flickered to life in my stomach. My back straightened at the same time as Kit's strong muscled arm tightened around me. Then he swung us both to face the man at our backs.

I gazed up into liquid gold eyes, which were as turbulent as an electric storm. They locked with mine.

My insides went from dismayed to annoyed as he scrunched his eyebrows at Kit and me.

Why was Bowie acting like this? He made his feelings about me very clear. He had no right to behave like I'd somehow wronged him.

My mind suddenly cleared. I knew I had to get through this day without any bad feelings. I racked up a bright smile and did the only thing I could think of, taking the testosterone level down a notch.

I greeted the beautiful asshole in front of me in a voice as sweet as a gumdrop while acting like he was my long-lost friend and sang, "Hi, Bowie."

Chapter Eight

Bowie

My hands clenched into fists. If there weren't kids around, I'd have yanked my brother away from Layla's side, then punched the smug little shit in the face.

My breath sawed in and out. "Get your fuckin' hands off her," I grunted.

Kit's eyes darted between us. He even had the fuckin' audacity to pull Layla closer.

Steam must've come outta my ears 'cause then, the bastard kissed her forehead, the exact same spot where I'd kissed her a week ago.

I closed my eyes to block out the sight of it. When I opened them again, I had to forcibly stop myself from losing my shit.

Kit smirked and quirked an eyebrow. What ya gonna do about it? His eyes challenged me.

Gonna fuck you up is what I'm gonna do about it, my stare promised back.

My sister bounced over and pulled Layla out of Kit's arms, the same arms I wanted to twist until they snapped clean off.

Asshole.

"Now, now, boys," Freya sassed. "Flex your pathetic muscles somewhere else. Us ladies stopped getting swoony over caveman antics about ten-thousand years ago."

"Speak for yourself," Rosie muttered from somewhere behind her.

"Amen, sister," Iris agreed.

Layla gazed up at me with those spectacular grey, doe eyes, and my mouth went dry.

"I-I-I'm just going to check on Sunny," she stuttered in her sweet voice.

My cock twitched.

"I'll go with you," Kit said, his wink directed at me.

A deep growl rose through my chest.

"Kit. Stop winding your brother up," Dad shouted from the gazebo.

"Absolute idiots," Freya said as she clomped over to where me and Kit were arguing.

Kit faced her off. "Not."

"Are too."

"Not," Kit bandied.

I turned my head to look back at Layla, and my gut jumped.

She wasn't there.

My head immediately swiveled around to see her walking arm-in-arm toward the play area with Cara. I bit back a groan as her tight little backside bounced seductively with every step.

My mouth watered.

"That's one fine ass," Kit blew out from beside me.

Anger flared and then erupted. I whipped around and shot my fist into my brother's face. He landed hard on his back. I followed him down and punched him a second time.

Hands grabbed at my shoulders from behind and hauled me up.

"Knock it off," Dad shouted. "You know the rules. No fightin' around the kids." He pushed me away by the collar of my tee, then stared at me at the same time as he gestured toward Kit. "He's doin' it on purpose. Ya fuckin' clown."

My little brother got to his feet. He raised his hand and swiped at the blood oozing from the cut on his lip with a flourish. "It's too easy," he said in an amused voice.

Simmering anger scalded my insides. "Don't you touch her like that again," I snapped.

"Sorry, bro. Didn't realize that the big, bad Bowie Stone had fallen for the pretty little mama."

I lurched for him again, my face twisted in anger.

"Bowie!" Dad bellowed in my ear as he dragged me backward. His eyes darted between me and my asshole brother. "If you can't act like grown fuckin' men, get gone."

Everyone stood silent, watchin' in amusement. People say women love drama, but these asshole bikers loved it more.

Colt had his head cocked to one side as he looked at Freya. Atlas was starin' at me, lips twitching. Drix and Ice were both looking at me too, but with thoughtful expressions. The rest of the brothers were quietly watchin' the show, muttering to each other.

A hand rested on my back.

I glanced down to see Iris with a soothing look on her face. "Ignore him, son," she said quietly. "She's not interested in him."

"Gimme one night, and she'll be into me. Guaranteed," Kit boasted.

My head snapped back toward him, glaring a promise of murder.

"This is why we can't have nice things," Iris gritted through her teeth.

Kit barked out a laugh.

"Incoming." Drix's voice rang out.

I turned to see Layla and Cara making their way back over toward us. Big Layla was clutching the hand of a cute little mini-Layla.

My heart swelled as mother and daughter looked at each other and smiled, the same way it did when I saw them together when I was sittin' in my truck.

Just like then, I couldn't tear my eyes away.

"You boys, behave," Dad ordered under his breath so that only me and Kit could hear. "Or I'll kick both of your fuckin' asses."

Rosie beckoned Layla, her daughter, and Cara over to the bench where she was sitting. My heart sunk as Layla's eyes caught mine, then immediately darted away.

I knew I'd been a dick to her that night, but how was I meant to make it up to her when she wouldn't even look at me? I rubbed at the ache of disappointment in my chest.

Dad had crouched down and was smiling at her kid. "Who's this little lady?" he asked.

"Sunshine Hope Hardin," mini-Layla beamed.

Dad took her little hand in his and gave it a gentle shake. "Nice to meet you, Sunshine, my name's John. I'm your momma's godfather."

Sunshine's eyes went big as saucers. "Does that mean that you're my Goddaddy too?" She breathed excitedly.

A chuckle went up. Dad threw back his head and let out a deep hooting laugh, and looked back at the little girl. "If that's what you want, darlin'."

She nodded enthusiastically. I watched Dad melt on the spot. She threw her arms around his neck, hugged him, then ran for her mom, who was now sitting at the picnic table with the other women.

A multitude of sensations hit me as my eyes locked onto her again.

Bowie

Dad stood slowly and clapped me on the shoulder. His eyes turned soft as he looked at the mini-Layla. "Make it right, Bowie," he ordered in a low voice.

I couldn't help gazing over at her and wondering what the hell I was thinking when I fucked her over the week before.

Layla was sipping a soda and talking to the women. Her kid was sitting on her lap and cuddling into her lovingly. My previous anger evaporated into thin air.

My woman was fuckin' beautiful. Her chestnut hair fell in waves down her back. Black shorts clung to tanned, shapely legs, and the cool as fuck vintage Floyd tee had slipped down one shoulder, showing the tie of a black bikini top.

Goddamned perfect.

My insides knotted so severely that I had to look away. I turned to my dad and jerked my head in a nod.

As I watched Layla with her little girl, I knew deep down that it was time to move forward. She brought out a yearning in me that I couldn't ignore.

"Consider it done," I vowed.

Hours later, everybody was fed and watered.

The music got turned up to blast a while ago, so most people were up dancing.

I was sittin' down at the picnic tables, still unable to drag my eyes away from Layla, who was being spun around by Atlas.

Dad and Cara were also kicking up their heels, along with Drix and Rosie.

Abe and Iris were slow dancing next to them in their own world. Every time I saw those two together, my chest gave a jolt.

They'd been in love for thirty-five years and were as much into each other now as they were the day they'd gotten married.

When I was younger, I used to think that I'd get that, but just when I thought I could reach out and touch it with my fingertips, it was ripped away from me.

A memory played in my head of rubbing a pregnant belly while laughter tinkled out around me. Then the edges of my flashback darkened as Samantha's unseeing blue eyes stared vacantly at nothing.

A wash of grief flowed through my chest.

I had to close my eyes so I could breathe through the familiar ache. Then I felt a tiny hand slip into mine, turning the ache into a tidal wave of warmth.

My head tilted down. Layla's little girl had climbed into the seat next to me.

Her innocent grey eyes blinked up at me with concern. "Why are you sad?" she asked gently. "'Cause my mama said, if someone's feeling sad, we should give them a hug."

My eyes darted back to the dance floor. My throat closed when I saw Kit swinging Layla around the dance floor. "Your mom won't dance with me," I muttered as I pushed the irritation down.

Sunny pulled on my hand. "Did you ask?"

"No."

"Then, of course she won't dance with you, silly. You has to ask."

I glanced down at the little girl. "She still wouldn't."

Sunny cocked her head, deep in thought. "My mama said that she thought you liked her, but then she said she was wrong."

"How do you know that?" I asked, disbelief lacing my tone.

"I heard her telling Auntie Cara," she admitted. "She thought I was playing in my room, but—" She turned her little body to face me. "Do you loves my mama?"

Bowie

My gut went jittery. "Whoa, whoa, whoa, Princess, dunno 'bout love, but I like your mom."

She gave me a knowing look and tapped her finger on her chin. "Maybe you should buy her flowers. Ladies likes flowers."

I shrugged. It couldn't make things worse, and there was a florist in town.

"Mama's working at Miss Anna's tomorrow," she continued. "You should send them there, and then all the other ladies will say 'ooh' and 'aah,' and she has to kiss you."

My chest warmed at the thought of Layla's mouth on mine. *Flowers it is, then.*

I turned back to the dance floor and studied Kit and Layla as they danced. A flicker of jealousy lit me on fire as I watched them laughing like old friends.

Confusion gnawed at my insides. Even Sam hadn't brought out these emotions in me. The compulsion to storm over there and pull Layla away from my brother was visceral and very fuckin' unsettlin'.

Kit turned Layla, giving me her back, then his stare veered to mine. He looked over at me and jerked his head. Was he finally losing it?

My face twisted as his head jerked again. Was he having a goddamned fit?

Kit's head gestured again. What the fuck?

Frustration moved through his features, and his eyes bugged out. Understandin' began to dawn on me. I got to my feet, winked down at Sunny,

then swaggered over to the dance floor.

Kit rolled his eyes. Then before Layla could say, 'fuck off, Bowie,' he quickly and very smoothly spun her outta his arms and into mine.

"You're very fuckin' welcome, asshole," he muttered quietly, then turned and walked away.

Layla blinked up at me, looking dazed. "How did that happen?" she asked, as if to herself.

"Hey," I smirked.

Huge grey orbs flashed with confusion. "I think it's time for us to leave," she uttered in a small voice.

My arms tightened around her. "You can't go yet. Cara's enjoying herself."

"Sunny's got school in the morning, and I start my new job."

"Then I'll take you home."

Layla stumbled slightly.

I caught her and pulled her into me. She stared up, finally meeting my eyes, and what do ya know? My dick woke up. He yawned, raised his head, realized Layla's pussy was close, then stood, ready for action.

She gasped as she felt my hardness pressin' into her belly. Her eyes locked onto mine, and my heart took a nosedive when I saw hers were full of hurt.

I laced our fingers together. "Baby. Don't go yet."

She pulled our hands apart. "Why are you doing this?"

"Doing what?"

"Staring at me, getting close to Sunny, dancing with me, telling me you're taking us home. I can't keep up with your multiple personalities."

"Look, about last week. I'm sorry."

"Thank you for the apology, but it doesn't change anything."

Her words made my gut clench. "Baby, look—"

"—I'm not your baby."

"No," I agreed, lifting my finger to her chin and tilting her face to mine. I stared into those huge eyes. "You're my Doe."

Her eyes grew, and I noticed her lips twitching like she was trying to bite back a smile. Everything inside me lit up like a Christmas tree.

"That's sweet," she said. "But I just want us to be friends."

Fuck.

Bowie

My eyes flicked over her face, taking in every feature. I knew I had to lay my cards on the table and make her understand. "I wanna be more than friends."

"No, Bowie."

"C'mon, Doe."

"Bowie, stop."

"Ain't never gonna happen, baby."

She blew out an exasperated sigh.

I pulled her closer until we were joined chest to chest, grasping her gently by the hips and tugging her to me so she was pressed against my dick.

The heat from her body scalded mine. I bent my head and gently scraped my teeth along her neck. Her pheromones sent a direct hit to my cock. I couldn't help letting a low moan escape.

My lips smiled into her skin. I kissed her, open-mouthed, just below her ear. My dick almost punched a hole in my jeans as I felt her shiver in my arms.

"I have to take Sunny home," she whispered.

"I know, baby. But dance with me for another minute. Please?" Her back stiffened, and I knew I'd lost her.

I loosened my arms, allowing her to pull away, then I lost her heat as her body abandoned mine, and it was my turn to shiver.

She looked lost for a minute before turning toward the benches. Her shoulders relaxed when she saw her girl leaning against Cara, sound asleep.

"I need to get home," she said in a firm voice.

My hand snaked to hers in an attempt to touch her fingers. She pulled it away. I watched as she folded her arms across her chest. She may as well have just screamed at me to get the fuck away because the effect was the same.

"Let me take you and Sunny out tomorrow for dinner," I pleaded.

She wrapped her arms around herself. "No. It's her last couple of weeks before the summer break. Now I work at the salon, she has to get used to a new routine. That's a step too far."

"Okay, so we'll wait until school's out?"

Her mouth turned down. "I don't think so, Bowie."

"Doe. Say yes. Please."

She looked over every inch of my face. I held my breath, waiting for her to agree.

"I'm sorry, I can't."

Self-hate pounded through me. I'd really fucked up, hadn't I?

"Trust me," I gritted through clenched teeth.

The sad look she gave me made my shoulders slump, then she

murmured something that made me want to shoot my own dick off.

"You hurt me."

My gut turned over on itself. Guilt had been eating away at me ever since the night I'd sent her home, but right at that moment, the regret was overwhelming. Black curls of shame crept through my chest, tormenting me.

"Give me another chance," I begged,

Her eyes flicked over me again. She brought her hand up and touched my arm.

"I'm sorry," she said, then turned and walked away.

Dejection gnawed at me.

I watched her say a few words to Cara as she gently shook Sunny awake. I couldn't tear my eyes away from them.

A hand clasped my shoulder. "How'd it go?" Kit asked.

"She fuckin' hates me."

"Jesus, Bowie, stop being a prick. If she hated you, she wouldn't have just let you leech on her neck."

I lifted one shoulder. "She says she can't trust me and won't give me another chance."

Kit let out a snort. "So, take it."

"What?"

"Don't ask her for another chance. Take it."

I thought about that for a second.

"You know where she works. You have an in with her best friend. Her kid likes you. What more do you fuckin' need?"

I half listened to Kit as I watched Layla take Sunny in her arms and set off with Cara to the jeep. As much as it pained me to admit it, he made sense. We followed a distance behind as they took the shortcut around the side of the building, probably avoidin' the bustle of the ongoing party, for Sunny's sake, to reach the jeep.

How could I expect Layla to fall at my feet when all I'd done was act like a fuckboy? She was a mother. She needed someone she could lean on.

The problem was, I'd never really needed to be that way.

Didn't know how.

The only time I'd ever had to step up, things went South. Since then, I ran for the hills any time responsibility came knocking.

A small voice nagged at me that Layla and Sunny Hardin would be worth any man risking his heart and soul for.

I pulled back my shoulders, determination washing away Layla's rejection. "Alrighty then. Guess it's time to pull all the stops out."

"What the fuck are you planning?"

I continued staring as the cherry red jeep drove slowly outta the clubhouse gates, its wheels kicking up dust clouds from the road.

"Brother," I said with conviction. "By the time I'm finished, Layla Hardin's not gonna know what's hit her."

Chapter Nine

Layla

Customers bustled through the salon door the second we opened Monday morning.

I'd rushed to work as soon as I dropped Sunny off at school to find Anna waiting for me with a latte and a smile.

My stomach whooshed with nerves, which wasn't good, seeing as it was still churning from the things Bowie had whispered into my ear the night before.

I loved being at the club and meeting everyone. Sunny couldn't stop talking about what a great time she had. Everyone had been so cool and welcoming, and I'd even managed to ignore Bowie.

Then he danced with me, and I was torn.

My head knew I should tell him to take a hike, but my heart didn't get the memo because it thudded to life as soon as I was placed into his strong arms. Then, the instant he kissed my throat, my pussy thudded to life as well.

While he was saying those sweet words, good Layla sat on one shoulder, pursed her lips, gave him the finger, then gave him her back.

But on the opposite side, bad Layla couldn't give two hoots because she blew him a big kiss, then beckoned him with one finger.

A half-hour after the salon opened, I made coffee for some of the ladies in the small kitchen at the back of the salon. I was preparing the pot when the bell above the salon door let out a loud jingle.

Weird, there were no more appointments due for another hour.

A minute passed then Anna's voice drifted through to the kitchen, "Layla, there's a delivery here for you, honey."

A delivery? For me? I poked my head around the door, face twisted with surprise. "Huh?"

"Get out here," Anna called to me. "We wanna see who they're from."

"I have no idea what you're talking about," I called back as I finished setting up the pot of coffee.

Quickly, I washed my hands, then returned to my desk where Anna whispered with the other stylist, Tristan, and two regular customers, Mrs. Fenton, and Emmie Dixon.

I'd known Emmie for years. She also lived down near the creek. Sometimes she watched Sunny on the rare occasions I got stuck at work. I liked her. You knew where you stood with Emmie.

"What's going on?" I asked as my feet carried me across the room.

Everyone parted like the red sea to reveal a huge bouquet of white roses and orchids as I got to my desk.

Emmie looked over her round spectacles and pointed a bony finger at me. "You're a dark horse, Layla Hardin. Didn't know you had it in you, walking around town like butter wouldn't melt, and you've got some poor sap wrapped around your finger all that time."

My brow wrinkled in confusion as I looked at her. "What. Who—?"

"—It's always the quiet one you have to watch," Tristan teased. "Come on, open the card. I'm dying to know who sent them."

I gaped at the abundance of roses and orchids. "They're for me?"

"Yes, they're for you." Anna chuckled.

Excitement lit me up from the inside.

Nobody had ever sent me flowers before. I'd never had a boyfriend, I didn't date. I'd even missed my own prom.

My toes seemed to float as they transported me over to my desk. Heart racing, I traced a fingertip over a velvety white petal.

A small white envelope sat in the middle of the arrangement. I took it, slipped the card out, and turned it over.

I blinked in disbelief. My mouth dropped open in shock as the words on the card registered.

Doe. Give me another chance. Bowie. X

My heart swelled to the size of Texas.

I read the words again, just to make sure I wasn't dreaming, then a noise sounded from behind me. I sensed somebody at my back and jumped out of my skin as Anna shrieked, "Oh my God!"

"Don't deafen the poor girl, Anna," Mrs. Fenton snapped, "at least not before she's told us who he is."

"Who sent them, Lay—?" Emmie began to demand, but Anna cut her off by holding up her hand to ask for silence.

Worry flashed behind Anna's eyes. She turned me to face her. "What's going on, Layla? That boy doesn't seem your type."

Resentment fired in my belly, and I straightened defensively. "I don't have a type."

"Who?" Tristan demanded.

Anna's straight, white teeth worried her lip.

Emmie let out a huff. "Spit it out, Anna. Who sent them?"

Anna's face twisted, then, on a breath, she said, "Bowie Stone."

"Bowie Stone?" three voices repeated simultaneously as the salon door flew open, making the bell above the door tinkle cheerfully.

"What?" a deep voice demanded.

I spun around to see Bowie strolling toward me. He looked like every woman's fantasy in his worn black jeans, white tee, and leather jacket.

My skin heated as his eyes caught mine.

He smirked, lifting a hand to brush his thumb across his lip as he gave me a heavy stare.

My blood warmed. I'd never seen anything so hot in my life.

The look he gave me was so sensual that I had to clench my thighs together. My nipples puckered against the thin material of my tee.

Bowie's eyes flicked down to my breasts and back to my face. A huge grin spread across his sexy, kissable mouth.

Tristan fanned his face with his hand as his eyes swept over Bowie appreciatively.

"Come to stake your hot biker claim, honeybee?" he asked in a sultry voice. "'Cause if Layla won't play, I will."

Everyone quietened as they looked at Bowie expectantly.

He rubbed the back of his neck nervously as he looked at each person, "Anna. Can my girl take a quick break?" he asked, his eyes never leaving mine.

I looked around the room dazedly. "Erm. Maybe we should do this lat—"

"—Now," Bowie ordered in a low voice. He grabbed my elbow and guided me toward the door.

I glanced back to Anna, Tristan, and the two ladies. They were all whispering together. "B—But it's not my break time," I stuttered.

Mrs. Fenton stepped forward, "Do you kids need condoms?"

My eyes filled with horror. "Oh, my God. No," I cried out.

"Only joking." She chuckled as Tristan snickered.

Bowie laughed quietly as he pulled the handle and swept me outside.

The bell jangled as the door swung shut behind us. Suddenly, we were face to face, alone on the sidewalk.

Outrage flooded through me as I stared at him in disbelief. My hands turned to fists as I jabbed them against my hips. "It's my first day at my new job. You can't just waltz in and boss me around," I snapped, then I turned to walk back inside.

Bowie gripped hold of my hand to stop me.

I pulled it away, but he grabbed me again, but that time by my belt loop, then he tugged me into him.

"What are you doing?" I demanded. "You can't come in and... and... Ugh!" I threw my hands up by my sides in frustration.

His eyes turned liquid gold. "You like the flowers?"

"Well, yeah. Thank you, but that's not the point, Bowie. I asked you a question. What are you doing?"

Bowie snaked his fingers up my back, gripped my nape, and angled my face toward his as his head lowered. "I'm taking what's mine," he growled, tugging me roughly into him. Our bodies crashed together, then, before I could say a word, he kissed me right there on the street.

I was rooted to the spot, paralyzed with shock, all while his lips moved against mine.

At first, my mouth refused to give way to his, but then his tongue stroked along the seam so expertly that my lips parted of their own accord.

A soft sigh of defeat escaped me, and he smiled against my mouth.

Skilled fingertips brushed down my spine, then dipped gently into the curve above my ass. Tiny sparks followed everywhere he touched.

His mouth left mine and began to trail down my neck. I sucked in the air I'd been deprived of.

"It's still there, baby. Can you feel it?" he groaned the words into my skin, and my heart stuttered. My mind registered that they were almost identical to the ones he said to me that night in his bed, and my belly filled with discomfort.

Just as I was about to pull away, my ears pricked up at the squeal of car brakes. Bowie froze and slowly lifted his head, looking over his shoulder toward the road.

Car doors thudded shut. "Yo, Bowie," a rough voice clapped out. "I know you like 'em easy, but watch it with that one. She needs a baby daddy."

I stilled as anger stabbed at my chest.

I recognized that voice.

Bowie's entire body stiffened against mine. I could almost see the fury pounding off him in waves as he turned slowly and began to stalk toward two guys leaning against the sleek black car.

Robert Henderson the Fourth, known to us as Robbie, was the asshole that Cara was engaged to. Rich, arrogant, and entitled. Robbie only ever bothered with people who had money.

I avoided him like the plague. He always said snide, mean things to me, but only when Cara wasn't looking, of course.

Robbie held up his hands defensively as he shot me a cruel smirk.

The guy with him, Brett Stafford, pulled up straight. "Hey, Stone." He grinned. "No need to get physical. We're only fucking around." He looked over at me. "Hey, Layla," he shouted. "Tell your guard dog we're all friends, yeah?"

Before I could utter a word, Bowie had grabbed Brett by his shirt collar, lifted him with one arm, and slammed him back onto the hood of the shiny, black Porsche.

Blood rushed in my ears. "No, Bowie," I screeched, but it was too late. He had already spun toward Robbie.

A muscle ticked in Bowie's jaw. "You ever say shit like that about her again, and I'll fuckin' end you." The tone of his voice made me shiver.

"What you gonna do, Stone, punch me?" Robbie sneered. "Go on. I'll make sure you end up in the cell next to your fuckhead brother."

"You're a joke and a fuckin' coward. What you gonna do when Daddy ain't around to fight your battles?"

Robbie's eyes flashed.

"Stop it, please," I begged as the bell above the salon door tinkled noisily.

I turned to see Miss Anna come storming outside. Mrs. Fenton, Tristan, and Emmie's faces were all glued to the window.

"Step back, Bowie," Anna ordered. "You know he'll go running to the sheriff."

Robbie shot her a sneer.

She turned toward me, then gestured for me to go inside. I shook my head. "I'm not leaving him."

Robbie was a troublemaker. I wouldn't put it past him to go to the sheriff's office and lie to get Bowie arrested. I wasn't going to let that happen.

Bowie glared at Rob before shoving him hard against the car. Robbie stumbled but was able to right himself. He stood and rolled his shoulders.

Scott slid off the hood, then stood at the front passenger side as Robbie walked around to the driver's door. "You should watch what friends you make in this town, Miss Bouchard," he warned. "My dad could make your life very uncomfortable if you align yourself with the wrong... type."

Tears burned in my throat. I looked helplessly at Anna.

"Don't you threaten me, Robbie Henderson," she retorted. "I eat little boys like you for breakfast. Get in your daddy's car and drive it away from my salon before I call Mayor Henderson and tell him you've been acting the fool."

"Come on, Rob," Brett muttered weakly. "He'll keep."

Bowie let out a hoot and held his arms out to the sides. "Yo, asshole. I'll make it fair. I'll take you both on at the same time, 'kay?"

"Bowie!" Anna reprimanded. "Not helpful."

Car doors slammed closed, an engine purred to life, then the purr turned into a low growl as the car began to pull away.

Bowie pulled himself to his full height, stretched his arm up, and gave the men the finger as they sped down the street. The instant they were out of sight, he lowered his arm and turned to me.

"What the fuck, Doe?" He growled, eyes flashing with temper.

I looked at him dazedly. "What did I do?"

"Those assholes gave you shit, and you just took it." His voice was soft but laced with anger.

Anna let out an impatient snort. "She took Richard Allen's nonsense last week too. Her card was declined in the store, and he was a pig to her."

Fury slid across Bowie's face as his hands turned to fists.

I tried to swallow past the tears that were still threatening to fall. "It wasn't his fault," I insisted.

"Maybe not," Anna replied. "But he didn't have to be such an ass about it."

Bowie reached his hand out and took my fingers in his. "Woman," he growled. "Anyone gives you shit again, you come to me. Got it?"

Frustrated tears scalded my throat. I tried to swallow past them, but they burned so hot that I struggled to breathe. "What about when it's you?" I croaked.

Shock moved behind his eyes. "What?"

"What about when it's you giving me shit? Like now, coming into my place of work being all... pushy."

"Baby. I—"

The tears in my throat morphed into rage. "—Baby?" I shrieked. "I've told you. I'm not your baby."

"Doe—"

An angry noise jumped out of my throat, and my fists clenched at my sides. "Oh my God," I yelled furiously. You are the most infuriating man I've ever met."

Bowie brought his hand up to cover his grin. "You're fucking cute when you're mad, Doe."

"Ugh!"

He grabbed my hand, tugged me into him, and kissed the tip of my nose. "I'll be over at seven," he said softly. "Don't cook. I'll bring dinner."

I pulled out of his grip. Frustration made me throw my hands in the air. "What did I just say?" I shrieked.

He walked backward for a few steps grinning at me, then he threw me a wink, turned, and walked over to a big black and chrome Harley parked in front of the alley.

I stood fuming on the sidewalk, so angry that I couldn't think straight, never mind respond.

He swung a leg over the seat, grabbed a black helmet off the handlebars, and put it on. "You like Chinese food?" he asked, pulling the strap across his chin.

"It's her favorite," Anna yelled over.

"Anna—" I began, ready to chastise her, but Bowie interrupted by shouting, "Later, babe," over the bike's roar.

He jerked a sexy chin lift toward me, then pulled away. Goosebumps trailed down my arms.

Anna's eyes danced with humor while she watched Bowie ride down the street. "I like him," she announced.

"What just happened?" I asked, watching him turn a corner out of sight.

"You've just been Bowie'd." She laughed as we made our way toward the salon doors. "I think you're in trouble, Layla."

My heart skipped a beat. As much as Bowie frustrated me, I couldn't help welcoming the warmth that spread through me as I recalled how he'd just defended me.

My lips curved into a small smile, and I shook my head, "I think you're right."

Chapter Ten

Bowie

Fury seared through my chest as I watched the video play out.

After Anna's outburst earlier, I'd asked Colt to hack into Allen's security feed. Now me, Dad, Kit, Atlas, and Colt were sittin' in church watching my woman bein' treated worse than a fuckin' thief.

I looked on in disbelief as Richard Allen had the nerve to tell Layla to put her groceries back. Seconds later, I ground my teeth together and watched her tearfully flee the store.

My hands clenched into fists. If I'd seen Allen in that minute, I would've killed him.

Colt tapped his phone, and the feed went black. "That's everything," he said quietly.

Silence fell over the room. Then Dad hauled himself from his chair and stomped to the window. "When was this?" he demanded.

"Monday," Colt replied.

"How's she fixed now?"

I ran a hand down my face. "I've got her."

Dad spun to face me. "But have you, Son? 'Cause she deserves someone who's gonna step up for her. If you're gonna fuck around like you always do, walk away now, 'cause there are men in this club who'd jump at the chance to claim her."

Jealousy scored through me. I'd never been a possessive man, but the thought of one of my brothers touching my Layla riled me so much that my vision blurred.

"If anyone tries, I'll see 'em in the ring," I gritted out, "and after I've broken every bone in their face, you can have my patch. Get me?"

Dad turned. His eyes searched my face, and a slow grin spread over his features. "Never thought I'd see the day." He walked over, pulled me from my chair, and clapped me on the back. "You claimin' her at the table, Son?"

Atlas barked out a laugh. "Someone needs to let Layla in on the joke 'cause last time I looked, she couldn't fuckin' stand him."

A muscle ticked in my jaw as I looked back at my dad. "Yeah, I'm claimin' her." I pointed to Atlas. "But that asshole's right. I need to bring her around to the idea first."

Atlas bellowed out a laugh, and Kit snorted.

Dad's lips twitched, "Good luck with that, Bo," he said. "Gotta say, the good ones are worth the effort."

"I want front-row seats to this shit." Kit chuckled. The smile slid off his face as Pop grimly stared at him.

"Dunno why you're mouthin' off," Dad said sarcastically, "you're the biggest dog's dick in town. Any woman who takes you on needs to make sure her shots are up to date." He turned to Atlas. "And are you done now?" More sarcasm.

"Yup."

"Then get Abe in here."

"Why?"

"Want him to make inquiries about the club opening our own grocery store?"

Bowie

Satisfaction coursed through me. I fuckin' loved this side of Dad.

If anyone was stupid enough to mess with the Demons, they got our prez's wrath, which extended to our women and kids.

Layla belonged to me now. She also belonged to my dad, seein' as he was her godfather.

Allen was gonna learn the hard way. He was fucked.

"How many friends have we got on the town council?" Dad asked Colt.

"Five out of eight," our tech guy replied. "The only ones who'll put the kibosh on it are Henderson, Barrington, and maybe Tucker."

Atlas let out a grunt. "Don't worry 'bout Tucker. I'll deal with that fucknut."

Dad rubbed his beard. "We'll get Abe to draw up a proposal. We'll get it pushed through," he looked at me, eyes glinting. "I'll teach that fuck not to mess with what's ours."

Two hours later, I knocked on Layla's door.

I carried a box for Sunny in one hand and a massive bag of Chinese food in the other.

I heard a loud shriek from inside. "Mama, it's Bowie. Can I open the door?"

Little feet pitter-pattered up the hallway. Then the door cracked open. Big eyes and a cute button nose looked up at me. "Hi," Sunny breathed. She noticed the box wrapped in pink paper under my arm, and her eyes went big and round as she opened the door wide.

"Mama," she shouted, "Bowie's got presents," then she turned on her heel and raced down the hallway.

I held back a chuckle and stepped inside, wrangling the door closed behind me. I turned to look in the direction that mini-Layla had gone and followed.

As I made my way down the hall, I could hear Layla's voice. "I know, but Mr. Barrington told me someone paid it off Friday afternoon." A pause, then, "Barrington said it was anonymous. He has no idea."

I had to bite back another laugh.

I settled her loan last Friday. Now Barrington would never be able to take advantage of my woman again. I had a growing list of names who'd dared to fuck Layla over, and he was the next bastard to be dealt with.

The kitchen suited her. It was light, clean, bright, and homely. Sunny's drawings covered the fridge, held on by magnets, adding a splash of color to the predominately white room.

Layla was talking on the phone, sitting at a big white wooden table. She looked up as I walked in. "Cara. I've got to go. I'll call you tomorrow," she murmured.

She stood as I put the parcel and food on the table.

Layla gasped as I pulled her into me. My cock thickened as our bodies connected. She was so small and soft compared to me that my chest crawled with the need to protect her.

I lifted her chin with my index finger and looked into her shocked eyes. "Hi, baby," I crooned, softly brushing my lips against hers.

Footsteps sounded down the hall.

Layla stiffened and pulled away just as Sunny raced into the kitchen with a doll in each hand.

She saw me and her mom and ground to a halt. Her eyes darted to the table and back to us again at the same time as her breath puffed in and out.

"Barbie and Petal have come to see what Bowie brought."

Layla put her hands on her hips. "Sunshine!" she reprimanded.

Mini-Layla ducked her head. "Sorry," she said as she looked up at me through her eyelashes with those grey eyes, just like her mom's.

I fuckin' melted. At that moment, if she'd asked to go for a joyride on my Softail, I'd have handed over the keys like a damned fool.

I grabbed the gift, crouched on my haunches, and beckoned Sunny over. She sidled toward me and beamed a smile.

"This is for you," I gave her a serious look, "but you gotta be good for your mom. Get me?"

"Gets you." She nodded seriously. I handed her the parcel and stood back up.

"What do you say, Sunshine Hope Hardin?" Layla prompted.

"Thank you, Bowie," Sunny sang as she began to rip at the paper.

I turned to Layla. "Get the plates, babe, yeah?"

She looked at me briefly before her gaze dropped to Sunny. Her eyes got soft and dreamy as they took her girl in.

Sunny's tongue was sticking outta the side of her mouth in concentration as she tried to get into the parcel.

My hand skated to Layla's hip. "Plates, babe, yeah?"

She startled like I'd bought her out of a daze. "Right, plates," she said under her breath as she approached a cupboard.

An ear-piercing scream cut through the air.

Layla stilled.

I froze and braced as a five-year-old juggernaut threw herself at my legs. My eyes caught Sunny's to see her staring up at me with tear-filled grey eyes.

My heart dropped to my ass, horror swirling through my chest. I held up my hands, "Whoa, whoa, whoa," I said defensively, "what I do now?"

Sunny's cute, tear-stained face transformed into a picture of joy as she beamed a smile. "You gots me a

Switch," she squealed, turning to Layla. "Bowie gots me a Switch, Mama." She jumped up and down, letting out an excited squeal before throwing her arms up in the air.

Horror morphed into relief as Sunny plopped on the floor with her console, looking at the two games I'd also bought.

"I gots a princess game and the one with the funny hedgehog," she said sweetly, eyes full of excitement peering up at me.

My heart swelled with pride. I puffed my chest out, stared over at Layla, and winked. "Think she likes it."

Layla shook her head in disbelief. "They're a lot of money, Bowie," she said, biting her lip worriedly. "The games are expensive too."

She carried plates to the table before going to the fridge for a pitcher. Her movements were jerky like she was pissed.

Unease crept through my chest at the thought that I'd gone and fucked up again. I never really thought about the cash I laid out. I'd just asked one of the guys what his kids were into and went with that.

I didn't want Layla to think I was tryin'a buy Sunny's affection. I legit just wanted to do somethin' nice for the girl. The last thing I wanted was for Layla to feel pressured.

"It's okay; I'll get 'em for her for her birthday and Christmas," I reassured Layla, grabbing her hand and slowly turning her into me. "Is it okay? I didn't mean to overstep."

Her head turned back to Sunny, still sitting on the kitchen floor, looking at her gifts. "It's really generous," she said. "Sunny asked me for one, but I couldn't afford it, so really, I'm very grateful."

I rubbed the back of my neck, blowing out a relieved breath. My chest constricted with a rush of emotion.

Bowie

I looked down at Sunny, then at Layla, who watched her girl with a small smile hovering over her lips. My heart twisted as a sense of belonging fell over me.

I was already gone for this woman and the kid.

For years I thought I'd been running scared, pushing everyone away because after what happened last time, I'd convinced myself that I didn't want this.

But maybe that wasn't it at all. Maybe I just needed to find the right one or the right ones in Layla and Sunny's case.

Layla turned back toward me, her eyes almost accepting. She shot me a nervous smile. "Thank you, Bowie," she said quietly. "Thank you for everything."

My hand snaked across the table, and I laced her fingers with mine. Warmth flooded me from top to toe as I looked into Layla's eyes.

"You're welcome, Doe."

Chapter Eleven

Layla

"Hot biker alert."

I looked up from my computer. "Huh?"

"He said hot biker alert." Emmie cackled from her chair under the window.

I looked at Tristan, who peered out the salon windows onto the street. "Your honeybee's on his way in, and one of his hot biker buddies," he said gleefully. "And he looks like he means business."

Excitement tingled through me. Was Bowie here? Since Monday, more flowers had been delivered, along with stuffed animals and a box of luxury chocolates. Without thinking, I fluffed up my hair.

Never in my life had anyone paid me this much attention. The fact that it was Bowie, the man I'd loved since I was a girl, just made it more beautiful.

The bell over the door jingled. I looked up, my eyes immediately locking onto Bowie's. He did that thing where he stroked his lip with his thumb, and I nearly came on the spot.

"Yo, Layla," another voice grunted.

Dazed, I looked behind Bowie to his friend. This guy had long hair and a full beard. I'd seen him in town a lot. Once in the coffee house, he forgot his wallet. The previous owners threatened to call the police. I felt terrible for him, so I counted out the last of the money I had on me and paid.

He looked around the salon to see Emmie and Mrs. Fenton eyeing him appreciatively, then turned back to me. "Can I get a cut and a beard trim?"

Tristan came bounding over. "Sure," he exclaimed. His eyes went to Bowie. "Do you need Tristan, the hair god, to give you a little touch-up, too, Honeybee?"

Bowie gave him a sexy wink. "Not today, Tris. Just tagged along with Hendrix to see my girl."

"You're a good boy, Bowie Stone," Emmie called over.

"I try my best, Em," he replied, eyes never leaving mine. "Got time to get a coffee with me, Doe?" he asked at the same time as Anna walked back from the office.

"Yes, she does," she replied, sending me a disapproving look. "Layla hasn't taken her lunch break all week. Can you bring some back for us?" She turned and went over to her purse by her station.

"I got it," Bowie growled.

"Honeybee's got it," Tristan called out to the room as he sat Hendrix down at the basins.

"Caramel latte for me, Bowie," Mrs. Fenton ordered.

Emmie nodded. "Same for me."

Bowie held his hand out to me. "C'mon, Doe."

I stood and walked around the reception desk and turned to Anna. "Won't be long."

The walk down the street to the coffee house was quiet. Bowie's thumb kept stroking over mine as he gripped onto my hand.

My pulse was thrumming, my skin prickling with awareness. There was something about Bowie that affected me. There always had been.

"How's Sunny?" Bowie asked.

I smiled. "You only saw her last night."

Bowie

We passed the window of Magnolia's; he grinned as he grabbed the door and pulled. "Just wanna know how my Princess is doin'," he said as the door swung open.

I ducked under his arm and walked inside. "Sunny's fine. Still your number one fan," I threw over my shoulder.

He barked out a laugh behind me as I heard the door close. "That's what I'm talkin' about."

The customer who had just been standing at the counter walked over to a table. My eyes followed him, and I frowned when I saw Sydney, her sister Paris, and Brett Stafford's sister Serena all glaring at me.

"Fuck," Bowie muttered.

I looked up. "Are you okay?"

"Yeah," he replied. "I just fuckin' hate those bitches."

"Bowie." Sydney's voice rose up. "Why are you hanging with the trash? I'll keep you company if you're lonely."

My blood turned to ice, freezing in my veins. I felt my cheeks redden as humiliation made my throat catch. What was Sydney's problem with me? And what was Bowie going to think? Embarrassment burned through my cheeks.

Bowie let out a low growl, turning slowly. "Shut your bitch mouth." His voice was quiet, but the anger that laced it made my stomach twist. My stare shot up to see that his face was furious.

The coffee shop fell silent.

A low grunt emitted from Bowie's throat. "Talk about her like that again, and I'll make you wish you'd never been born. Do you fuckin' hear me?" Bowie's voice rang out clear, true, and absolute.

"But—"

"—I said, shut your mouth. There's nothin' you gotta say that I wanna hear."

You could cut the tension in the room with a knife.

I looked ahead, unseeing, wishing I was invisible.

"I think it's best you go, girls," another voice said. I peeked down the counter to see Magnolia, the owner, standing at the coffee machine, looking over at Sydney and her girls.

"I'm not going anywhere," a woman huffed. It sounded like Serena.

"Come on, Syd." Paris, that time. I couldn't forget her voice.

Chairs scraped, and footsteps scuffled across the wooden floor. I kept facing the counter, not wanting to see the hate I knew would be reflected in the girl's faces.

I held my breath until I heard the door open and closed. My shoulders relaxed as I let out the air I'd been holding.

Relief flowed through me.

I looked up at Bowie, a little awestruck. "Thank you," I whispered gratefully.

Liquid gold swirled down at me, thawing out the cold. "Don't let anyone talk down to you, Layla. You're better than them. No contest. You feel me?"

He gripped the back of his neck. "Got more fuckin' class in your pinkie than all those bitches put together. They bother you again. Tell me, got it?" His tone left no room for argument.

I beamed up at him, heart swelling and thudding with happiness. Nobody had ever stuck up for me before like that.

"Yeah, Bowie. I got it."

Chapter Twelve

Bowie

"I'm nearly there. Go inside and wait for me, baby," I rasped as I sped down the road in my truck.

"Okay," Layla's sweet voice sounded through the speaker. "I'll see you soon." The line went dead.

I looked through my windscreen at the car ahead of me, goin' no more than fifteen miles per hour. "Come on, what the hell is this? Drivin' Miss fuckin' Daisy?" I muttered, irritated as all hell.

It was the weekend after the barbeque, and in that week, I'd seen Layla nearly every day.

At first, she dug her heels in, but after the coffee shop incident, she seemed to thaw and finally agreed to a date. Now here I was, running late 'cause I was stuck behind this joker.

Fuck. My. Life.

I asked her if I could pick her up from her place—do it properly—but she said if Sunny heard me there, she'd never go to sleep.

Reluctantly, I agreed that she could meet me at the restaurant in town, but now I regretted letting Doe get her own way seein' as now I'd left her hangin'.

"Thank fuck for that," I snapped as the old Caddy finally turned off down a side street. Shakin' my head, I finally stepped on the gas.

A few minutes later, I pulled up fifty feet from the restaurant.

I parked, jumped down from my truck, and closed the door with a thud. The locks beeped, and I put my keys in my jeans pocket.

My gut jolted when I spotted Layla. She was up the street, standing outside Giovanni's with her head bowed.

Annoyance pounded through me. I didn't like the thought of Layla standin' out at night waitin' for my late ass.

"Thought I told you to wait for me inside," I called out as I approached her.

Layla kept her head down.

"Doe, what the fuck's goin' on?" I tipped her chin up with my finger and froze.

Her eyes were filled with tears.

Fury roared through my chest. What the hell happened? She was fine when I'd just spoken to her. I looked up and down the street to see if I could spot anyone suspicious, but it was deserted.

"Who upset you?" I demanded.

She quietly sniffed. "She wouldn't let me wait for you inside."

Anger must've pounded off me 'cause Layla winced. I took a calming breath. "What the fuck?" My voice was like death.

My girl wrapped her arms around her waist, and something cracked deep inside me.

She looked so lost.

I heaved out a breath, trying to calm the fuck down. The last thing I wanted was to upset Layla anymore.

I ducked my head and caught her eye. "Baby, tell me what happened."

"The hostess doesn't like me," she whispered.

My face twisted with surprise. Layla was the most likable person I'd ever fuckin' met. "Why?"

Bowie

"She has a son in the same class as Sunny. She and some other moms think I'm trash because I have a child, but I'm not married."

I wanted to punch a wall, but something in her tone stopped me from losing my shit. "Layla, it's not the nineteen-fifties. America's full of single moms and dads."

Her face fell. "I know, but it's only ever been me in Hambleton, and people can be awful."

My throat thickened. I reached down and took my girl's hand in mine. "Baby. Don't listen to their bullshit. You're a fuckin' queen."

She slowly looked up at me, eyes confused.

I lifted my hand and traced my fingers over her forehead, smoothing the frown lines. "You're fuckin' everythin', Layla. You work hard. You're a kick-ass mom. And you're sweet as fuckin' candy."

A small smile hovered over her lips. "You think so?"

"Baby. I goddamned know so." I tugged at her hand and pulled her toward the door. "C'mon."

Her mouth twisted with embarrassment. "Can we go somewhere else?"

"Nope. I'm sortin' this shit."

I grabbed the door, swung it open, and ushered my girl through it.

The air inside Giovanni's was cool. It was a nice place, exclusive and expensive. Personally, I thought it was a bit overrated. Still, I wanted to bring Layla here anyway 'cause I wanted to make her feel special.

And maybe I wanted to impress her just a bit.

A tall, dark-haired woman stood at a wooden podium. As I walked in behind Layla, her eyes flicked to me. She straightened her shoulders; the move pushed her tits out while her fake lips smiled at me seductively without even glancing at my woman.

"Good evening, Sir." Her eyes roamed my face. "Do you have a reservation?"

I gave Layla's hand a reassuring squeeze, then let it go while I leaned forward. "Yeah, sweetheart," I said, flashing her a smile, "but can I speak to Giovanni first?"

Triumph flashed through her eyes, "Of course. What name shall I say?"

"Bowie Stone."

"Wait here, Sir," she said breathily.

I nearly gagged at the cloud of the strong perfume that hit my nostrils. A shudder ran through me as she set off toward the restaurant, swinging her ass.

The restaurant was busy; every table was occupied. The Barrington's were eating in silence over by the window.

On the table next to theirs, Robert Henderson Senior and his wife, Elise, were sipping wine and chatting.

Elise looked up and smiled.

I nodded a greetin'. Nice lady. Shame about her fucknut husband.

I led Layla over to the bar, my eyes narrowing when I noticed Rob Junior on a stool at the far end. He was talkin' to Serena Stafford.

Serena glared at me and whispered something to Rob. He looked over, his eyes hardening.

I smirked and gave him a cocky finger wave.

The main doors opened, and in walked his sidekick, Brett Stafford. His lips thinned when he saw me, and he made his way over to Robbie.

Good, a full house. The perfect time to make a statement.

Layla was mine, and from now on, this town would treat her with some fuckin' respect.

"Sit," I ordered, gently taking her elbow and helping her onto a stool.

"What are you going to do?" she asked, biting her lip nervously.

I stroked a finger over her cheek. "Somethin' I should've done two fuckin' weeks ago."

Bowie

"Bowie!" a loud voice boomed from behind me. I turned to see Giovanni, the owner, make his way over.

I held out my hand. "Good to see ya, Gio."

Giovanni grabbed my head and shook it eagerly. "Are you eating with us tonight?"

"Yup," I replied. "But I got a problem." I helped Layla off the stool and wrapped my arm around her shoulders. "Was runnin' late, so I told my girl to come inside and wait."

Gio smiled down at Layla. "Of course. She's welcome."

"Welcome, is she?" I said, voice loud so everyone could hear. "So why did that stuck-up bitch ass hostess throw her out?"

Giovanni's face fell as silence fell over the restaurant.

The Demons had a lot of investments in town and further afield. Eight years ago, when Giovanni opened this joint, he needed backers, and guess who stepped up. Yup. The Speed Demons were the proud owners of fifty percent of this fine establishment.

"Fire. Her," I stabbed out the words, voice unyielding.

Layla coughed quietly from beside me.

"She's my niece," Giovani said quietly.

I ducked my head and stared at Gio so he knew I wasn't fuckin' around. "Don't. Give. A. Fuck."

"Bowie—" Layla began. I held up my hand, and her voice trailed off.

"Couldn't care less if she was the Queen of fuckin' England, Gio," I snapped. "She's bad for business."

His shoulders slumped, then he looked over back over his shoulder. "Giana," he bellowed.

The bitch came walkin' over, hips swayin'. "Yes, Uncle?"

"Why did you turn this woman away?"

She looked at Layla. "W—W—Well…" she stuttered, lost for words.

"I've told you about this," Giovanni hissed.

"Uncle, I—"

He slashed his hand through the air. "You cannot treat customers this way, Giana. I have to let you go."

Her lips pursed.

"Get your things and go home. I'll see you tomorrow."

Triumph flowed through me, makin' my lips tip up in a satisfied smile. My arm snaked around Layla's shoulders. A public claiming.

Her eyes narrowed at Layla. "This is your fault," she spat accusingly.

My girl froze like she was rooted to the floor.

Possession roared through me. I pulled Layla behind me to shield her. My feet stepped forward of their own accord, and the woman shrank back. "No, bitch. It's your fuckin' fault. What did she ever do to you?"

I straightened and glared around the room.

It was Saturday night. Every stuck-up asshole in this town was here. It seemed like the perfect time to lay down the law.

"Layla Hardin is my woman," I announced. "John Stone's her godfather. That means she and her daughter are protected by the Speed Demons." My face twisted with a silent threat. "Anyone who gives them shit from now on will answer to me."

I turned and looked down at Layla. My heart bounced in my chest when she gazed up at me with huge, shining eyes.

"Hungry, babe?" I asked gently.

She let out a half laugh, half sob, and nodded.

I looked at Gio. "Is our table ready?"

He grinned. "Yes, tonight it's with my compliments." He looked gently at Layla. "My apologies, Layla. In Giovanni's, you are always welcome."

She beamed at him.

We followed Giovanni through the restaurant to our table. I felt a tug on my sleeve. I glanced down to see my girl staring up at me with adoration.

I swear the bottom fell outta my world.

She was fuckin' killing me.

"Thank you, Bowie," she whispered.

I puffed my chest out, a lion defending his lioness. Pride swirled through my blood, along with a sense of rightness.

A thumb came up to rub my lip, and Layla's eyes went soft.

"Anytime, Doe," I murmured. "Anytime."

Chapter Thirteen

Layla

"We're just friends," I insisted.

Cara looked at the twelve red roses on my reception desk and turned back at me. "Never had a friend send me a dozen of them before," she murmured.

"Girl, you ain't seen nothin'," Tristan said as he sprayed Mrs. Fenton's hair. "Last week, it was white roses and orchids, a stuffed toy, chocolates, and a date at Giovanni's. This week orchids, cupcakes, and lilies." He hooted out a laugh. "He should have shares in *Blooms*, the amount of dough he must've laid out this week alone."

"Friends, my ass," Emmie muttered from her chair by the window. "How many times was he at your place last week?"

"Six out of seven," Tristan crowed.

Emmie looked at me knowingly. "And this week?"

I bit my lip. "Umm, twice."

"And it's only Thursday now," Mrs. Fenton butted in. "Protest all you want, Layla Hardin, but we know better."

"He won't be over anymore this week," I protested. "He left for Colorado this morning. He won't be back until the weekend."

Tristan hooted out a laugh. "Expect your phone to blow up, girlfriend. That boy's a smitten little honeybee."

My cheeks heated. "Oh, my God. Stop." I rolled my eyes at Cara, who shook her head, smiling.

It had been nearly two weeks of bliss.

After Bowie's speech at Giovanni's, I invited him in for coffee and made out with him on my couch for an hour.

His relentless pursuit of me, and his kindness to Sunny, had already made me half forgive him. After he had my back in Magnolia's and the restaurant, I couldn't lie to myself anymore.

We were much more than friends, but I wanted to keep him to myself for a while.

Anna walked through from the kitchen. "Leave her alone. If she says they're friends, then they're just friends."

Mrs. Fenton twisted her head slowly and grinned at me. "You must be those friends with benefits that I keep hearing about?"

My cheeks went from warm to burning. I covered my ears with my hands. "La la la la la," I sang, trying to block out Mrs. Fenton's words.

"What's that?" Emmie called over to her.

"It's what the young'uns say nowadays when they want a roll in the hay without getting wed."

Emmie snorted. "Well, Bowie must like Layla's hay. The man's gone gaga." She turned to me again. "Does Bowie like your hay, Layla?"

My eyes bugged out at Cara. "Help," I mouthed.

She grinned, then got up from her chair next to me. "Sorry. Lunchbreak's over. I have to go." The bell over the door tinkled as it swung closed behind her.

Mrs. Fenton watched Cara walk down the street. "Did you tell her what that idiot man of hers did last week?" she asked.

I shook my head. How could I tell Cara what Robbie said to me? I didn't want to get in the middle of their relationship, and he'd just laugh it off as a joke like he usually did. This wasn't my first rodeo with him.

"Bowie will handle it," Anna reassured her. "Now he knows what's going on. He'll look after our girl."

My stomach went warm and fuzzy.

Tristan fanned his face. "That man is fine," he said in a low voice. He turned to me. "Are you going to go with him on Saturday?"

Bowie told me last night that some of the club members were hitting the bars in town for Freya's birthday. He asked if I'd go with him, well, more like told me I was.

A pang of disappointment hit my belly. "I don't think so. I haven't got a sitter, I don't have anything to wear, and I don't want to blow my first paycheck in one night."

"I'll sit with Sunshine," Emmie offered.

"I know. Thank you, Emmie," I said. "But I'll be late home, and I don't want you out past midnight."

Emmie nodded. "Fact is, I'm usually snoring by ten these days anyway. I can't seem to keep up."

I gave her a small smile. "Thanks for the offer."

"Well, if you do go out, you can come and raid my wardrobe," Anna said. She turned and looked me up and down. "I'm a size bigger than you, but I have some dresses that would still look good."

Defeat made my heart sink. There was no way I could go without a sitter. "Thanks, Anna, but I don't think it will happen."

"Bring 'em in tomorrow," Tristan ordered. "If I know anything about men, Layla's honeybee won't take no for an answer."

"I will," she replied. "They're too small for me now anyway, so you may as well have them."

Excitement washed over me. "Really?" I asked.

Anna shot me a huge smile. "Yes. Really."

Gratitude swelled in my chest. Anna had been so good to me. In a way, I was grateful for that day at Mr. Allen's store because if it hadn't happened, I'd still be cleaning the Barrington's house.

"I can't remember the last time I had something nice to wear, Anna," I mumbled. "Thank you."

Anna's eyes shone as she quickly turned back to her workstation and straightened her combs and brushes.

She cleared her throat. "What time's my next lady due?" she asked.

I opened the diary on the computer. When I saw who was next, my heart sank. Turning back to Anna, I murmured, "It's Sydney Barrington."

"In that case, it's time for me to go," Mrs. Fenton announced.

Emmie stood with her. "Me too," she said with a nod. "That girl makes my teeth itch."

Tristan looked up from his phone. "Is that friend of hers booked in for an appointment too?"

I checked the computer, and my heart sank further. "Yeah. Serena Stafford's with you at the same time."

"Please tell me it's not highlights," he pleaded. "Not today."

I bit back a smile. "No. Both of them are booked in for a blow-dry."

"Halle-fucking-lujah. There is a God," he muttered.

Emmie looked out of the window and grimaced. "Time to go, Clarice," she announced. "Let's go to the coffee house and see Magnolia." She grabbed her purse from the counter.

"Bye, y'all," Mrs. Fenton called out.

As they approached the door, it opened, and the bell jingled.

Sydney strutted inside with another blonde girl. Serena Stafford was Brett's sister. Their dad was the lawyer I used to work for before he fired me.

Sydney's eyes darted to me at reception, and she did a double take. Her footsteps faltered. "So, this is where our cleaner defected to," she said nastily, putting her hands on her hips. "You know I had to scrub my own bathr—"

"—Sydney," Anna interrupted. "Come sit here, and we'll make a start. We've got back-to-back appointments today."

I frowned, then clicked on the calendar to check. We only had four appointments this afternoon, and two of them were with Tristan.

I looked up at Anna, who led Sydney to the basins. She glanced at me over her shoulder, and her eyes went huge.

I smothered a laugh with my hand, then clicked on the accounts tab to pay some invoices.

The girls were chatting with each other while they were getting their hair washed. I was glad to be sitting behind reception because their conversation was so shallow that my eyes nearly popped out; I rolled them so hard.

Anna and Tristan finished at the basins and sat the girls in front of the mirrors.

"Are you going on Saturday?" Serena asked. "Sound like he's desperate to make everything up to you."

"We never really broke up," Sydney replied. "We just had a break."

Serena let out a low giggle. "When was the last time you—you know."

"Last night."

"Is that when he asked you to go out with him?"

"He's been asking me on a date for months," Syd shrugged. "I may throw him a bone. I mean, he's such a god in bed. Why wouldn't I?"

The girls giggled. I wondered exactly what kind of guy would fall for Sydney. She was a spoiled brat at the best of times. All she did was boast about how much her clothes cost and how her daddy would buy her anything she asked for.

Admittedly, having a decent car and nice clothes would be nice. Still, the satisfaction for me came from earning it myself, and that was exactly how I would raise Sunny too.

"What will his sister say if you crash her birthday drinks?" Serena continued. "You two don't get along, do you?"

My ears pricked up. *Birthday drinks?* My mind went to Freya.

"I can't stand her. She's the reason my guy wanted a break," Sydney replied nastily. "You think I care what that bitch thinks?"

I sat up straight and looked over at the girls. I saw Tristan give Anna a pointed stare. He glanced over at me. When he noticed me watching, he avoided my gaze and returned to Serena's hair.

"True." She shrugged. "But you know how protective Bowie is regarding his sister. He'll dump you if you upset her."

I froze.

Bowie?

The wires in my brain must have overloaded because I was sure Sydney said Bowie had asked her to go out on Saturday.

I retraced the conversation back from the beginning. As I played Sydney's words back, burning tears rushed up my throat.

She said they had sex last night. Okay, so she only implied it, but—

Bowie came over Monday and Tuesday night. He brought dinner, played with Sunny, and talked for a while. Both nights he kissed my cheek and left.

Yesterday he called and said he couldn't come over, that he had things to do. He also told me he was going to

Colorado to pick up Freya's furniture and he'd catch up with me on Saturday.

Had Bowie bumped into Sydney at some point and changed his mind? Or maybe, he was seeing both of us. It's not like he made me any promises.

Confusion tugged at my mind. After the coffee shop last week, I thought he didn't like her, but from what she'd said, it sounded like they had history.

I tried to swallow past the lump in my throat; I blinked furiously as my vision began to blur with tears. I had to keep it together until tonight when Sunny slept; I could break then.

I looked unseeingly at the roses on my desk. When the guy from *Blooms* delivered them this morning, he said they represented love. Now all they represented was betrayal.

Anguish hijacked my chest as memories of Tuesday played through my mind.

Before Sunny went to bed, he came over to show her how to play her console.

When she finally slept, I grabbed some drinks, then we went out back and looked up at the stars.

He'd pulled me onto his lap and wrapped a blanket around me. His fingers left mine, and he turned my face to his. "I'm fallin' for you, Layla," he'd mumbled. Then softly kissed my cheek.

It meant everything to me. I knew down to my soul that I loved him. I always had, always would.

But he was a liar. Every word, every touch, every kiss, an untruth. He didn't want me, and why would he? He was Bowie Stone.

I was just Layla Hardin, single mom, the town joke.

My heart ached painfully, and a single tear rolled down my cheek.

Why did I keep doing this to myself?

Chapter Fourteen

Bowie

"C'mon, c'mon," I muttered under my breath. The phone rang and rang. "Fuckin' goddamned women."

"Still ghostin' your ass?" Reno asked.

I heaved an exasperated breath, hung up, and began pacing the motel room.

It had been days since I last spoke to Layla, and I was beyond worried. I knew she was alive and kickin' 'cause she picked up when I called the salon. When I said her name, she huffed and slammed the phone down.

I was fuckin' stunned. My woman was the sweetest girl in the world. She forgave all my past bullshit pretty much overnight, or so I thought.

"She was good as gold Tuesday." I brooded.

"Didn't you see her Wednesday night?" Reno asked.

I stopped pacing. "No, I went to see Leah with Callum and ensured she was all right. Then we headed to the hospital to talk to Frey about the blood results."

"Well, somethin' must've happened between then and now, Bo, 'cause it's pretty obvious at this point she wouldn't give you the steam off her piss."

My gut churned. "I can't fuckin' sort it from here. I'll see Layla tomorrow. It's Frey's birthday, and we're going out."

"We gonna get back in time?"

We had tomorrow morning to pack up, then a five-and-a-half-hour drive home. "Don't see why not," I told him. "Most of the boxes are on the truck. We've only got to get the furniture on tomorrow, then off we fuck."

We'd driven over to Colorado Thursday afternoon to pack up Freya's shared apartment. She'd organized her own place for next semester, so she'd given notice.

I wished I hadn't agreed to it now, what with Layla's radio silence. There was nothin' worse than being miles away when shit hit the fan, especially when you had no clue what shit had hit what fan.

I was goin' fuckin' crazy.

I racked my brains. What could Layla be pissed about?

Unease licked inside me. Surely she couldn't have found out about Sydney.

Could she?

A feeling of impending doom settled in my gut.

Fuck. I should've gone to my woman's place and told her about it right after it happened, but it was late, and I didn't want to wake Layla or Sunny. Especially as I knew she'd be upset. I thought it would keep until I got back. I needed to explain in person.

For the first time in years, I was fearful.

I lost everythin' that mattered once, and now I was at risk of losin' everythin' again, but this time I only had myself to blame.

Panic cracked through my chest. I rubbed at the sharp pain that shot through me, then began to pace the room again.

"Fuck, fuck, fuck," I chanted to myself. I looked over at Reno, who was lounging on the bed, looking at me like I'd lost my fuckin' mind. He was probably right.

My feet ground to a halt. "I may know why Layla's pissed."

Reno lifted one eyebrow enquiringly. "What the fuck did you do?"

Bowie

My hand snaked up and clutched the back of my neck. "Wednesday, I went over to see Frey at the hospital. We were talkin' outside about Saturday night, and I told her I'd asked Layla to go with me." I paused as I tried to think of a way to explain.

"Go on," Reno told me.

"Sydney must've been somewhere eavesdropping because she heard everythin'. When Freya went back inside, Syd strutted over."

"And?"

"She tried to kiss me. I stopped her and said I wasn't into it, but she wouldn't take no for an answer, so I told her straight."

Reno shook his head. "What the hell did you say to her?"

"Told her to fuck off, said that she was just convenient, and I wouldn't fuck her again if she was the last pussy on Earth."

Reno grimaced.

"Yeah," I continued. "Told the bitch if she touched me without my say-so again, I'd get one of the ol' ladies to break her fingers."

Reno's lips twitched. "Bet she loved that."

"She said she'd make me regret I'd ever met her."

"Looks like she succeeded, brother."

Blood pounded in my ears.

I had to explain to Layla. I had to make her understand that I didn't want anyone else and that she and Sunny were it for me. But how the hell could I? She wouldn't even pick up the phone.

I wracked my brains, tryin' to think through the rushing in my ears.

I grabbed my phone, dialed, and waited for my sister to pick up.

There was a click. "What do you want, Bowie? I just finished a twelve-hour shift. I'm tired," Freya said.

"Have you seen Layla?" I asked.

"No."

I had to do some damage control, but my woman needed to get with the program too.

Layla and Sunny belonged to me now. I was claiming 'em at the table. Club life could be tough, but I'd shoot myself in the dick before allowing Layla to walk away. Doe was way off the mark if she thought I'd let her shut me out.

"Bowie. What's going on?" Freya demanded. "Bowie?"

"Sis," I said, tone serious. "I need you to do somethin' for me."

Chapter Fifteen

Layla

The Lucky Shamrock was wall-to-wall packed. We'd been waiting at the bar for ten minutes and were still waiting to get served.

Cara gave me a pissed-off look. "This may take a while," she murmured. "Seems if you want a drink around here, you've got to have big hair and most of your tits hanging over your top."

"Watch, and learn," Freya smirked, ducking under some guy's arm and stepping up to the bar.

I watched in amazement as she pulled her red corset down slightly, fluffed her hair, and leaned over. "Hey, boys," she called out in a sultry voice, running a fingertip down her chest. "I'm feeling a little faint here. Can I get a drink?"

Within minutes, three cocktail pitchers were lined up before her, ready to go.

"On the house," the bartender shouted over the music as he gave her cleavage an appreciative glance.

"I wanna be her when I grow up," Cara whispered in my ear.

"Me too," I agreed, stepping forward to help Freya.

We all grabbed the pitchers and a tray of glasses, then swerved the crowds as we made our way over to the table where Rosie, Tristan, and Anna were waiting.

Freya had called me that morning, begging me to meet her at the salon. My plan for the day was to curl up, eat ice cream, and cry, but she wouldn't take no for an answer.

The second Sunny and I arrived, Tristan swept me over to the basins and began washing my hair.

"You're coming out tonight," Freya had insisted. "I've asked Anna and Tristan to come too."

I argued I didn't have a sitter, and Freya told me she'd arranged for Sunny to stay overnight with Abe and Iris. Sunny had squealed in delight. And that was that.

Then I said that I needed that week's paycheck for bills.

Freya laughed and told me that her dad had put a stack of cash behind the bar to cover our night, seeing as it was her birthday.

My stomach fell as she looked over at me sadly. "I know you're not happy with my brother," she'd said gently. "So, I've made it a girl's night."

My heart squeezed in my chest. It had been two days since I learned about Bowie and Sydney Barrington, and I'd cried myself to sleep both nights. I was lost without him, and now I'd had time to think. I was beginning to realize that things didn't add up.

"Come on, Layla," Anna said kindly. "A girl's night is exactly what you need."

I glanced at Tristan. "Honey," he drawled. "I'm more woman than all of you ladies put together, so don't think for a minute that you're gonna leave me out of the shenanigans."

I'd smiled at each one of them. I was blessed to have these people in my life. As heartbroken as I was over Bowie, I was also relieved that I had so many people at my back. Maybe they were right.

"Why don't you wear the black dress I gave you?" Anna suggested as she removed a roller from Freya's hair.

I'd winced. The dress was a beautiful satin sheath with tiny straps that held it up, but it was so short that it skimmed the tops of my thighs.

"Pretty please. For me?" Freya pleaded.

And here we were.

I looked down at the shiny material, took another sip of my cocktail, and smiled. It felt so light and smooth against my skin. Tristan had put honey lowlights through my hair, then layered and straightened it to touch the top of my ass.

I felt pretty for the first time in years, confident even.

"Let's toast the birthday girl," Rosie said.

We raised our glasses and yelled, "Happy Birthday, Freya!" The DJ played the 'happy birthday song,' and the crowd roared.

As the night went on, more cocktails were consumed. We got louder and louder and laughed harder and harder.

Tristan was hilarious. He scared away every guy that approached us. He told them we were all his women, though I'm not sure they believed him, seeing as he was wearing silky black culottes, and black high-heeled pumps, with red soles. Regardless, they left us alone.

More cocktails hit the table courtesy of John Stone. Our glasses didn't stay full for long. A couple of hours later, we were all pretty drunk.

Freya and I laughed at Tristan, who was flinging Anna and Rosie around the dance floor in time to *Havana* by Camila Cabello.

"He should go on Dancing with the Stars," Freya giggled. "Look at his ass move."

My head twisted to see Tristan grind his hips against Rosie, samba style. "Oh my God, he's amazing," I breathed.

Freya nudged my arm. "Bet he's a god in the bedroom."

"Yeah," I agreed as I watched him gyrate his ass. He took Anna's hand in one of his, Rosie's hand in the other, then expertly twirled them around.

Freya gestured with her head toward the bar. "Do you think she's okay?"

I craned my neck to look back at Cara.

Robbie and two of his cronies had arrived about an hour ago. He'd sent Cara an angry stare, then began to flirt with Sydney Barrington, who was standing at the bar with her sister, Paris.

Cara stayed put, ignoring him. Eventually, after failing to get the reaction he expected, he stomped over and pulled her away to talk.

Cara gestured angrily with her hands as her fiancé leaned against the wall, a smug expression on his face.

My chest went tight when I saw her throw her arms in the air in frustration.

He just shrugged and laughed in her face.

She spun around and tried to walk away, but he pulled her back by the arm. Cara tugged it out of his grip, looked back, and gave him the finger before approaching us.

"Robbie is such a dick," Freya ground out as she sat back. "Can you believe she's marrying him next month? I know what Xander did was wrong, but they used to be happy. I know he disrespected her horribly, but it was so out of character…." She trailed off as my best friend stomped back to the table.

Cara plopped down into her seat, grabbed her drink, and took a huge sip. "Fuck him," she spat.

"You, okay?" I asked her softly.

"I'm fan-fucking-tastic," my friend replied. Slamming her cocktail back on the table, she stood and swayed on her feet, grabbing Freya with one hand and me with the other. "Letsss dance," Cara slurred. She pulled us from our seats and toward the others.

Bowie

I didn't know if it was the drinks, the company I was with, or my new

found confidence, but I let loose as soon as I stepped on the dance floor.

Usually, I was too shy to dance, but as the music played, my hips began to sway in time to the bass.

Tristan turned away from Anna and Rosie and pointed. "That's my girl," he yelled as he danced toward me, crooking his finger, Patrick Swayze style. "Come to daddy." Before I knew it, he spun me so his front was to my back, shaking and grinding into my ass.

Freya and Cara danced around us, laughing. I was enjoying myself so much that I didn't see Robbie and his goon's approach.

Someone grabbed my arm hard and jerked me away from Tristan. I whipped around and saw Robbie squeeze Cara's arm so roughly that she stumbled and cried out in pain.

My heart leaped into my throat as a familiar voice slurred into my ear from behind. "Why you dancing with him when you can have a real man?"

A cold shiver ran down my spine.

I turned slowly to see Brett Stafford staring down at me, blue eyes glinting dangerously.

"Nice dress," he leered as he pawed at me. "If I'd known you cleaned up this well, I'd have given you a shot years ago."

Panic rose in my chest as he tried to pull me away from my friends. "Let's get out of here." He smirked.

"Get off," I cried. I tried desperately to pull away, but Brett's strong fingers dug into my skin. My eyes veered to the red marks he left. "Please, you're hurting me," I begged, but Brett ignored me and dragged me off the dance floor.

"Let her go!" a voice yelled.

Suddenly my arm was free. Tears sprang to my eyes as I rubbed at the spot where Brett's fingers had dug into me.

"If you touch her like that again, I'll cut your tiny dick off." I looked up and saw Tristan holding the back of Brett's shirt.

Brett managed to get out of Trist's grasp and spun around. "Fuck off, you fa—" Brett shouted as the music was shut off. He realized everyone was watching him, and his voice went quiet.

"Don't you dare call him that!" The tornado called Freya stomped toward Brett. "You're disgusting!" she yelled, launching herself toward him.

A strong arm shot out and grabbed the back of Freya's top. A loud ripping sound split the air. I turned to see Robbie grasping onto her. "I don't think so, bitch," he rasped threateningly.

I turned to see the entire bar staring, and my cheeks reddened.

Freya glared at Robbie, "You ripped my top," she yelled. Gripping her top with one hand, she swung around, slapping Robbie hard across the chest with the other.

Shit, this was getting out of hand. I was about to try to reason with Robbie when a deep voice shouted from behind me.

"Henderson. You've fucked up for the last time. Get your buddies, get your shit, and get the fuck outta my bar."

Robbie's face turned to stone. I looked over my shoulder to see Callum O'Shea glaring at Robbie, arms folded across his muscled chest.

Silence reigned over the bar. My face burned as I saw everyone staring.

"You've got thirty seconds to fuck off, or I call the sheriff," he warned. He looked at me, then Freya. "You, ladies, okay?" he asked.

Bowie

Freya huffed. "I'm fine," she snipped. "But Brett hurt Layla."

"You dirty fucking biker cun…." Brett began, voice trailing off as his eyes flicked to a spot behind me.

The air turned oppressive. It was so heavy that it felt like I was being weighed down. Everybody's eyes seemed to zone into the same spot, over my shoulder.

"Oopsies," Tristan said.

"It's about time," Freya grumbled.

The air turned to electricity as a deep voice boomed, "Is that my sister you're calling a dirty biker cunt?"

My heart began racing as I slowly turned to look behind me again.

Bowie stood next to Callum with Atlas and Kit by his side.

His face twisted into an angry scowl. My stomach turned to ice when I realized how much he'd seen. I watched, fascinated, as his eyes turned to hard flints.

It was surreal. Part of me wanted to run for the hills. I'd wanted to throw up after what Sydney boasted in the salon, but the young girl who'd loved him for years wanted to jump in his arms.

Freya pointed at Brett. "He hurt Layla," she accused. "He tried to drag her outside."

"Fuck," Kit muttered. He sprang toward his brother. Atlas was right behind him.

Anger pounded off Bowie as he began to stalk toward Brett. "You're a fuckin' dead man," he snarled.

Brett's eyes darted fearfully around the room. He started scrambling backward, trying to escape the storm he knew was about to hit. I winced as he banged his hip hard into a table. "I—I didn't mean to—" he stuttered, but it looked to me that Bowie was past caring about what he had to say.

Bowie's arm began to reach out toward Brett's throat. Atlas appeared at his back. His arms reached around Bowie's body, binding him so he couldn't touch the other man.

"Brother, you better get the fuck off me," Bowie snapped back at his friend.

"C'mon, Bo, he's not worth the jail time," Atlas said quietly. "Think of your girls."

Bowie's head turned toward me. A shiver ran down my spine, but that time, it wasn't from fear.

"You okay, Doe?" Bowie demanded, his jaw clenching so tight a muscle ticked.

I bit my lip nervously as Bowie's eyes darted to my mouth, and his eyes turned soft.

"You and your boys better get gone, Henderson," Kit bit out. "Or next time, we won't stop him." His voice had a hardness to it that I'd never heard before.

"Can't wait," Robbie spat. "I'll see the lot of you locked up on assault charges."

"It'll be a fuckin' manslaughter charge if you or your lapdogs ever touch my woman again," Bowie growled.

Robbie nodded toward the door. "Come on, B. This place is starting to stink."

Atlas laughed. "Jesus. You're a fuckin' embarrassment." He looked Robbie up and down. "I reckon your ma left you on the tit too long, ya whiny ass prick."

Tristan and Freya burst out laughing. I lifted my hand to smother the giggle that bubbled through my throat.

Robbie's face turned almost purple with anger. He turned, kicked a stray chair across the room, then stalked to the door. "Fucking biker assholes," he shouted over his shoulder. He swung the exit door open, then held it ajar as Brett followed behind him.

The room went silent.

My brain was muddled. I hated confrontation. I turned back to Freya as I rubbed the spot on my arm again, where Brett had pulled me.

"Are you okay?" I asked Freya.

Bowie

Bowie growled, slowly turned, and pointed his finger at me, eyes flashing angrily. "What the fuck are you wearing?" he demanded.

A spark of anger ignited in my chest. Were we in some alternate universe? Did he really think he could tell me what to wear?

Indignant, I put a hand on my hip and cocked it. "Look here, Bowie Stone. What I wear is none of your business. Go boss your girlfriend around and leave me alone." I turned my finger inward and pointed to my chest. "I've had enough of your crap."

Bowie's eyes narrowed to furious slits. He turned toward the bar, searching. "Sydney!" he shouted.

My heart sank.

Was Bowie turn up here for Sydney? I tried to swallow past the tears in my throat. The thought of seeing them together punched a hole through my chest.

"Just saw her leave," Callum called out.

Bowie's hand snaked up to rub the back of his neck. "Fucking perfect," he snipped under his breath. His gaze darted back to me. "Look, baby," he began. "Sydney's lying. I would never touch—"

A high-pitched scream cut Bowie off. A chair clattered to the floor, and a loud *thump* banged through the air.

"Someone help!" Rosie screamed.

Anna kneeled on the floor by our table, bending toward someone sprawled out on the ground. Panic swirled inside my chest when I recognized the black skinny jeans. Something was very wrong. My heart raced so fast that it was pounding in my ears.

I tried to clear my mind and think back to how much Cara had to drink, but instead, hysteria rose. "Help her, please," I begged.

Somebody raced past me, a flash of red, Freya. She ran to the commotion, falling to her knees on the floor, checking the woman's pulse.

Tears filled my eyes.

Freya lifted her head. "Somebody call nine-one-one," she shouted. Her head turned, and her worry-filled eyes found mine. "It's Cara," she confirmed.

Chapter Sixteen

Bowie

"Xander's gonna fucking flip," Kit muttered from beside me. "It's bad enough for him in there without worrying about this fuckin' disaster."

"She'll be okay," I replied.

"He made us promise to look out for her."

I stifled a groan. "Yeah."

I looked across the room at Layla. She was leaning her head on Tristan's shoulder. I had to keep myself from stompin' over and pulling her off him. My woman should've been depending on me.

"She'll come around, bro," Atlas said quietly from my other side. "You just have to tell her what's what."

I tore my eyes away from my girls and stared at my boots. "I fuckin' know she will, she won't get a choice, but I'm not gonna start any shit in here, am I?"

We were at Baines Memorial. Cara was rushed here by ambulance after she collapsed. We called the club and got the prospects to bring a couple of SUVs to take the girls and Tristan to the ER. Me, Kit, and Atlas followed on our bikes.

We'd been here about thirty minutes. Layla called Cara's folks, who were on their way. Reluctantly, she called Robbie from Cara's phone and left a message.

I fuckin' hated hospitals. They filled my mind with dark thoughts.

I waited in a room like this for hours while Sam was dying just a few feet away. I breathed in my nose and outta my mouth, tryin' to fill my lungs and ease the anxiety clawing at my insides.

The sound of footsteps clattered up the hall. I turned to see a tall man with grey hair and a dark-haired woman race in.

Cara's parents.

"How is she?" the man asked.

"What happened?" the woman asked at the same time.

Layla stood, then rushed toward them. My girl's eyes shone sadly as she shot Cara's dad a worried look. "I'm so sorry, Seth. I should have been keeping a better eye on her."

Cara's mom took Layla's hand and squeezed. "You didn't do this, sweetheart. It's not your fault."

I got to my feet and walked across the room to take my girl's back. Seth Landry caught my eye and gave me a nod. Cara's folks used to come over to club cookouts back when she was with Xan. I liked Cara's dad. He was cool.

"Where's the Doctor?" he asked.

"Freya'll be back out soon," I reassured him. "She went to see if she could get us an update."

Deborah Landry put her hand through her husband's arm. "Cara knows to be careful when she's out, Bowie. She knows how to take care of herself." Her voice was thick with worry.

Cara had grown up in New York and lived in Wichita for a while. She was more streetwise than most other girls in Hambleton, so the fact she got spiked was a bit of a headfuck.

The sound of more heavy footsteps came crashing up the hall. I turned to see Robbie Henderson storm into the waiting room. "Where is she?" he demanded. "Is she okay?"

Layla's body stiffened as Rob's eyes turned to her and narrowed.

I put my hand on my girl's back, a silent show of support. His eyes flicked up, and he shot me a glare. "This is your fault, Stone. If you hadn't forced me to leave that shithole, I could have kept an eye on her."

My skin prickled. "Cara was drugged well before we got there, asshole."

"Alright, boys," Seth cut in.

"But he—"

"—Robert! Stop!" Deb screeched, face pink with anger. "This isn't helping Cara."

Henderson's shoulders slumped. "I'm sorry. What if she doesn't..." his voice trailed off. Both hands raised to clutch the back of his neck as he looked painfully at Seth. "We're getting married in a few weeks."

My stomach twisted at the concern on his face.

When Cara passed out, I'd suspected Robbie had somethin' to do with it. From what Frey had told me, Rob had been an asshole to Cara before I walked in. I didn't like the prick. There was somethin' off about him.

Lookin' at him now, it didn't ring true. In fact, he looked wrecked, broken even, which was weird. Either he was innocent or a fuckin' good actor.

The tap of shoes on tiles sounded from the direction of the cubicles where the patients were assessed. Freya emerged with a guy wearing a white coat. He looked around the waiting room. "Family of Cara Landry?"

Freya gestured toward us, and the doctor made his way over.

"We're Cara's parents," Deborah explained. She searched the doc's face for a clue. "Is she okay?"

The man smiled and held out his hand. "I'm Doctor Sullivan."

"How's my daughter?" Seth questioned as he shook other the man's hand.

A grim look spread across the doctor's features. "Cara's responding well to treatment. We found flunitrazepam in her system but were able to counteract the drug with a dose of Flumazenil."

Deborah frowned.

"Rohypnol," Freya explained quietly. "Doctor Sullivan gave her a dose of another drug, which acts as an antidote."

Deb's hands flew to her face, and she sobbed.

"She's gonna be okay," Freya said, squeezing Deb's arm. "She'll have to stay here tonight for observation, but all being well, she should be able to go home tomorrow."

"Who would do that to her?" Deb cried.

"The Sheriff's going to send someone down in the morning to get a statement," Doctor Sullivan said drily. "With any luck, they'll catch whoever's doing this."

Robbie stepped forward. "When can we see her?" he demanded.

"Immediate family only for tonight," the Doc replied. "Cara's still sedated. When she wakes up, she'll probably be very distressed."

Seth's face fell. He ran his hand down his face, then turned to face the room. "Thank you, all of you, but there's nothing more you can do tonight. We'll take Cara back to our house tomorrow. You can all come and see her there."

"Will you let me know if anything changes?" Layla pleaded. My gut churned as I looked down at my girl. Her face was ashen, and her eyes shone with tears.

"Of course, sweetheart," Seth replied. "But you need to get some sleep."

Everyone stood and went over to Cara's folks. After hugging Deb and murmuring our goodbyes, we started to leave.

Bowie

I held Layla's hand firmly in mine and leaned down. "I got ya, baby," I said quietly as we walked down the corridor.

My girl just looked up at me blankly.

"She'll be okay," I assured her as I guided her through the main doors.

Silence.

Shit. I needed to get her home. What if she was in shock or somethin'?

We all walked through the revolving doors to the parking lot. I took a big gulp of crisp, night air. It was a godsend after sitting in that waiting room. Hospitals were a reminder of death for me.

My hand went to Layla's back, about to guide her to my bike, when a deep voice called out my name.

I tore my eyes away from my girl to see Dad and Hendrix stalking toward us. "How is she?" Pop asked, worry drenching his voice.

"She's gonna be okay," I said. "They're keeping her in tonight, but hopefully, she'll get discharged in the morning."

Dad cursed quietly under his breath. "Church tomorrow, at noon." His voice was steely. "We're gonna flush him out."

I jerked a nod of agreement.

"We had to send Sparky back to the clubhouse," Hendrix said. He looked at Tristan, then Rosie. "You two live north of the town. Boner's taking you both home." He turned to Anna. "You're with me."

Rosie nodded. "Come on, honey," she said, grabbing Tristan's hand. "It's been a long night, and I need to get back to my kids."

Anna turned to my girl. "Will you be okay?" she asked softly.

"I've got her," I bit out, back snapping straight.

Anna's eyes spat irritation at me. "According to Sydney Barrington, Layla's not the only one you've got," she accused.

I glanced down at my girl. My chest burned as I saw her dip her head. Anger at Sydney fuckin' Barrington made me clench my hands into fists.

"Pipe down, Woman," Hendrix retorted. "Mind your own fuckin' business."

Anna put her hand on her hips, popping one out. "You gonna make me?" she said accusingly. "'Cause I'm telling you, handsome. It'll take a better man than you to shut me up."

Dad grinned. Kit and Atlas smothered their laughter.

"Just get on my bike, woman," Hendrix ordered.

Anna huffed, then swung her eyes back to Layla. "Will you be okay?"

Layla kept her eyes on the ground.

Anna's face was fiery. She cocked one eyebrow at me. "You better look after her," she warned.

"Always," I vowed.

Anna patted Layla's shoulder, then walked with Hendrix to his bike.

I saluted Dad loosely with two fingers, then grabbed Layla's elbow and led her to my Softail. "You're on the back of my bike," I told her as we drew level.

She finally looked toward my black, and chrome, Softail. "I can't get on that," she whispered.

Her eyes looked down at that lame fuckin' excuse for a dress. She looked stunnin'. All soft golden skin, innocent doe eyes, and pouty lips. My sweet siren put on Earth to drive me insane.

I shrugged off my leather jacket, then stooped down and tied the arms around her waist, leaving the back hanging down. "That'll cover your ass. But unless you're with me, you don't wear that dress again, baby. Ya feel me?"

Layla froze. Big, grey eyes swept up to search mine. My gut swirled at the hollow look in them. At that moment, if I could've kicked my own ass, I would've been bouncin' off the cold hard ground.

I grabbed my helmet off the handlebar and put it on Layla's head. The state of Wyoming didn't require us to wear brain buckets, but we did anyway. I only had one with me, but it was more important for me to keep my girl safe.

I swung my leg over the saddle and grabbed Layla's hand, helping her on behind me. She wriggled backward. I reached behind and pulled her legs toward me so she sat flush at my back.

"Make sure your ass is covered," I insisted. I flicked a switch, and the bike roared to life. "Hold on tight, baby," I shouted over the engine as I pulled away.

My chest swelled as Layla's hands gripped hard around my waist. I nearly groaned out loud as her soft fingers brushed against my stomach.

My cock woke up immediately. It grew so hard that I thought it would punch a hole through my fuckin' zipper.

Layla squirmed behind me. My jaw clenched as her gorgeous little tits rubbed against my back. Images of her spread out on my bed, waitin' for me to fuck her sweet pussy until she screamed my name, swirled through my brain.

My dick throbbed.

My thoughts went to the Sydney bullshit, and my cock deflated. Layla wasn't very fuckin' happy with me at all. The thought of losing her made me wanna throw up. What if she didn't believe me?

Somehow, I had to make her see that Sydney was out to cause shit. The thing was, I knew enough about women to realize that I had a fuckin' mountain to climb. It was my word against the lying bitch's.

I was still ponderin' this when we pulled up to Layla's cottage. I slowed down, then stopped and switched off the engine.

Silence fell over us.

Behind me, Layla fumbled as she took off the helmet. "Thank you for the ride. I'll see you around." Her voice held a tinge of sadness, which triggered a myriad of emotions to rob my breath.

My hand flew to her knee. "We need to talk, Doe."

"No!" Layla said emphatically, pressing down on my shoulder as she swung off my bike.

She turned to walk into the house, but I grabbed her hand and pulled her back. "Sydney was lying, baby." My voice was desperate.

Layla's head jerked up. Her eyes went glassy. She pulled her fingers out of my grasp. "Why would she lie, Bowie?" she asked. "What would she have to gain?"

My gut began to twist as her words registered.

My girl didn't believe me. The thought of her walkin' away from what we had, made anger burn in my chest. I'd only known her a few weeks, but the thought of losing her was unbearable.

"She's a spoilt bitch who always wants her way, baby," I pleaded. "But I swear on everythin' that means somethin' to me. It didn't happen."

Layla's eyes flickered over mine like she was searching for something.

"I did see her Wednesday," I admitted. "I went to the hospital to talk to Freya. When I jetted, Sydney called me over and tried to kiss me, but I didn't fuckin' entertain it. You gotta believe me."

"She said you asked her out for Freya's birthday. How would she know about that?"

I put the bike on the kickstand and dismounted. "Me and Freya were talkin' next to the loading bay," I explained. "Sydney was in one of the ambulances. She overheard us talkin' about it. I didn't ask her. Why the fuck would I when I'd already asked you?"

"I admit, I thought about that. It did seem weird," Layla murmured as her brow furrowed.

"That's 'cause it didn't happen, Doe."

Layla thought for a minute, and then she blinked up at me. "Okay," she said.

Relief sank through me.

I looped my index finger into her belt loop and gave her a hard tug. She stumbled into me.

I quickly caught her and looked deep into her eyes, tryin' to convey the truth with my stare. Agony moved behind her gaze, and a thought glimmered. If she was hurtin', it meant she felt something for me too.

I leaned down so that my mouth brushed against her soft cheek. "You're it for me, Doe," I mumbled against her skin. "I ache for you, baby."

Soft arms snaked around my neck. Joy poured through me so fast that I wanted to punch the goddamned air. I pulled away a little, so I could see her face properly. "You believe me, baby?"

Layla's eyes never left mine as she smiled. "Let's go inside."

I pulled her to the door. "Key," I demanded, as a huge grin split my features.

She fished inside the little purse that crossed over her body, pulled out a ring of metal keys, and handed it to me. "It's the gold one."

I turned the key in the lock and ushered her inside. As we walked to the kitchen, I watched as she removed her purse and placed it on the table.

She leaned her hip against the wood and looked at me thoughtfully. "If Sydney tries anything again, will you tell me?"

"I had every intention of tellin' you, Doe, but it was late. I thought it would keep until I got back from Denver.

I didn't know she'd drop a fuckin' axe on my neck while I was away."

I stepped toward her, then reached out and tilted her chin up to see her pretty face. "If we're gonna do this, baby, then we're both all in. Both feet. No dickin' around. It's you and me against the world. Ya feel me?"

Layla laid her hand across my cheek. "Will you stay here tonight with me?"

"Yeah, Doe. But we're not fuckin'."

"Why?"

"'Cause you've been drinking."

A bemused look moved across her face. "I'm sober now."

"Don't care," I replied. "Just gonna wrap you up in my arms all night, baby. The next time I fuck you, I want you with me all the way."

She cocked her head at me, and a small smile played around her lips. "Bowie Stone," she declared softly. "I think that underneath that bad boy biker exterior, you're really a gentleman."

My eyes turned serious. "Swear to me that you won't tell anyone."

She let out a laugh, and I was mesmerized. It was the most magical fuckin' sound I'd heard in my entire life. I bent my mouth to hers, "Missed you, baby," I muttered into her lips.

"I missed you too," she replied, her sweet breath mingling with mine.

My heart jerked in my chest, then thumped hard behind my ribs, and I knew right then that I was done for.

It was like she'd breathed my soul back onto me, a soul that had abandoned my body years before.

For the first time in a long time, I felt alive.

Chapter Seventeen

Layla

I blinked at the morning light shining brightly through the cracks in the curtains.

I warmed when I felt Bowie's face snuggled into my neck.

Soft stubble tickled my skin as puffs of heavy, rhythmic breath skated along my throat.

Fingers twitched across my nipple, igniting a flame between my legs.

Bowie's sweet words from the night before played through my mind. My heart flipped inside my chest, and I smiled contentedly because he was with me.

Sydney was lying all along, so Bowie said. Was I a fool for believing him? Maybe.

When Sydney's mouth spoke those lies, it cut me deep. A dark part of myself whispered *Why would he want you anyway? You're nobody, and he's everything.*

It rocked my soul because believing the bad things about myself over the good was always easier. It was easy to lose confidence.

The shock had worn off by Friday night, and I could think more clearly. I realized that many things that Sydney said didn't add up.

Bowie wasn't the type of man to send flowers or buy gifts for a woman he didn't want. He'd been kind and attentive. He'd bought Sunny her console and brought dinner. Ate with us. Spent time with us.

Bowie could have any woman he wanted with just a click of his fingers, so if all he wanted was easy, why did he pick me when I was anything but?

Apart from that one time, he'd shown me that I could trust him, whereas Sydney, well, all she'd ever shown me was that I couldn't.

I had to go with my heart, and the fact was, my heart lay smack bang in the direction of Bowie. It had since I was fourteen years old.

Now I had him. I wasn't going to waste my chance.

My skin prickled as fingertips brushed over my nipple again. My heart stuttered as it puckered under my man's touch.

Soft lips skated over the back of my neck, causing goosebumps to run down both arms like tiny little flickers of air.

Bowie sucked softly on the skin below my ear. "Morning, baby," he said sleepily.

A smile glimmered on my lips. "Morning, Bowie." My voice held a note of contentment just because I was in his arms.

I tried to move, to turn my body toward him, take in his beautiful eyes, but his hand pressed down against my hip, a silent command to stay where I was. The bite of his touch sent sparks of pleasure licking between my legs, making my pussy flood with moisture.

His fingertips trailed down over my thigh, then lower. I moaned as he pressed down again, then gasped as his fingers delved under the lace of my panties and slipped inside. "You're so fuckin' tight, Doe," Bowie groaned.

Long fingers gathered the moisture from my core and moved up to circle my clit slowly. "I love how wet you are for me, baby. Let me in. Let me make you feel good."

I obeyed without hesitation. My legs fell apart, desperate for Bowie's touch. "That's my good girl," he said into my throat, voice rough with need.

Happiness bloomed like a flower unfurling in my chest because all I'd ever wanted to be was Bowie's good girl. Fingers pressed down hard on my clit, then began to stroke across it. "Oh, my God," I sighed.

"I love you, Layla," he murmured.

The uttered oath made my heart stop just for a beat. Then it grew to double its size as bliss washed through me, causing years of sadness and frustration to melt away. All that mattered was us. I knew that every moment of pain I'd lived through was worth it because it had led me to this moment, to him.

My breath increased as my hips began to grind against his hand.

"That's it, Doe. Take what you need," he rasped. Heaviness began to build in the pit of my stomach as he growled. "Take it all, baby."

Bowie's lips skated down to nuzzle my throat. His fingers continued circling my tiny bundle of nerves, sending sparks of pleasure through me. My hips rocked up to meet his touch, but I couldn't quite reach where I needed.

I mewled softly. "More, Bowie. Please," I begged.

"That's it, baby, come for me," he commanded.

My body must have been waiting for permission because as soon as he growled the words, my pussy clenched around his fingers.

The orgasm that just before was out of reach slammed through me.

I let out a sharp cry, my hips bucking harder. "Yes, yes, yes," I chanted as tiny lights exploded in my brain. All thoughts flew into the ether. All I could do was feel the bliss that coursed through my being.

The cold was the first thing I noticed when I came back to Earth. Bowie wasn't holding me anymore. My limbs were so heavy that I had to roll onto my back. I sucked air into my lungs, trying to calm my thudding heart.

I opened my eyes, searching for him. Strong hands gripped the back of my knees, jerking me down the bed. My eyes snapped open.

Bowie's hair was mussed from sleep, his eyes lazy but blazing with heat. Fingers tugged on my panties. I lifted my ass, and he pulled them down off my ankles.

"You on birth control?"

"No," I replied. "But I'm clean. I've only been with you since I had Sunny."

His lip quirked at that. "I was tested six months ago, and I've only fucked you since. I'm going bareback, baby, I wanna feel your cunt, but I'll pull out. Okay?"

My eyes skated over his muscled arms, hard pecs, and prominent abs. My pussy clenched with need again at the sight of his hard cock. "I want to feel you, too," I breathed.

He laid his body over mine, settling between my legs.

Liquid gold eyes stared into mine as Bowie's hands slid to the back of my thighs, tugging them wider apart. "This'll be quick, Doe, but I'll make it up to you."

He slid the head of his cock through my folds, notching it against my opening. I closed my eyes, waiting for the pleasurable burn.

He thrust his hips, sliding into me with one hard stroke.

His voice was a ragged groan as he pushed one word through his clenched jaw. "Baby."

Bowie's warm hand rested on my heart before he began to push his cock inside me, gently at first, with hard, rhythmic strokes.

I hissed as his strong thrusts stretched my core, an invasion of the best kind.

After a few more thrusts, the bite of pain began to subside. "You're so fuckin' beautiful," he moaned, his strokes becoming more urgent, deeper. "You're strangling my cock, "baby," he rasped. "I can't hold it much longer."

A spark of fire began to swirl in my stomach.

Bowie let out a long groan as his hips began to snap forward faster. "Fuck," he groaned.

A familiar pressure began to build. I pushed up to meet his thrusts. "Please, don't stop," I begged.

You're so fuckin' tight," he grated out, thrusting into me harder, brutally, grunting every time his hips pounded against mine.

This time the build wasn't gradual; I went hurtling over a cliff's edge.

The air crackled in my ears as I called his name repeatedly. His hand lowered to rub my clit, and my entire body arched up toward him as my world tilted on its axis.

"Fuck, yeah," he moaned, riding me through my orgasm. Then as my heart rate began to slow, he swiftly pulled out.

The loss of his weight made my eyes jerk open.

I watched as he kneeled and bowed his head while furiously stroking his hard length. A deep feral groan sounded deep in his throat as warmth splashed onto my belly.

"Fuck, fuck, fuck," he rasped, all while his hips jerked uncontrollably.

I watched, fascinated, as ropes of cum spurted onto my skin until Bowie's hand slowed and eventually stopped.

Hooded eyes swept down my body, then softened. "I've made a mess of you, Doe," he said. His fingers snaked onto my belly, and he rubbed his seed into my skin, anointing me.

I looked up at the ceiling and smiled at the contentment warming me inside. The bed dipped. My head twisted to the side to see Bowie sprawled out next to me, the arm furthest away flung over his eyes.

I stilled as he began to laugh. Deep, throaty sounds emitted from his chest. The infectiousness of it made me smile wide as I watched his chest rise and fall with mirth.

His chuckles faded. His hand found mine. "Me and you against the world, Doe. Feel me?"

I nodded.

My soul had waited for him, never wavering, never giving up, because it knew, even as a fourteen-year-old girl, that it would always belong to him.

I was his, and he was mine.

Bowie Stone, my man.

Chapter Eighteen

Bowie

My eyes locked onto Dad and Atlas the second I rode through the gates to the club. They were outside the main doors talking.

I raised my hand in greeting as I slowly pulled up next to them.

The morning sun reflected off the smooth fiberglass of my helmet as I removed it, hung it from the handlebars, then switched off the engine.

A sense of peace settled over me.

After Samantha and the baby, I didn't think I'd ever feel so alive again, but I was wrong. Now I had Layla and Sunny it was glaringly fuckin' obvious that something had been missing for a long time.

My girls not only made me happy, but they settled me down.

Looking after them gave me a sense of achievement that I hadn't felt in, well, ever, honestly. Not even with Sam.

I dismounted, making my way toward the clubhouse.

Atlas lifted a hand and pointed. "That right there, Prez. That's the look of a man in love."

Normally I'd be pissed at SAA's attempts to get under my skin, but right then, I couldn't bring myself to care a fuckin' hoot.

Jules Ford

I *was* a man in love. So fuckin' what?

This mornin' had just cemented what I'd already known for weeks. Layla was mine.

A satisfied gleam shone in Pop's eyes, a grin splitting his face. "About fuckin' time. Adele will be over the moon when she finds out she's got a ready-made granddaughter."

I quirked an eyebrow. "Tell Ma to hold on tight, Pop, 'cause this ride's just beginning. I want more kids. Wanna be a young dad."

Dad barked out a laugh and clapped me on the back. "You're a chip off the old block, son. Can't wait to take it to Church."

"Today?"

He shook his head thoughtfully, his hand reaching for the door. "Nope. Today's an open meetin' in the bar. Time to step our game up. We've been too goddamned laid back." He swung the door open and stepped into the clubhouse.

Satisfaction rolled through me. Finally, we were gonna get this shit sorted, and last night had hit a bit too close to fuckin' home.

Cara being hurt was the last straw. Now the prez was really pissed. Cara was one of ours.

It was Sunday, and all the tables were full of dudes shootin' the shit. Some had club girls on their laps or hanging off their arms.

The games area was packed. The crack of a cue ball clattered through the air as I made my way through the bodies toward the bar.

I saw my first naked woman. Hell, I saw my first blowjob in this room. Xan and I sneaked into a club party. I was thirteen.

A year later, everything changed.

Freya woke up one night and came down looking for Pop. Gramps had just finished railin' a club girl over a

Bowie

pool table. He was pullin' up his pants when my sister stumbled through the door, rubbin' her eyes.

From that day on, if you wanted to fuck, you did it in a room. I was glad for it. The thought of seein' some of these men's dicks wasn't exactly at the top of my wish list. I'd stick to seein' Layla naked all day long.

Memories from that mornin' flickered through my mind, and my cock twitched.

After I'd shot my come all over Layla's belly, I'd pulled her into the shower to wash it off. My fingers stroked over her stomach, touchin' the cute little pooch where she'd carried Sunny.

I wanted to worship it 'cause I knew soon, I'd put another baby in there.

I'd been waitin' a long time for my woman. I'd already fucked things up once. I knew she'd forgiven me, but I needed to tie her down and make her mine in every way.

Babies, rings, vows, happily goddamned ever fuckin' after.

My chest puffed out proudly at the thought of her stomach swollen and round with my kid. My woman's life was mapped out for the next five years 'cause she'd be knocked up for most of it.

We already had Sunny, but I wanted another girl. And a boy. And a girl.

I swaggered up to the bar, where beer bottles were already lined up, so I grabbed one and made my way toward the stage, where a few tables had been pushed together. Chairs were lined up behind them, facing the room.

I looked at the placements. The VP to the prez's right, symbolic cause Dad always said that the VP was his right-hand man, then the SAA, Enforcer, Road Captain, Secretary, and Treasurer.

Our Treasurer's chair had sat empty for two years. My brother, Xander, had lost his way a while back, but I had faith that he was sortin' his shit. While he'd been locked up, he'd smashed his CPAs and became a qualified accountant. He was a whizz kid with numbers and money, hence his road name, Cash.

Colt covered his duties but never sat in Xander's seat. That was reserved for the man himself.

Ice and Atlas stepped up to the stage and took their seats.

Hendrix and Colt followed soon after, then Dad and Abe.

Pop eased himself into his chair, then slowly picked up his heavy, wooden gavel and crashed it onto the sound block.

Silence fell over the room.

"Brothers," he began. "Last night, Cash's ol' lady passed out in the O'Shea's pub. She'd been roofied."

Mutters rose through the room.

Dad lifted his hand for silence. "She's gonna be okay. But the fact that it happened to one of our own means that now, it's on us to stamp out the scumbag who's fuckin' with our town and, by extension, our club."

Shouts of agreement went up.

"Had a powwow with the Sheriff this mornin'. We've agreed that three groups of Speed Demons'll patrol different areas in town from Thursdays through to Sundays until we catch the sick bastard. We've narrowed down the places where we think the deals are takin' place."

Dad stopped, then nodded to Atlas.

The SAA stood slowly and looked around the room. "We need volunteers. Some'a you men got families and need to be with 'em, so, we ain't gonna force it on ya, but we need ya brothers. If you can spare us your time, then stand."

Kit, Reno, Chaps, and Shotgun all stood.

They prospected together and were close buds. One of 'em didn't do anythin' without the others also doin' it. Partyin', workin'. I sometimes suspected that it even extended to fuckin', too.

Iceman and Abe stood simultaneously when I got to my feet.

One by one, men began to rise from their seats. Fender got to his feet. His wife just had twins. I gave him a chin lift, a sign of my gratitude.

Within a minute, every single man was on their feet.

Atlas looked around the room. "Well, lookee here, we've got enough men to do a rotation. The brothers who ain't got kids will be scheduled for one shift per week, the ones who have, once every two weeks. We may call on you if we need extra bodies patrolling at weekends, but I think we're sorted."

Dad looked around. "First sign'a danger, you shoot first, ask questions last. I'd rather visit you in the big house than visit your grave. Make sure all your gun permits are up to date. Any problems with 'em, see Colt. He'll sort it."

Dad leaned across the table, palms flat. "I'd rather you didn't shoot to kill 'cause I'm lookin' for some club justice, but if it's a choice between you and him, always choose you. Ya get me, brothers?"

Multiple voices called out in reply.

"Yeah, Prez."

"Got ya."

"Will do."

Dad nodded. "I appreciate ya, brothers." He stood up straight and bellowed our club motto. "Mess with a Demon?"

I joined in with all the other voices, shouting our reply. "And we'll raise Hell." A loud roar went through the room.

This club, these men, were in my blood. They were part of me.

I stood, snapped my back straight, and joined in with the raucous cheers.

"Meetin' adjourned," Dad shouted over the din before smashing the gavel down.

Music began to thump through the speakers. Men surged to the bar to snatch up the bottles of beer that Boner was quickly poppin' the tops off.

All of us officers weaved through the crowd, heading toward the far couch reserved for us only.

As I headed over, I caught sight of Kit and did a double take. He was kissin' April, one of the club girls. That in itself wasn't the issue. The issue was that she was the one Xander cheated with back in the day.

We didn't blame her for what happened. If we did, she wouldn't be here. Xan was the one with a girlfriend. He was the one who should'a kept his dick in his pants. She was doin' her job, though I suspected she wasn't as innocent as he made herself out to be. I didn't trust her at fuckin' all. Kit needed to watch his back.

I slumped down onto my seat and looked over at my brother again. He was talkin' to Hammer with his hand glued to April's ass.

Fuck's sake. My little brother had a fuckin' harem of women. Why the hell would he pick the one who fucked Cara over? This was precisely like Kit though, thinkin' with his dick.

It's not that Kit wasn't loyal, but sometimes he didn't think. He was a pure hedonist.

"Every team needs a leader," Atlas said, his eyes following mine to Kit. "Think Breaker's ready?"

"Nah," Dad replied. "Kit's not ready. He'll get there, but for now, it's a no. What about Reno? He won't let you down."

Atlas nodded thoughtfully. "Already had him in mind. The officers can lead along with Fender and Reno. I was also gonna suggest Riggs."

"Good choice," Drix agreed. "He'll do well."

Dad looked at me. "Layla gonna be okay with you patrollin'?"

After what happened to Cara, I knew my girl would want me to move mountains if it'd help catch the fuckers who hurt her friend.

I gulped down a mouthful of beer. "Layla understands."

"That's why she's gonna be a good ol' lady, Son."

"Yeah."

Ice turned to me. "How's Cara doin'?"

"Spoke to Seth before I came here. She's awake, but she's not right. Layla said she'd head over there before she picks Sunny up from Iris. I'll get the lowdown from her later."

Dad took a swig of his beer. "Your brother's callin' tonight. This'll send him apeshit."

"So don't tell him."

"And when he finds out I kept my trap shut? He'll hulk out."

"Better at home than in lock-up."

Dad thought for a few seconds. "Maybe."

"He's weeks away from getting' out, Pop," I said, peeling at the label on my bottle. "If he pops off in there, he won't get parole."

"Bowie's right, Prez," Drix agreed. "Play it safe. Once he's out, he can hunt the fucker down with the rest of us."

Atlas let out a grunt. "If we haven't caught him by then."

"Hope it's me who gets to shoot him up the ass," Dad muttered.

Ice snorted. "Ditto."

I took another pull of my beer. Xander had a short fuse. It was the thing that landed him inside in the first place. That, and Robbie fuckin' Henderson.

If he found out what had happened to Cara, he'd flip. He still called her his ol' lady and was convinced she wouldn't go through with the wedding.

My gut dropped at the thought of Xan gettin' out, then gettin' sent back in. His sentence would be a nightmare. They'd lock him up and throw away the key.

Fingers of trepidation curled in my chest as I came to a realization.

It was clear we had to catch the sick fuck, yesterday.

Chapter Nineteen

Layla

Cara was napping when I arrived at her parent's house.

She'd been discharged from the hospital that morning. The doctor told her dad they should keep a close eye on her but let her sleep it off.

Her parents were worried sick. Seth was more stoic than Deborah, but I could tell that underneath his calm exterior, he was concerned.

Deb pulled me inside, ushering me into the kitchen. I loved her house. The kitchen was huge and modern, with slate floors and countertops.

She looked dead on her feet. Her face was pale. Brown eyes, identical to Cara's, were hooded with fatigue. "Are you hungry?" she asked.

"Starving," I said as I sat on a stool at the counter.

I'd built up an appetite that morning with Bowie.

I never knew sex could be like that. Our first time was good, but earlier, when he whispered all those dirty words, it blew my mind.

My pussy clenched at the memory of his fingers stroking my clit. I rubbed my thighs together discreetly, trying to alleviate the ache.

Deb had her back to me. She opened the fridge, pulled out a plate, and set it in front of me. "I made a sandwich for Cara, but she doesn't want to eat."

"Thank you, this is amazing," I said, lifting it to my mouth.

Deborah bit at the inside of her lip worriedly. "It's not like my girl not to eat. She loves her food."

I swallowed down my bite and grinned. "Cara would kill you for saying that."

"I don't know why it's so embarrassing for you girls to eat these days," she muttered. "My Cara's so clever and talented. She shouldn't be worrying about her image. It speaks for itself."

I chewed thoughtfully. I would have given anything to have a mom like Deb. She was Cara's biggest cheerleader. She gave her support when needed and space when not. It was probably a big part of why my friend was so strong and confident.

Cara was the most discerning person I knew. She was intelligent and quick-minded, which, when mixed with her beauty, was a lethal combination. I couldn't work out how this could have happened to her.

She made teenage boys cry when they thought they could screw around in her class. Well, the ones who weren't crushing on her, at least.

"You can go up if you want," Deb said, voice quiet with exhaustion. "Can you take some water up with you? She needs to drink fluids."

I ate the last bite of my sandwich, then washed my hands at the sink. Deb took a bottle of water from the fridge and handed it to me.

I walked up the stairs. Cara's bedroom door was closed, so I gave it a light rap.

"Who is it?" she called, her voice groggy.

I turned the handle, opened the door, and poked my head around it. "It's just me. Your mom said that you need to drink some water."

Bowie

The light in the room was dim, but I could still see Cara slowly sitting.

I stepped inside the room and closed the door behind me. "How are you feeling?"

"Honestly? Like I've hit with a truck." Her voice was tired and a little slurred.

I made my way over to her, then sat on the edge of the bed. "Here, drink this." I held the bottle out.

She took it from me, unscrewed the cap, and sipped. Her skin was tinged with grey. Her usual silky hair was limp and dull. Her eyes were bloodshot, and half closed. She put the top back on the water and handed it to me.

I shook my head. "More."

She rolled her eyes but drank some down.

"Better." I took the bottle from her and placed it on the bedside table.

Cara dropped her gaze. "I'm sorry," she murmured.

"No. No, Cara. You didn't do anything wrong." I took her hand, heart twisting as she began to cry softly.

"It's just the drugs," she sobbed. "Freya said that I'd have a comedown."

"Move over," I commanded.

She shuffled across the bed. I positioned myself next to her and wrapped my arm around her shoulder. "I'm the one who's sorry. I could see you were upset about Robbie. I should have been keeping a closer eye on you."

"It's not your fault," she cried.

"And it's not yours either."

She sniffed. "It's just… I can't stop crying."

My heart clenched for her.

I remembered feeling the same way after the night I got drunk and passed out. The only difference was I'd been left with something more than a hangover.

"It will pass," I crooned in her ear.

"I know I'm being a big baby." she sobbed. "But my head hurts so bad. I'm confused and disorientated. I've lost hours out of my life."

155

Something pinged in the back of my mind, and unease crept through me.

"Mom keeps making me drink water. But I'm scared in case I have to get up and go to the bathroom. I get so dizzy."

My brow furrowed as I tried to think.

Cara hiccoughed. "There's no food in my stomach, but it's cramping. I try to vomit, but nothing's there."

A memory hit me like lightning. Crawling to my kitchen, guzzling water. My stomach turned, making me stumble for the bathroom.

Cara described the symptoms I'd had after the night I blacked out, the night I got pregnant with Sunny.

A shudder went through me.

"And I miss Xander," she wailed.

Shock at her words pushed the memory away. "What?" I asked, voice stunned.

"I know I'm weak, but he always looked after me when I was sick." Another sniff. "I won't get back with the cheating pig, but it's at times like this that I wish he were here."

My arm tightened around her. "I think it's natural to feel that way, Cara. You guys were so much in love." I rested my cheek on her head. "Do you love Robbie?"

"No."

My eye widened in surprise. "Then why are you marrying him?"

"Because he'd never cheat on me."

My mind wandered back to last night when Robbie was flirting with Sydney at the bar. "Even if that were true, Cara, it's not a reason to marry someone."

"It is," she argued. "Xan broke me. I was a mess. I couldn't eat, I couldn't sleep, I couldn't function. I was lost."

"I don't understand."

"I never want to go through that again. The first time almost destroyed me. Robbie's good to me, his family is nice. He'll be a good husband, and that's all I need."

I touched her hand. "But you don't love Robbie."

"Exactly. If I don't love him, he can't hurt me."

Sadness for my friend swept over me. "Cara, you can't marry someone you don't love. You're not being fair to Robbie, and you're not being fair to yourself."

A thought hit me, and I gave her a concerned look. "You're supposed to be getting married in a few weeks."

"Robbie knows, and he doesn't care," she said quietly.

"Why would he want to marry someone who doesn't love him?"

She lifted one shoulder. "I care about Rob. He says the love will come later."

"Will it?" I asked.

"No," she murmured. "I'm done with love."

Tears filled my eyes. I pulled my arm from her shoulder and moved around to face each other. My chest twisted again when I saw the heartbreak stamped all over her features. "Cara. Please don't marry someone you don't love. It'll be disastrous."

Her back slumped. "Now's probably not the best time to discuss it, Layla. My head's all over the place."

I knew how she was feeling. I remember waking up in a strange bed at the party, not knowing where I was. It took me a while to even remember that I'd gone somewhere that night. I was so confused, disorientated, and sore.

"Tell me what happened with Bowie? I don't even remember them being there," Cara asked, interrupting my thoughts.

I couldn't stop a big smile from stealing across my face.

Her mouth dropped open. "Oh my God, did you—?"

"—Yes," I grinned. "This morning."

"Will he not see Sydney anymore?" The question hung in the air.

My lips pursed. "She was lying. He went to the hospital to see Freya, and Sydney tried to kiss him. He pushed her away."

"That bitch," she snipped, eyes turning hard. "She's such a snake. I'm sure she tries to hit on Robbie too."

I winced as again I recalled Robbie with Sydney last night.

"So, how was it?" she asked, voice curious.

My heart sped up as I thought about her question. "Amazing."

"Your eyes have gone all gooey," she smiled. "Did Bowie make you…. You know?"

My cheeks heated. "Twice."

"Sounds just like his brother. It must be a family mantra."

"What?"

Cara smiled. "Ladies first."

A laugh escaped me. Cara joined in but grimaced, raising her hands to rub her temples. "Don't. It hurts when I laugh."

Another laugh bubbled up my throat. Cara joined in and winced again. "Sweet Jesus. My head's going to explode," she whined. Then she yawned.

"I'll let you get some more sleep." I leaned forward. "If you need anything, you call."

"I will."

We hugged, and she settled back down in bed. I stood, headed for the door, opened it, and looked back. "Love you, Cara."

"Love you back."

I walked out and closed the door quietly behind me.

After saying my goodbyes to Deborah, I set off for home. I was glad for the walk. It would give me time to think.

Bowie

My memories of the night Sunny was conceived were sketchy at best. It was Brett Stafford's birthday. He was home for the Summer, and his dad let him invite some friends over.

I remember arriving late and talking to a group of girls I knew from school. I didn't really notice who handed me the red solo cup of beer, then another, and another.

After a while, my limbs began to feel heavy. I felt nauseous, so I went to the bathroom. The next thing I remembered, I woke almost naked, aching all over.

It took me almost a week to recover.

At the time, I thought I was suffering from a bad hangover. I didn't question it because I had no point of reference to compare it to. I'd hardly drunk any alcohol before.

At the time, I asked around to see if anyone knew what had happened. Brett said he remembered seeing me all over some guy from his college. I assumed we'd both been drunk and had sex. I felt sick that I'd lost my virginity to a complete stranger.

Someone whose name I couldn't even remember.

Later, when I found out I was pregnant, I asked Brett for his friend's number or address. He said the guy had already graduated and had left.

I had no way of contacting him, so I put it down to experience. Soon after, I lost my job, and my pregnancy got tough. I had bigger things on my mind, so I pushed it all down and accepted it for what it was.

But now, after speaking to Cara, something felt off.

I'd had hangovers since, but none like that. I knew my alcohol tolerance wasn't high, but three beers? No, something wasn't right.

Tendrils of anxiety began to wrap around my chest. They squeezed so tight that my breathing became rough.

Confusion, nausea, feeling low emotionally, tiredness, and a considerable chunk of time lost. It all stunk of the same familiarity.

Deep down inside, I knew that there was more to the story. I think I always had. I was just too terrified to face it. At the time, I knew nothing added up, but I stupidly ignored it. I think I was frightened by the truth.

Now, I had no choice. I had to start going over the events of that night.

Something had happened to me, and it was bad.

Chapter Twenty

Bowie

I was heading out to my bike when my phone chimed.

Abe *Your OL's at mine. Y the fk hasn't she got a ride?*

I frowned down at my cell. My gut tightened as I began to wrack my brain.

I'd never seen Doe driving. The only time I'd seen her in a car was when she was in Cara's or Anna's. There wasn't a vehicle at her house, either.

Guilt tugged at my chest. I should have been paying attention. Layla was mine to look after. It was my responsibility to make sure she was okay.

I swung my leg over my saddle and mounted my bike. "Way to fuckin' go, asshole," I grumbled to myself. I strapped my helmet on. When it was secure, I flicked the switch and pulled away.

It took me just under five minutes to get to Abe's place.

His house was built on club land, right at the edge of the acreage we bought along with the warehouse. Abe said he liked living outta town 'cause he was away from all the bullshit. I was beginning to understand where he was comin' from.

I pulled up outside his sprawling ranch house and switched off my engine. I looked up as the front door slammed and saw Abe descending the porch steps.

Our secretary prospected into the club under my grandpa's rule. He was sixty years old but looked ten years younger. He always said club life aged you, but you wouldn't know it by looking at him.

"She turned up for Sunny just after I got in," Abe said as he walked toward me. "I asked her where her car was. She said she walked." He folded his arms across his chest and glared at me. "Nearly three fuckin' miles."

I gripped the back of my neck and looked down at my boots.

"What the fuck, Bowie? Why hasn't she got a vehicle?"

My gut twisted. "I didn't know."

"It's your fuckin' job to know. You're her ol' man, ain't ya?"

"Yeah, but only just."

"You think I'd let my Iris walk miles around town? Especially with all this drug business goin' on."

"No," I began, "But—"

Abe glared. "—But nothin', boy. Get it sorted."

I jerked a nod and made my way toward the porch. He was right. I needed to get a fuckin' grip on what was happening around me.

As I walked past him, his big hand clasped my shoulder. "How did you miss it, Bo?"

I scraped one hand down my face. "I don't fuckin' know. We only went out once, and I assumed she got a cab 'cause I was takin' my girl home. She never mentioned it. I never thought to ask."

"She's proud and works hard."

My chest puffed out slightly. "Yeah."

"I like that about her."

"Me too," I said as the door flew open, and a mini tornado crashed down the porch.

"Bowie!" Sunny shrieked. "Mama's sad." She stumbled slightly, and a little hand went around my knee to steady herself.

I looked down into big grey eyes, my gut clenching. "Why?" I asked.

"She said she's fine, but when Mama says that, it means she's sad, or I've done something wrongs."

I gave her the same look my dad gave me when I'd been up to no good. "Have you been good for Iris?"

She looked up at me with a pout, then took her hands from my leg, punchin' 'em onto her hips. "I'm always good."

"That's my girl." I shot her a grin. Then, I crouched down so we were eye to eye. "I need to take your mom somewhere urgent, Princess. Would it be okay if you stayed with Iris a bit longer?"

She put her finger to her lip, takin' a few seconds to think. "Yes," she said decisively. "'Cause I can helps Iris with dinner."

"How about tonight I take you and your mom out to eat?"

Her little face lit up, and she punched the air. "Yes!" she shrieked and began to twirl around with her arms out by her sides.

I gave Abe a 'what the fuck' look. "Is she okay?"

"She's a little girl, Bo," he snorted. "They do this kinda shit."

"You said a bad word," Sunny sang. "You're a naughty man."

The door swung open as I barked out a laugh. I looked up to see Layla, and Iris, making their way down the steps.

I approached Layla, grabbed her hand, and helped her down the last few steps, pulling her into me and kissing the top of her head.

Her shoulders slumped. I pulled back, tilted her chin up, lookin' into her eyes. "Why didn't you tell me you haven't got a ride?" I demanded gently.

Confusion flashed across her face. "Why would I?"

"You need a car."

Her forehead scrunched up. "Yeah. I'm saving up for one."

"I've got a car you can have."

"No."

"Yes."

"Bowie, I—"

"—Yes!"

Her mouth went tight. "You're so bossy," she exclaimed.

Iris threw her head back and let out a short laugh. "You better get used to it, Layla, girl. These men don't take no for an answer." Her eyes softened slightly. "He's right, though. You do need a car."

Sunny grabbed her hand. "Please, mama, my foots might fall off if I haves to keep on walking a lot."

"I thought you liked walking?" Layla asked, eyes narrowing.

Sunny shrugged. "I didn't wants you to be sad that my legs hurt."

Layla's face paled. "Oh my God," she mumbled, voice laced with guilt.

I looked at Iris. "Can we borrow your brain bucket?"

Iris nodded and ran back up the steps to the house. Seconds later, she came out with a silver helmet. She clattered down the porch steps and handed it to Layla. "There you go. Sunshine can help me peel potatoes while you're gone." She looked down at the little girl. "Right?"

Sunny furiously nodded her head. Iris grabbed her hand and led her back onto the porch.

Sunny stopped, looked back, and waved. "Bye!"

I saluted her loosely with two fingers, then got on my bike. "C'mon." I held out my hand.

Layla grabbed my fingers and got on behind me. We both pulled on our helmets and secured them.

"What are you up to?" Layla asked from behind me.

I grinned and patted her knee. "You'll see."

An hour later, I followed Layla, who was driving her new car.

When we left Abe's, we rode to my place. I led her inside the garage and told her to pick anything she wanted. Well, anything except my other bike and my truck.

Sayin' that. Her other choices weren't too fuckin' shabby.

My garage housed a nineteen-sixty blue Chevy convertible, which I'd restored from scratch, A two-year-old silver Tesla, and a four-year-old black Impala.

In my mind's eye, I pictured my two girls cruisin' around town in the Chevy with the top down with the wind blowing through their hair. The image made my chest warm.

I slowed to a stop and pulled up behind the shiny black Impala. Layla got out of the driver's side and shut the door.

She went for safety. Go figure.

I removed my helmet, kicked on the stand, and jogged over to my girl, who was about to open the back passenger side to get Sunny out.

I pulled her gently outta the way, opened the door, then bent inside to pull Sunny outta the new car seat, which was fitted just before we picked her up from Abe's.

"It smells like candy," Sunny squealed.

Layla let out a soft laugh from behind me. "She has a thing about car smells. She says Anna's smells like perfume."

"And Cara's smells like flowers," Sunny added.

I undid the straps and gently took her arms out. I lifted Sunshine from her seat, stepped back, and gently placed her on the ground. She ran straight off toward the house.

"Thank you," Layla murmured. "Are you sure you won't need the car?"

I grabbed onto her belt loops and pulled her into me. "It's yours, Doe."

Somethin' moved behind her eyes.

I gently palmed her face and gently kissed her.

She let out a sigh.

"You okay?" I asked.

Her mouth turned down at the corners. "Yeah."

"I'm hungry!" Sunny yelled out.

Layla pulled away, looking down.

I frowned. "Doe. Have I done somethin' wrong? Is the car too much?"

"No. No. No," she assured me, grabbing my hand. "The car's amazing. Honestly, I think I'm just tired."

Relief made me grin. "Well, we did have one hell of a mornin'."

"Yeah," she said absentmindedly, starting toward the house.

I frowned. What the hell was goin' on? My woman was sweet and funny. She always had a cute little comeback when I made one of my quips.

My eyes followed her as she walked away. She unlocked the door, then swung it open for Sunny, who ran inside. Layla disappeared behind her, leaving the door open for me, not even looking behind her to see if I was following her. It was like she was in a dream state.

What the fuck had I done? I gripped the back of my neck and thought back to earlier.

Bowie

When I left her, she seemed okay. In fact, she was all smiles, seeing as I'd made her come twice. She'd been to see Cara. Maybe she was worried? I quickly nixed that idea, seein' as Doe already told me she was on the mend.

Somethin' had happened between this mornin' and now.

She wasn't herself; It was more than bein' tired and preoccupied. It was clear as day that she had somethin' big on her mind.

And I was gonna find out what it was.

Chapter Twenty-One

Layla

Bowie was angry with me, and I couldn't blame him one bit.

It had been nearly a week since I'd talked to Cara in her bedroom at her parent's house. It was almost a week since I'd begun to suspect things weren't as they seemed.

I couldn't stop thinking about the night I'd passed out.

For the first time in years, things were beginning to make sense. My blackout, my symptoms, the way I was for days after. It all pointed to me being drugged.

Dark thoughts hijacked my mind as I weighed everything up.

Had somebody taken advantage of me? Had someone walked into that party intending to hurt me? Or was I just unlucky and in the wrong place at the wrong time?

The only thing that made me question myself was the timing.

Sunday night, I asked Bowie—casually, of course—if he knew exactly when the assaults had begun. He told me that it was about three years before.

The night in question was six years ago. Years before, the police had picked up on any crimes being committed.

I wondered if the assaults began before Bowie said, but the authorities hadn't picked up on a pattern. I hadn't reported what had happened to the police. It never even crossed my mind. So, maybe I wasn't the only one.

The questions were starting to affect my well-being.

I was a mess. I couldn't eat. I was having nightmares. Everything felt wrong. Sunny kept me functioning, but it was evident to Bowie that I had something on my mind.

He repeatedly asked me to talk to him, but I couldn't. We'd been together for just weeks. How could I tell him what was going through my head when I didn't know for sure what had happened myself?

The week had started off okay. Sunny was on summer break.

I took her to the salon with me for a couple of days, then Iris and Rosie stepped in, and she also spent time at their houses.

I was going through the motions at work but also at home. Every time Bowie touched me, I couldn't help wincing. Every time I pulled away from him, his face fell.

He looked bewildered by it all. I felt like such a bitch.

By Thursday, he'd had enough of my horrible mood.

He told me he was swamped with work and club business and needed to stay at the compound for a while.

It broke my heart, but I couldn't blame him.

I spent the days and nights cursing my memory. I needed to know what had happened; it drove me crazy. Then I'd cry because the thought of actually knowing, of reliving it, made me sick to my stomach.

I kept up appearances at work. The salon was the only place where I could get my mind off things, so on Friday, when Anna asked me to work overtime the next day, I jumped at the chance.

After a busy week, Saturday morning had been busy at the salon with ladies wanting to be pampered. When lunchtime came around, I'd offered to go to Magnolia's coffeehouse to pick up lunch for everyone.

After a week of thinking about that night, I'd concluded that I had to speak to Brett Stafford again. The thought of it made me uneasy, but he was my only lead.

When I walked into Magnolia's and glanced around, my heart stopped.

Brett was in sitting in the back corner, tapping on his phone.

All week, I'd made myself crazy thinking about Brett and what he'd told me back then. I was convinced he was lying. He'd been so cagey about everything.

Did I want to talk to him? No, I didn't like or trust him, but what other choice did I have?

I gave Magnolia my order, paid, and turned to face where Brett was sitting. I took a deep breath, then weaved between the other tables of people relaxing with their coffees.

As I stopped next to him, he looked up. His eyes flashed with surprise, and his features turned into a sneer. "Look, it's the biker bitch coming to ruin my day." He looked back down at his phone and said in a bored tone. "What do you want?"

Stomach swirling, I pulled out the chair opposite him and sat down. My fingers shook slightly, so I folded them into my lap.

I hated confrontation,

"Don't remember inviting you to join me," he muttered.

"I want to talk to you about that night, Brett, and what happened."

He froze for a few seconds. "We already talked about it."

I smiled, trying to take the edge off what I was about to say. "Your friend, the one you said I was with at your party, Sunny's dad. I need to get in touch with him."

"Sorry, sweetheart." A cloud of nonchalance settled over him. "No can do."

Desperation tugged inside my chest. "I need to know, Brett. You said his name was Justin Smith, but there are a thousand Justin Smiths in America. I need to track him down." I tried to keep my voice low and not scream at him the way I wanted to.

Brett shrugged, "Can't help you."

"What town is he from? What state?"

Another shrug. "You're wasting your time."

"Why won't you tell me?" I pleaded.

"Because I don't know."

"Please, Brett…" My voice trailed off. An idea began to grow in my mind. I looked up into his eyes, searching, then went for gold. "I-I think he may have drugged me."

I was looking for a reaction, for any clue that he knew more than he told me, and I got it. The color drained from his features. It would have been comical if the situation wasn't so serious.

He cleared his throat, unsure, then stuttered. "Don't be stupid." His voice was a croak. "Who'd want to drug you?"

"Somebody did it, Brett."

"Stop lying."

"I'm not lying."

"You are."

He was the one lying through his teeth. I could sense the agitation coming off him in waves. "What if I went to your dad and told him what happened to me in his house? Would he help me?"

I sat back and waited.

Brett's face turned from white to red. I could almost feel his irritation morph into anger. "You say one word to my dad, and I'll come after you, bitch."

I blanched at the vein of threat in his voice. Why was he so angry? If he was innocent, wouldn't he want to get to the bottom of what happened? To rule himself out, at least.

"Look, Brett," I said, leaning toward him. "Something happened to me at that party, and you know what it was. I won't stop until I find out."

A muscle ticked in his jaw. "Layla. You drank too much and threw yourself at an innocent man." He curled his lip into a smirk. "Why're you doing this? Is it about money?"

Exasperation rose through me. "It's got nothing to with money. I've been supporting my daughter since the day she was born. That won't change. The only thing I want is justice."

Brett snorted. "Justice? You're looking for an easy payout."

"I don't care about money," I told him, my voice rising.

Brett's eyes darted nervously around the room. "Keep it down," he hissed.

I craned my neck to see a few people at nearby tables looking at us.

"Sorry," he called out as he held up his hands. "Just friends having a disagreement. Didn't mean to disturb you."

My head whipped back to him. "Now, who's the liar?"

Brett's entire body stiffened. He pushed his chair back against the wall with a loud scrape, then stood. "I don't need to listen to this. I'll give you one last warning. I'll sue you for defamation if you mention your pathetic lies to anyone else." His lips twisted into a mocking grin. "I know a good lawyer."

His words made me shrink back into the chair. My insides curled, but then a flicker of something burned in my stomach. Resentment.

This was my life, my body. I wasn't a commodity for his friends to use whenever they felt like it. Why did everything have to be at my expense? Where were their morals?

Back then, when I realized that I'd had sex that night, I felt used and cheap, but I thought maybe we were both drunk, and perhaps I was to blame too.

Now, things were different.

Somebody set out to take advantage of me that night. They drugged and violated me. I was guilty of being naïve and stupid, but they were guilty of much more. Why should they get away with it?

"I'm not letting this drop, Brett," I warned.

"Then you'll be sorry." He put his phone in his pocket and sidled past me. "Remember, Layla. Say a word about me, and you'll suffer."

And with that, he weaved through the tables and out the door.

My hand went straight to my heart.

It was thudding so hard I imagined my skin pumping in and out in time to its rhythm. I breathed in slowly, then out, repeating the action, trying to calm down.

Dazed and even more confused, I stood and went to the counter.

I took hold of the coffee Magnolia had put in a cup holder for me, thanked her, and walked outside. I was on autopilot.

My eyes squinted in the bright sunshine. It seemed harsher somehow. Maybe the universe was trying to tell me that the world wasn't safe, that I needed to wake up and see the light.

I glanced across the street and spied Brett on his phone.

He was talking to someone animatedly. He was shouting, but not loud enough that I could pick out the words.

His eyes lifted to mine and even from across the street. I could see the stern glare he sent my way. His entire body was wired in anger, or was it fear?

Bowie

I ignored him and pulled my shoulders back, beginning the short walk back to the salon. Adrenaline coursed through me, making my fingers shake.

My senses screamed that Brett was somehow involved. His reactions and emotions made it obvious.

All I wanted to do was call Bowie and tell him what I knew, but I didn't. Instead, I made a plan. I'd call him after work, ask him over, make dinner, apologize for how I acted, and then tell him everything.

Regret burned in my chest when I thought about how I'd pushed him away. I knew in my bones that he'd understand, even help me. I'd just needed space to get things straight in my head.

My heart sank when I thought about how much that night six years ago had cost me and how close I'd come to losing everything. The repercussions were still affecting me.

I couldn't let what had happened take me down.

I had to speak to someone, maybe, the police. My only issue was that it had happened six years ago. I didn't know if they'd even take me seriously now.

It was time to take the bull by the horns and work through it.

Bowie had been there for me, begging me to talk to him, and I would.

When I thought of how long it had taken us to get together, I knew one thing above all else.

It had cost me enough. I couldn't also let it cost me, Bowie.

Chapter Twenty-Two

Bowie

The orange and red sky cast a colorful hue over the whitewashed buildings as we walked through town on Saturday night.

It was gettin' on for nine pm, and the sun was just settin'. A sure sign, along with the warmth, that summer was upon us.

Colt had scheduled me to lead one of the patrols.

Shotgun was walking at my side, Boner taking our backs. Our footsteps echoed up and through the narrow alleyways that ran up behind Main Street.

I probably should've cried off seein' as my mind wasn't on the job. It was consumed by Layla.

Last weekend, after we picked up her car and returned to her place, she was quiet and withdrawn.

Initially, I'd let it go, thinkin' she'd come round soon enough.

We went to bed and got under the sheets. I reached for my girl, but she turned her back on me. I tried to pull her around, to hold her, but she said she wanted space.

I lay there in the dark, hands behind my head, brain whirring with questions. Was the car too much? Fuck, was I too much?

I put it down to her bein' tired from Cara's ER trip the night before, so I closed my eyes and went to sleep.

Monday night, it was like Layla was there physically, but mentally she'd checked out. She pushed her food around her plate, eyes misty, deep in thought, distant. I helped with the dishes. Afterward, she played quietly with Sunny until bedtime.

She gave me her back again that night.

Tuesday was the same.

By Wednesday night, we were hardly talkin'.

Even Sunny picked up on the weird vibe. She became sullen, whiny. A different kid than what I was used to.

A dark cloud sat over the house, casting its gloom over everyone.

Layla was so distant that I may as well not have been there.

Later that night, I woke up to her crying in her sleep. I tried to comfort her, but she pulled away again and said it was nothin', just a bad dream.

I lay awake for the rest of the night, sick to my stomach, just thinkin'.

By the time six am came around, I'd been awake for hours, thinkin' the worst. Anger and confusion nipped at my insides, and I knew I'd blow if I stayed around.

I tried one last time to get through to her. I begged her to let me in, but she kept sayin' she was fine and that it was nothing.

I went to stroke her cheek, cup her face in my hands, and make her see that she could trust me, but she shrank away.

Pain exploded in my chest, and I knew that was it. I couldn't do it anymore. I told her I had shit to do, so I'd sleep at the club. I couldn't stay there while she was freezin' me out. I didn't wanna argue in front of Sunny and end up losin' her completely, so I walked.

The jury was still out on if I'd done the right thing, seein' as I hadn't heard a thing from Doe since, even though I'd left countless messages.

Bowie

And it was fuckin' killin' me.

I was hardly sleepin'. My nights were spent workin' up a sweat in the ring. Atlas picked up on my restlessness and appointed himself as my shadow while we lifted weights and sparred in the club's huge gym.

The Demon's SAA could be a mouthy fuck, but he had my back when it counted.

I was pulled outta my thoughts by the sound of our boots scuffling over the sidewalk. I checked the inside of my cut when my Glock-17 sat nestled comfortably in my body holster, then glanced back to make sure Boner was still at my six.

My feet ground to a halt when I saw that he'd stopped ten meters back and was looking somewhere behind him.

I gave Shotgun a nudge. He turned, and we both made our way toward the prospect.

We were down an alley past the salon, a ten-foot gap between two buildings. Anna's place sat at one end of the alley, the other end leading onto Main Street, comin' out near Magnolia's coffee shop.

A musical beat thumped through the air.

The Lucky Shamrock sat about two-hundred meters from our position, on the same street as Mag's place but further up to the right, out of sight from where we were standing.

The sound of the music, and people having a good time, was comforting somehow. Reminding me that civilization was just around the corner.

The night was beginnin' to wrap us up in her cool arms.

Darkness had begun to descend. It cast shadows up the walls of the buildings, which now appeared dusky grey without the light of the sunset's colorful rays.

Boner turned to us as we approached. "Heard somethin' behind me, boss."

My wits immediately went on high alert. Boner had done three years in the Marines. If he heard somethin', I was takin' it very fuckin' seriously.

I closed my eyes, stretchin' my neck from left to right, gettin' in the zone, takin' in my environment, and honing my senses.

My ears picked up at the eerie echo of a glass bottle rollin' on concrete in the distance. I could've ignored it if the sound came from Callum's place to my rear, but it came from the direction of the salon.

Me and Shotgun looked at each other.

"Did you hear that?" His voice was a rasp.

A shiver of awareness went from the top of my spine to the bottom.

"Could'a been a cat," Boner muttered.

Then the echo of running feet sounded down the alley, drawing our eyes back.

That feelin' hit me again, Icy fingers strokin' down my back. "That's no fuckin' cat," I growled. "C'mon."

My body poised and ready, I began to run.

The thud of my footsteps pounded off the concrete path that led up toward Anna's shop. Boots slapping on the ground sounded from behind, reassuring me that Boner and Shotgun were at my back.

My heart raced, adrenaline making the blood roar in my ears. I pumped my arms hard, adding momentum to my sprint.

Years of training had bulked me up, but boxing was also about speed and endurance. Boner trained too, but he was more about adding muscle mass. Shotgun was fit, but he didn't spend much time workin' out.

I burst out of the mouth of the alley and onto the street by the salon, the shallow breaths of my brothers puffing hard behind me.

I slowed down, looking around, desperate for a sign.

Movement caught the corner of my eye. My head jerked to the right. A flash of somethin' turning down another alley on the opposite side of the street, between *Blooms* and the bookstore, *Turning the Page.*

I raised my arm and pointed toward the alley. "There," I yelled. Then I took off again, gathering pace as I sprinted across the road.

My chest was fit to burst. My breath sawed in and outta my chest. I breathed through my nose and out of my mouth, desperately tryin' to get air into my lungs.

Boner and Shot were just hitting the sidewalk when I reached the end of the alley. I pulled up to a stop and peered down into the darkness.

All I could see was black. A dark void of nothingness.

I was about to walk away when what sounded like a quiet grunt came floating through the ether. My heart jumped into my throat.

I took deep breaths, tryin' to calm my thudding heart, to tamp down the adrenaline coursin' through my veins.

I wasn't fearful or even nervous. I just wanted to get it done, then go talk to Layla.

"Who's there?" I called out. "Show yourself, and nobody'll get hurt."

A quiet laugh drifted from the darkness.

Footsteps drew up behind me. I glanced around and saw my brothers. "Stay here. I'm gonna find out what the fuck's goin' on." My voice was low, quiet, and angry.

"You sure, Bowie?" Shotgun asked, "I can back you up."

"Nope," I replied. "It's time to pay the fuckin' piper. I want you both up here in case he gets past me."

Shotgun's hand clapped my shoulder, then fell away as I began to stalk slowly into the darkness.

My pulse began to quicken again. "Who's there?"
Silence.

I walked further into the alley, my heart thumping outta my chest, makin' the blood rush through my veins.

As my eyes adjusted to the darkness, I saw movement again. I was slowly picking my way further down the alley when the body of a man loomed in front of me.

He was dressed in black, head to toe. A black baseball cap covered his hair. A black balaclava hid his face.

"You better fuckin' stop right there, asshole." My voice came out with a menacing growl, making the man freeze on the spot.

My hand snaked up my chest toward my gun.

As my fingers touched the coldness of the barrel, the man spun quickly and held an arm out, pointin' it in my direction.

I caught the glint of metal.

"Don't be stup—" I began. A spark from the gun blinded me simultaneously as a loud *bang* punctured the air, and the earsplitting volume pulsed through my ears.

A sudden, burning pain raged through my chest.

My hand flew to the skin that seemed to be on fire, but when I pulled it away and looked down, blood coated my fingers instead of flame.

Deep shouts rang out behind me. Someone bellowin' my name, Boner, I think. Then the pain seared through me again, making me drop to my knees.

The rattle of a chain fence jarred me to look up. The shadowy figure climbed up and over the top. My eyes were glued to the masked man as he dropped to the ground, vanishing into the night.

A hand on my back. Then a shout. "Call an ambulance!"

The edges of my vision began to darken, and I was falling. My head hit the cold, hard ground as a vortex began to suck me into its murky, black depths.

And as I tumbled into its deep, dark hole, one name fell from my lips.

Layla.

Chapter Twenty-Three

Layla

A loud *bang* on the door woke me.

I must have fallen asleep on the couch. The book I'd been reading was lying open across my chest. I'd probably dropped it there when I drifted off.

Bang, bang, bang.

I sat up with a start and glanced at the clock. It was just after midnight.

Bang, bang, bang.

I swung my legs off the couch, planted my feet on the floor, and stood.

My stomach fluttered. *Bowie,* I thought as I quickly started through the hallway and stumbled to the front door. I'd messaged him earlier, but he hadn't replied. I tried to call, but no answer. Why was he knocking when he had a key?

I looked through the peephole, and my brow furrowed when I saw Iris and Abe waiting.

My stomach gave a sickening clench.

Something was wrong.

I turned the key and released the chain with trembling fingers. Slowly, I pulled the door open. My heart sank despairingly when Iris' eyes lifted to mine. They were bloodshot as if she'd been crying.

Fear prickled through me. Somehow, I knew what she would say even before she said it.

"It's Bowie," she murmured.

My throat closed up. Suddenly, I couldn't get any air. Iris stepped inside the house and rubbed my back gently, her warm hands sending heat through me.

"Is he alive?" I croaked.

She nodded. "Yeah, but it's serious. I'll stay with Sunny. You need to go to him."

A sob burst out of my chest.

As I got to the threshold, Iris hissed, "Layla."

I stopped.

"You tell him he's not going anywhere. Tell him he's not to give up, that if he doesn't come back, you'll hunt him down and nag him for eternity. Tell him, Layla."

My heart began to shrivel up in my chest. A tear dripped from my chin.

"Layla," Iris said quietly. "Keep it together. Go."

I was still wearing my jeans and shirt from earlier. I slipped on my sneakers and wordlessly followed Abe to the door, then to his truck.

The fifteen-minute drive to the hospital seemed to take forever. The air inside was thick and black. I could almost touch the fear that weighed down the atmosphere.

"He's strong, Layla," Abe muttered.

"I know." My voice was flat.

"You keep talkin' to him. If anyone can pull him back, it's you."

Fear made my chest tight. He had to be okay because I'd never be the same if he left me. I'd stay on the earth for Sunny, but I wouldn't be me without him.

The lights from the hospital loomed ahead. Abe parked the truck and got out. I swiped at my cheeks, trying to put on a brave face while I waited for Abe to open my door.

Bowie

He took my hand, helped me down, then kept a tight hold of it through the reception, up in the elevator, and into the waiting room.

I was terrified. What if Bowie had already gone? What if he died thinking I didn't love him? Regret for the past week slammed into my chest, bringing more tears to my eyes.

A dozen faces turned to me. There was a second of quiet before I was swept up into strong arms. John.

I was like a rag doll, weak and limp. My legs trembled, and I itched all over. It felt like something crawling under my skin, something foreign and nasty.

"What happened?" My voice was muffled as I mumbled into his chest.

John released me, then stepped back. "He was patrollin'. He followed someone down an alley. Got shot."

I'd messaged him earlier. I told him I was sorry and asked him to come over, but he didn't reply. I thought he was busy. Thought maybe, it was his way of teaching me a lesson for not speaking to him for days, but all along, he was out getting shot.

My chest crumbled. More tears slipped down my cheek. "Will he die?" My tone was dead, like my soul.

"Bowie's lung collapsed. They took him into surgery."

"Will he die?"

"Layla—"

Frustration ripped inside me. "Will. He. Die?" I screeched, every muscle taut.

John's face smoothed out, expressionless. "I don't know."

I squeezed his hand, and with trembling knees, I turned and saw Freya sitting at the end of a row of hard plastic chairs secured to the wall. My throat burned as I walked over on trembling knees and sat beside her.

For the next hour, I went over every memory I had of Bowie, even the bad ones, because even though at the time they ripped me apart, now, I cherished every one of them. Any thought starring Bowie was a comfort.

I remembered years ago; I saw him in town. He was with a stunning blonde woman. My heart collapsed when he snaked his arm around her neck and pulled her into him. He kissed her hair, smiling.

I remember going home and thanking the universe that he was happy because I loved him enough to want that for him, even if it wasn't with me.

After that, I conceived Sunny.

I thought it was God's will. Maybe the love I'd prayed for since I was a girl wasn't meant for me, so, He gave me another great love in my daughter. Then, a few weeks ago, He gave me everything. I said a silent prayer and begged Him not to take it away.

My head lifted, and I stared around the room.

John was sitting opposite me, his head in his hands. Kit, next to him, stared into nothing. Atlas was pacing, his hand gripping the back of his neck. Other men I knew by sight but not by name were waiting silently.

How could I feel so alone in a room filled with people?

I glanced at the woman next to me. Freya, quiet and subdued.

I was numb, in limbo, lost to the fear that swirled around my head, infecting me with its darkness.

Footsteps echoed up the hall. More club brothers.

Reno first, then Colt murmured something to John. Hendrix walked over to us, squeezing my shoulder, then Freya's.

The room began to fill up until all the chairs were taken. Some men sat on the floor with their backs to the wall, heads bowed.

My stomach clenched with dread, then the squeak of sneakers on a tiled floor squealed from the other corridor.

Heads jerked up.

A woman dressed in scrubs entered the room, pulling a surgeon's cap from her head. "Family of Gage Stone?"

John stood, followed by Kit. Freya gripped my hand and stood, pulling me up with her.

Tension gripped my heart as we walked forward. My knees almost buckled. I desperately wanted to hear the words, but a small part of me shied away, fearing the worst.

Instead of retreating into a dark corner, I straightened my back and stood with Freya, John, and Kit. I had to do this.

"I'm Doctor Green. Gage is in recovery."

Relief spread through my blood at the words, then ebbed away again when she continued. "But he's not out of the woods yet."

John's eyes narrowed. "Tell us," he demanded, tension gripping his shoulders.

"The bullet caused a pneumo-hemothorax. I've repaired the damage, but Gage lost a lot of blood." She looked at all of us in turn, face sympathetic. "Tonight will be critical."

John's shoulders slumped. "Can we see him?"

The doctor smiled warmly. "He's being transferred to the ICU. We'll be a while setting him up, but yes. You can see him soon."

Kit's chest contracted like he'd been holding his breath for hours and could finally let it go. He bowed his head.

Freya grabbed my hand, leading me back to the chairs. "Sit," she murmured, "It's going to be a long night. We'll need our strength."

John murmured words to the men, and they started to leave one by one. They all clapped him, then Kit on the shoulders, before filing out.

It was strange. I heard John address the men and tell them the news, but I couldn't have told you what words he spoke if my life depended on it.

"I'm stayin'," Atlas gritted through clenched teeth. "I'll wait here a while before I go see him. Gonna give that shithead a piece'a my mind."

A slight grin played over John's mouth, although his eyes were sad. "Bowie would like that," he said sadly.

I turned to Freya. "When can we go in?"

"Soon," she replied, her voice a whisper of pain. "The nurses need to set the room up first."

I waited, all the while wondering if my heart would ever beat the same if he wasn't here to cover it with his hand and keep it safe.

If he left me, that would be it. I would never love another man. I'd be an empty shell. I would be there for Sunny, always, but at the same time, just waiting for the day we'd be together again.

Pangs of regret jabbed in my chest. Why did I close off from him? I should have talked to him. If I'd told him what was on my mind, maybe he wouldn't have gone out tonight. Perhaps he would have been home safe with me.

A few minutes later, a nurse came out. She led us down a hall and into a room.

My hand flew to my mouth when my eyes rested on Bowie. He was hooked up to machines, with tubes coming from his chest.

His usually healthy, tanned skin was grey. He seemed too big for the bed somehow. The big dick energy he did so well was nowhere to be found.

"Oh my God," I breathed. Panic rose through me. My throat tightened in fear, and I fought for breath for the second time that night.

Freya walked over. She looked at his chart and turned to me. "His vitals are good. Blood pressure's not bad, considering. Now, it's just a waiting game."

That relaxed me somewhat, but not much.

Bowie

John pulled out a chair from under the window, Kit the one next to it. I sank into a seat to the right of the bed and watched as Freya sat on the opposite side.

My hand clutched onto his. His skin was cold and clammy. It didn't feel right. He was usually so warm.

Everything felt off, like the universe was somehow out of whack, jarring.

"Do you remember when Bowie threw me into the pool that time? Then he felt guilty, so he jumped in after me and fished me out." Freya's voice was wistful.

Kit let out a quiet chuckle. "He always was a pussy when it came to you."

John grinned. "In the ring, he's a beast. But when it comes to the women in his life, he's a kitten." He looked over at me, his sad eyes earnest. "He's gonna be okay."

"Yeah," Freya agreed, her voice suddenly determined. "His recovery won't be easy, but we'll all be there for him."

I smiled at the same time that I wanted to cry. "Sunny will love using that toy medical kit you gave her."

Freya laughed softly. "He'll love it."

I nodded. "She'll be heartbroken. She loves him." My voice cracked as I spoke.

The room fell silent.

My chest burned with fear as I took in Bowie lying in that bed, hooked up to those machines.

How could someone do this to another human being? To him? "Have they caught who did it?" I asked.

"Nope." John's voice was stern.

"Boner reckons it could'a been the one we're after," Kit muttered. "It makes sense. Maybe he had a load of drugs on him. Bo got too close and…" Kit's voice trailed off. I looked up and saw John shooting him a glare.

I should have told Bowie everything that I'd discovered last weekend. Maybe I could have helped somehow. If I had, maybe he wouldn't have been out there.

My throat burned with tears, guilt flashing through my chest.

Freya huffed. "Dad, stop with the club business. It's family business, too. Layla's his ol' lady, and I'm his sister. We've got a right to know what's going on."

John's eyes swung to Freya. "The less you know, the better. You know how it works; women stay clean."

Freya's face hardened. "Good enough to give you all the information the cops wouldn't. Not so clean then, right, Dad?"

"Stop bustin' my balls, Freya. It ain't the time or the place."

Freya sighed. "I'm just saying we have a right to know."

Something tickled against my hand, and my head flew down to see what touched me.

Did his fingers move? My heart stilled.

Please, please, please. Let him wake up.

Joy hit me when it happened again. I saw his finger twitch. My heart jolted.

"Guys?" The word was a question.

Then I jumped as a loud buzzer began to wail.

Beep. Beep. Beep. Beep.

Freya's face went white. She flew out of her chair and into the corridor.

Doctor Green came rushing into the room, a nurse at her heels. She ran to the bed and checked Bowie over.

My heart cracked open. "No! Please help him!" I screamed.

"Son!" John bellowed.

Doctor Green looked over her shoulder at the nurse. "Get them out of here," she demanded. She turned back to my Bowie and cracked his eyelids open, shining a small medical torch into his eyes.

The nurse grabbed hold of me. Freya began to guide John out. "Let the Doctor do her job, Dad."

I looked around. Somehow, we were in the corridor.

Bowie

Tears welled up. I stared through the window to see the Doctor's hands pushing down on Bowie's chest. She was doing CPR.

I let out a small sob. "Please, Bowie. Don't go," I cried.

Doctor Green kept pumping Bowie's chest with her hands while shouting directions to the nurse.

I dug the heels of my palms into my eyes. *No, no, no.* Bowie had to be okay.

He had to.

Chapter Twenty-Four

Bowie

I was trapped in a sea of darkness.

Now and again, voices penetrated through the watery depths, but I couldn't make out who was speakin'.

At some point, I could sense light, but then the darkness came rushing back and enveloped me, and I was trapped again.

Voices again, on and off, cryin'. My girl was screaming my name.

Then nothin'.

I thought I heard Doe saying she'd chase me through Hell, but that couldn't be right. They didn't allow angels down there.

I tried to fight my way up to the surface. I was desperate to burst through the dark waters and take in a massive breath of air, but somethin' kept dragging me back down, and down, and down.

It seemed to go on forever. Cold fingers grabbed my leg and pulled me back down each time I got close to the top.

I kept fightin' my way up, though. Every time, I seemed to get closer and closer to where I needed to be, and suddenly I was floating.

The dark began to fade, and the light shone through, getting brighter and warmer.

Dad's voice. *Wake up, Son. She needs you.*

And that made me fight even harder 'cause I needed her too. I needed her if I was ever gonna breathe easy. There was no me without her, and vice versa.

Then the pain hit me.

It was agonizing. Every muscle screamed for relief. The ache of it made me want to go back under. At least there, I couldn't feel it eating at my flesh.

Son. Wake up! Dad again. He sounded pissed this time.

The world rushed back in like the vortex that had sucked me in was spittin' me back out. I could feel the air on my skin, then the most fuckin' irritatin' beeping of a machine.

I tried to groan, but somethin' stuck in my throat.

I panicked, and my eyes opened.

I was in a room, bright sunshine streaming through the windows.

The light hurt my eyes. I tried to lift my hand to shield them, but the pain in my chest stopped me.

I tried to breathe, but I couldn't. Chokin' noises escaped my throat. I wanted to gag.

"Bowie." Dad's voice was calm in my ear. "Relax. You've got a tube down your throat. Calm down, Son. I'll get the doctor."

My face was wet. Was I crying? Jesus, I hadn't cried since Sam died.

I closed my eyes again. The pain began to recede as the world faded again, but then I heard footsteps runnin' and her beautiful, sweet voice. "Bowie, I'm here. Wake up."

Then a different voice. "Relax, Bowie. There's a tube down your throat. I'm going to take it out. It won't hurt, but it will be uncomfortable. Are you ready?"

I think I nodded.

Bowie

Then the pain in my chest began to stream up my throat. Jesus fuckin' Christ, I thought she said it wouldn't hurt?

But then a soft hand grabbed hold of mine, and the pain seemed to fade.

"Love you, Bowie," she said.

"Love you, Doe." But my voice was nothing, just a graze through the air.

A whirring noise sounded, and my body moved. My back slowly elevated to the sky. Fuck me sideways. It hurt.

"I'm sitting you up, Bowie." Was that Freya? "Try to open your eyes."

I tried, but I couldn't. My eyelids felt like they had been coated in sticky tar, black and gritty.

My body went weightless. I felt myself falling again, but not into a dark sea. The waters were sparkling clean. I knew I needed to swim in their clarity for a minute.

I'd be back soon.

Chapter Twenty-Five

Layla

Bowie had been out of it for two days.

He'd coded twice that first night. Both times, I lost a piece of myself.

I couldn't eat, couldn't sleep, couldn't breathe freely.

My place was at his side because if the worst happened, at least I'd be there with him at the end.

Somehow, he got through the night. The doctor, Freya, and John heaved a sigh of relief, but I still couldn't breathe.

On day two, I clung to him, talking, remembering what Iris told me.

I did it. I told my man that if he left me, I'd chase him through the stars, and even if he went down there, I'd chase him through Hell.

His fingers twitched, and my heart nearly burst with joy.

On day three, John made me leave him. He said I should shower, change, go for a walk, and get some food.

I went reluctantly. After about an hour, I rushed back through the main hospital doors when my phone beeped.

My heart stopped beating in my chest.

I grabbed the cell, looking at the words that filled the screen.

I began to run. I shot past the elevator because who wanted to wait for that? I banged through the doors to the staircase and ran up, taking two at a time.

Should I have slowed down? Probably, but I was beginning to think clearly. I completely controlled my mind and body for the first time in days.

My feet didn't touch the ground. Suddenly, level three was looming ahead. I burst through the doors, into the corridor, and ran to Bowie.

Doctor Green was already in the room, checking his pulse. John was sitting in a chair beside the bed, muttering something urgently in Bowie's ear.

I went to the side of his bed. "Bowie, I'm here. Wake up." My voice came out breathless.

Doctor Green said something about a tube, but I didn't hear. Honestly, I didn't care to. All I could see was him, and all I could hear were his soft groans.

Although I knew he was in pain, they were like the sweetest song I'd ever heard.

Relief flooded my veins, melting the ice that had taken up residence inside. It washed over me, warming my blood.

Bowie's eyes flickered open and closed again. I was next to him, clasping his fingers in mine. I couldn't help smiling at their warmth, the cold and clammy, all gone.

Another groan left Bowie when the doctor pulled the tube from his throat. My gut clenched as I watched a tear run down the side of his beautiful, courageous face. I said what I should've been saying to him through all the days I'd stupidly pushed him away from my side, where he belonged.

"Love you, Bowie."

He croaked. The words couldn't come, but I heard them in my head and my heart as clear as day because whenever I told him I loved him, he always replied to me the same way.

Love you, Doe.

He woke up throughout the day, just for a few minutes, then fell back asleep again.

I was there—every time.

By the evening, my eyes began to close of their own accord.

Doctor Green had just rechecked his vitals and recorded the readings onto the tablet she carried everywhere.

"Go home, Layla," John said. He looked at Freya. She was slumped in her chair. "You too, Frey. You both need to get some sleep and come back in the morning. I'll stay with him tonight. Keep an eye."

"I don't want to leave him," I replied.

"He'll be more alert tomorrow," the doctor said while she continued to tap. "He'll have more strength by then. He'll need you awake and alert."

John tapped on his phone and looked up. "Abe's on his way. He'll take you home. Sunny's desperate to see you."

I realized then that I hadn't seen my girl for nearly two days. My hands flew to my mouth again. "Sunny," I gasped.

John shook his head and grinned. "Iris has been in her fuckin' element, Layla, don't worry. She's good. We got her, and we got you, too."

My lips tipped up, calm washing over me. "I know."

The next morning, Bowie woke about half an hour after I arrived. John had gone home to sleep, and so had Kit and Atlas.

Freya was down at the cafeteria, getting coffee and something to eat.

I sat next to him, holding his hand, His fingers twitched, and my eyes flew to his face.

He was awake, staring at me, eyes half-mast.

My heart thudded hard. Joyous relief swept through my insides.

"Baby," he whispered as his liquid gold eyes roamed my face.

"Sshhh," I said quietly. "You don't have to speak. Do you need some water?"

He gave me a weak nod.

I reached across to the small cabinet beside his bed, poured water into a beaker, put a straw in, and brought it to his mouth.

He took a small drink and another and nodded.

"Do you remember what happened?" I asked him.

His eyes turned hard, and he nodded again.

Freya swept back into the room and squealed. She ran over, checked Bowie's pulse, then leaned down and hugged him.

That girl was a force of nature. She began to fuss over him, pulling his blankets up and smoothing his hair. Ever the carer.

His eyes darted to mine, and he winked, then that sexy smirk of his transformed him into my man again.

I let out a sigh of relief.

Bowie was back. He was going to be okay.

Can you believe it? On day three, Bowie got out of bed.

I didn't know whether to laugh or cry. He was determined to test my patience.

Before I left the house, Sunny put her little hand on her hip, then cocked it for all she was worth.

"I's going to see Bowie, Mama," she announced. "He needs me."

Iris had to hide her laugh behind her hand.

Bowie

I rolled my eyes. "I'll try, Sunny," I assured her.

"No, Mama," she sassed. "Tell the doctors that Sunshine Hope Hardin is comin' to's the hospital, and Bowie said yes."

Iris turned away as a noise released from her throat.

I crouched down and hugged my girl.

I entered his room, Sunny's declaration still on my mind, and froze. He had already managed to swing his legs over the bed. He was just about to get on his feet, Kit by his side, holding his elbow.

"No!" I demanded.

He looked up at me and laughed, his voice still croaky from under-use and also from the tube that had helped keep him alive. "I need a piss, babe. The doc took my catheter out."

Charming!

"Stay in that bed, Bowie."

"Doe. C'mon," he cajoled.

"Bowie!"

He laughed again. "Wanna hold my dick while I pee, baby? He missed you."

My eyes bugged out. Oh my God.

Kit began to laugh. A giggle rose through my chest and burst out. For the first time in days, I was happy.

It took him a couple of attempts, but with Kit's help, he did it. He stood on both feet, looked at me with a cocky 'told you so' grin, and shuffled into the bathroom, his brother by his side.

I didn't go with him.

By day four, Bowie was walking everywhere by himself.

I went to talk to the doctor about his medication. I was asking questions when her gaze fell somewhere over my shoulder.

I spun around to see Bowie walking down the corridor in the opposite direction. His shoulders were stooped forward, and he was hand in hand with Sunny.

Yes, she got her way.

Panic swirled through my stomach. "What are you doing?" I screeched.

"Goin' to the vendin' machine," he threw over his shoulder, his voice still a rasp. "My baby girl's hungry." He turned back to me and smiled smugly.

"It's okay, Mama, I'll looks after Bowie," Sunny called over.

"Ugh!" I exclaimed, my hands clenched into fists. "That man drives me crazy."

A soft hand patted my shoulder. "Don't worry." Doctor Green laughed. "If he collapses, he's in the right place."

I spun to face her as my body went cold. "What?"

She smiled. "Just a doctor joke. He'll be fine. It's good for his recovery to get up and about."

"He's just been shot," I whispered.

She grinned. "Don't worry. He's got a good Doctor."

By day five, I'd given up trying to keep him in bed.

Sunny had come to the hospital with me again that morning. Iris had arranged to pick her up just after lunch and take her swimming at the clubhouse.

My eyes jerked to her as she crawled all over Bowie, grasping her toy medical kit while he lay patiently on the bed. "Sunny! Get down," I demanded.

"Leave her alone," he mumbled through the plastic toy thermometer poking out of his mouth. "She's takin' my temperature."

"Yeah, Mama. I's gonna makes Bowie all better." Sunny leaned down to the foot of the bed, fumbling inside her plastic medical briefcase. She pulled out a toy stethoscope and walked on her knees back over to Bowie.

I looked up to the heavens, begging God to give me strength.

Day six, and Bowie was in a foul mood.

"I'm bored outta my fuckin' skull," he grumbled.

"You could try sleeping," I snapped. "Then you won't be bored.

His eyes narrowed at me. "Slept for three fuckin' days nonstop, Doe. I wanna get the fuck outta here, go to the club, have a beer."

Irritation stabbed at my chest. "You can't drink alcohol with your medication."

"I don't need any goddamned medication."

Doctor Green swept into the room. "Yes, you do, Gage. The medication will help you heal. If you stop those painkillers, I guarantee, you'll cry like a baby."

I threw my arms up in the air. "Thank you."

"But all being well, I'll discharge you tomorrow."

My eyes darted to her. "What?"

"Nothing else I can do for him. He can continue his recovery at home."

My throat went tight. "But he'll overdo it."

Doctor Green shrugged. "We'll see him back here very soon then, won't we?" She patted Bowie's shoulder.

He seemed to slump further down the bed. "Sorry, Doe. I just wanna get outta here."

I took his hand. "I want you to be well, Bowie. I thought I was going to los…" the words stuck in my throat.

Bowie leaned over and pulled me by my hand.

"What?" I asked.

"Get on," he ordered.

"I can't."

"Yes, you can." Doctor Green informed us. "Hugging therapy is good for the soul. Just make sure you take your shoes off," she said before disappearing through the door.

Bowie shuffled across the bed.

I sat my ass on the side and lay down next to him. My skin tingled, happy that I was back in proximity to my man. Goosebumps traveled down my arms making me shiver in delight.

His eyes stared into mine, liquid gold swirls pulling me in. "It'll be okay, Doe," he promised.

My heart stuttered. Guilt had been stabbing my chest ever since the night Bowie got shot. Now it was screaming at me to tell him everything.

What if I'd told him something that may have helped catch the man doing the assaults? What Kit had said that awful night by Bowie's bedside rang true? What if Bowie did get too close? And that's why he got hurt.

Could I have stopped it?

I had spent a week being a bitch, not talking to him or trusting him. I imagined, over and over, how I'd feel if he kept something like that from me. The thought sickened me to my stomach.

It was time to put my fears to one side. I knew I could trust Bowie.

"I need to explain why I pushed you away. There's a lot we need to talk about," I murmured.

Bowie snaked his arm slowly around my neck until my face was snuggled into his chest. "We'll talk, Baby. I wanna know what happened to make you shut down. But for now, just for tonight. Let's just be."

He was right. There was nothing we could do at that moment. As soon as I told him what I feared had happened to me, I knew he'd grow angry and frustrated. Deep down, I wanted one more night with us like this before things changed.

"Okay," I breathed, inhaling his scent, the familiarity of it relaxing me.

"We've got the rest of our lives to talk, Doe. It'll keep for one night."

I nodded, my body relaxing against him. I felt safe again for the first time in days. Nobody could hurt me when I was with him.

"Love you, Doe," he breathed.

"Love you, Bowie."

My heart thudded back to life as he whispered. "Me and you against the world," as I drifted off to sleep.

Chapter Twenty-Six

Bowie

The doc discharged me three days ago.

Anna had given Layla more time off to be home with me.

My girl wouldn't let me lift a finger, which I was glad for. It was weird. When I was in the hospital, I seemed golden, but as soon as I got my ass outta there, I crashed.

Layla was worried that Sunny was cooped up in the house too much, so she arranged for her to go to Rosie's for a couple of days.

Dad visited daily with at least one'a my club brothers in tow. Freya also showed up every day, sayin' she needed to check my blood pressure.

It was cool that everyone rallied, but between all the visitors, and Layla, I was dead to the world by eight most nights.

I was startin' to realize that bein' shot in the chest was no walk in the park. Not just physically but mentally, too.

I napped a lot but still found myself wakin' up in a cold sweat, recalling the glint of a metal gun and burnin' pain. One time I dreamed that it was Layla the gun was trained on, but I couldn't get to her to help.

My woman was okay but subdued.

The whole ordeal seemed to affect her more than me. She was constantly fussin', makin' sure I was okay. Sometimes when she came close, I'd see a flash of guilt behind her eyes. Her fingers would reach out like she was compelled to check that I was still whole.

I knew we had to have a conversation, but my subconscious recognized that whatever she had on her mind was big. My gut told me things would never be the same when the words were uttered. So, I shied away from it like a coward.

I was lyin' on the bed with Layla tucked into my side. Every time she breathed out, a small puff of air skated over my chest, bringing me peace.

Instead of doin' what I should'a been doin', insisting that she talk to me, I found my fingertips trailing up and down her spine. Goosebumps skated over her skin, and she shivered.

Her hand went to my stomach, playin' with the trail of coarse hair that disappeared into my sweatpants. My cock twitched at the close contact.

We hadn't fucked since the mornin' after Cara was drugged.

A gunshot to the chest didn't cool my libido. If anythin' it made me hornier. I'd had a wake-up call, and because of that, I knew life was for livin'.

My cock grew harder. Layla noticed, then froze.

"Don't stop, baby," I pleaded quietly into her hair. "Touch me."

She lifted her head from my bare chest. "We can't, Bowie. What if I hurt you?"

"We'll go easy. Please, baby, I need you."

She began to protest, "Bowie, no"—

"—Yes," I demanded. I pulled Doe on top of me, and my hand went straight to her nape, and I pulled her mouth down hard over mine.

My girl felt soft and pliant beneath my touch.

Our tongues tangled for a minute as I kissed her slowly and deeply. Eventually, I pulled back, sucking gently on her bottom lip.

She sighed softly, and her body pressed deeper into mine until our breaths mingled into one.

My cock began to pulse like it had its own heartbeat. I pulled back. "Jesus, Doe. I need to fuck you so bad."

Her face fell. "What if I hurt you?" she asked. She let out a small moan as I ground my cock against her jean-clad pussy.

"We'll be careful," I assured her, fingers tapping gently on her ass. "Strip. Let me see you."

Her hooded eyes met mine. She groaned quietly as my fingers traced down her back again. My hand swept over her shoulder, then down to her firm little tits. I plucked at her nipples through her shirt.

She arched her back, the sexy little whimpers she made sendin' blood rushing to my cock.

It grew so hard that an ache tugged at my groin. The need to thrust into her, to feel her tight, wet heat surrounding me, was overwhelming.

Layla planted a kiss on my chest, and she shuffled across to the edge of the bed. I watched intently as she stood, slowly unbuttoned her jeans, and slid 'em down over her hips, legs, and feet.

Her arms went to the hem of her shirt. In one fluid movement, she pulled it up and over her head and stood there naked before me, all apart from her red lace panties.

My dick throbbed as I took in her beautiful body.

Her tits were firm. Round little cherry red nipples grew hard, beggin' to be sucked. Her breathing was harsh. Every time she huffed out, her chest thrust toward me. I couldn't take my eyes off her.

"You're fuckin' perfect, Doe," I croaked.

"So are you." She smiled, then bent down toward me, pulling at the waistband of my sweats until I lifted my ass slightly, allowing her to pull 'em down and off. The air hit my dick, making it grow even harder.

Layla's eyes flicked over it. Then, fuck me, she licked her lips before peelin' her panties off and walkin' down to the bottom of the bed.

My mouth watered as I watched her tight little ass bounce. I ached to reach out, touch the curve of her hips and cheeks, and stroke over the tight little hole.

I thought I'd died and gone to heaven as I watched her position herself at the foot of the bed, on her hands and knees.

I nearly moaned at the sight of her crawling up my legs until her mouth was level with my burgeoning cock.

She was a fuckin' temptress, born to put me under her spell.

My hand snaked down my body to grip hold of my cock. I was desperate for some relief. "Lick it, baby," I demanded, offering it to her. She smiled and obeyed.

Her pink tongue licked the underside hard in one movement, going from base to tip, tasting all along the large vein that protruded through the middle.

I nearly blew there and then. "Jesus," I groaned.

Layla looked up at me, eyes wide and innocent. Without breaking her stare, her tongue darted out to lick away the pre-cum that gathered at the tip.

I couldn't drag my eyes away from her.

Never had I witnessed anything more erotic or so fuckin' hot. The love that wanted to burst outta my chest just made the whole experience better and more intense.

I couldn't help letting out another groan, the need for her clawin' at my insides. I grasped the base tightly, then tapped the head of my cock gently against her lips, seekin' entrance to her warm, wet mouth. "Suck me, Doe," I grunted. "Open up wide for me. Be my good girl."

Her jaw went slack. Inch by inch, I fed her my cock, my hand still gripping the base.

She began to suck gently. Her warm mouth pulled me into the back of her throat, and I wanted to weep with joy.

"Harder," I demanded. I grabbed the back of Doe's head and arched up. She eagerly complied, and I began to thrust up into her mouth. "That's my good girl," I praised. Her soft moan of reply vibrated through my length and buzzed through my skin.

All sense of pain floated away, replaced by raw hunger. I opened my eyes to watch as I fucked Layla's mouth.

Watching her suck my cock was the greatest show on earth.

My hand tugged at the base while Layla's mouth pleasured the rest by sucking and slurpin' like a woman possessed.

Her long chestnut hair fell over my thighs. The brush of it across my legs only added to the myriad of sensations my brain was tryin' to process all at once.

A tingle began at the base of my spine, the familiar tug of euphoria working its way through my system like raging wildfire.

I pulled back, pulling myself out of the warm, wet recess of her mouth. She gazed up again, then released me with a pop that fizzed through my veins.

"Ride me," I growled, voice thick with need.

My entire body pulsed, sending me lightheaded. When I looked down and saw Layla crawling up my body, I nearly passed the fuck out.

A goddess sent to earth just for me, cheeks flushed, lips swollen from suckin' hard on my cock. She sat up, swung a shapely leg on either side of me, then nestled her wet little pussy against my cock.

"That's it, Doe," I muttered, dick hard as steel as her hips circled mine.

My eyes fell on the red flush across her chest, leading up to her neck. My finger reached out, tracing it from bottom to top, marveling at its rich hue.

My hand descended, tracing over one nipple and circling it gently. Layla's head jerked up, and she moaned to the sky as I moved across to the other.

"That feels good," she groaned, eyes flying back to mine.

"You ready?" I scraped out.

She jerked a nod and lifted her hips. My cock rested against that tight little notch that was put there just for me. I was captivated by the sight of her sinking slowly on it. She let out a strangled moan when she was fully seated.

Black dots swum behind my eyes. The pleasure was so fuckin' intense.

I clenched my jaw while my Layla began to grind against me. I grabbed her hips to help her along, guiding her movements.

Her eyes shone with pleasure. I reached up and ran a hand over her slack jaw. My other hand dug into her hip, controlling her speed.

"I'm so close, Bowie," she mumbled as she arched her back, placing both hands on my knees.

My fingers trailed down between her breasts, her legs, and over her clit, circling her erect little bud, making her cry out with pleasure.

Her thighs began to shake. I watched, fascinated, as she rode me faster, hips grinding against mine, pussy sheathing my cock in its warm, wet heat.

I clenched my jaw, tryin' just for a moment to disassociate myself from the sensual thrust of her hips, willing myself not to cum.

As her pussy clenched around my length, I felt it in every nerve ending. The tingle in my spine returned with a vengeance, this time not allowing me to will it away.

"You need to cum, baby," I gritted, rubbing her clit harder. My dick kicked hard as it engorged inside her core.

"That's it, Layla. Cum on my cock."

The tingle spread to my groin. I let out a shout as Doe's pussy clenched harder and harder. I began to thrust my hips hard up into her, ignoring the stab of pain in my chest, awareness only for the ecstasy that enveloped me.

She began to whimper louder and louder. Then she let out a keening cry. Her pussy clenches around my cock so tight I nearly blacked out.

Narrow hips rocked hard against mine. I snapped mine up faster, meeting Layla thrust for thrust, fuckin' her through her orgasm, watching as her entire body seized up.

My dick throbbed, "I'm gonna cum," I rasped. She groaned and went to move off me, but I dug my fingers into her hips, forcing her down as my balls drew up tightly.

"Fuck. Yeah," I groaned.

My seed gushed into her pussy like an erupting geyser. The orgasm ripped through me, shaking me to my core.

Layla's movements began to slow until finally she let out a sigh and collapsed down onto the good side of my chest, mind, body, and soul finally spent.

After a minute of her face in my neck, she pulled up and off.

My arm fell across the bed, and my woman collapsed on top of it. My fingers trailed loosely up and down her spine.

"You're amazing, Doe," I said, voice still low.

She snuggled into me. "It gets better each time," she said lazily. She looked up at me with big grey eyes. "Love you, Bowie."

I shuddered out a breath, still feeling the high from how hard I'd just come up her sweet little cunt. "Love you, Doe," I replied.

This woman was mine. Nothing was clearer to me at that moment; she belonged to me. Our souls knew each other, maybe from a past life. When my heart found hers, I knew I was home.

As her finger skated up and down my chest, my gut twisted as she whispered the words that would forever change our lives.

"We need to talk, Bowie. It's about Sunny's dad. I'm ready to tell you now."

Chapter Twenty-Seven

Layla

I sat upright on the bed, shrugging my shirt and panties back on.

Bowie grabbed his sweats from the floor beside the bed, then pulled them up his legs and over his ass.

He held my hand in his, allowing my mind to return to six years before.

My first memory from that night was the ache between my thighs. That's what made me wake up. It was so intense that I sat with a start.

Nausea gripping my stomach. I blinked into the dark, unfamiliar room, trying to remember how I got there.

The soreness that burned across my skin penetrated my muscles, and I began to cry. I looked around the room, sniffling quietly. At the same time, I desperately willed my eyes to grow accustomed to the pitch-black surrounding me.

I didn't feel good. My head was about to split with the thudding pain hammering through it.

"Think, Layla, think," I said out loud. I was startled because my voice sounded sharp, like cracked pieces of broken glass.

Bass thumped through the walls. The room seemed to thrum with it.

Memories suddenly raced back into my mind, and I groaned out loud when I remembered that I was at Brett's party.

Pain lurched inside my stomach. A shriek sounded through the room. It sounded like a dying animal. I began to cry again when I realized it was me.

I was disorientated, and so, so cold. I looked down, then began to sob. I was naked apart from the bra I remembered fastening when I dressed for the party earlier that night.

My mind went back to my arrival. Brett, smiling down at me. Somebody handed me and red solo cup, then another.

I must have had too much to drink. I'd had a glass of champagne at Cara's mom's birthday party. The next day, my brain felt like cotton wool. The way it felt then was similar but so much worse.

My legs scrambled across to the edge of the bed. Searing pain ripped through me, again, pulsing from the place between my legs.

Everything from head to toe felt wrong, like I'd been displaced somewhere foreign, and my memory couldn't keep up.

It was frightening. I couldn't remember how I came to be in that bed.

The room was suddenly flooded with white light. My head whipped to the side. A wall made of windows and a door led out to a swimming pool. Moonbeams danced over the water, making it glisten.

I let out a relieved breath. I wasn't trapped.

The room seemed to vibrate around me. I wondered if I was tripping. I seemed to be in a dream state, but I knew it couldn't be because the ache making my teeth chatter felt all too real.

I groaned as I slipped off the side of the bed. The sharp ache in my stomach splintered through me again, and I doubled over with the intensity of it.

After a minute, it passed. I hobbled across the room toward a door that was slightly ajar. I could have cried with relief when I saw it was a bathroom.

My hand felt for a light switch. As I grabbed onto the wall, my fingers trailed over a small button that I pressed. The buzzing from the strip light sounded in my ears.

The first thing I did was go to the mirror.

My heart dropped when I saw the state of myself. Despair tugged at me, and suddenly I wanted to cry again.

My eyes were dull, my pupils' huge voids. My long, curled hair was mussed. A trail of black ran down my face where my mascara had run.

My fingers turned on the taps. I was startled by the sound of the water whooshing out. I quickly splashed my face, appreciating the coolness of it against my skin.

I think it helped wake me up because I began to notice the pressure in my stomach that indicated my bladder was full.

My feet stumbled over to the toilet, and I flopped down.

A painful burning sensation took my breath away, but I gritted my teeth through it, then fumbled for some toilet paper.

My heart froze when I saw the blood. It looked diluted somehow, mixed with another sticky substance. Dread pounded through me. I chanted. "No, no, no. Please, no."

Deep down, I knew I'd had sex. Now, I had the physical evidence.

Devastation washed over me because I was a virgin up to then, saving myself for the boy I knew was 'the one.'

I began to cry again because it suddenly hit me that I'd thrown something precious away through alcohol and one wrong drunken decision.

One of life's milestones I would never get back.

My skin itched almost painfully. I scratched down my arms in an attempt to drive the sensation away. Unfortunately, the self-disgust that swirled through me wasn't as easy to eliminate.

I washed my hands, then splashed more water on my face, stopping myself from screaming out loud.

My feet hobbled back into the bedroom. I gathered the clothes that someone had thrown haphazardly on the floor and dressed.

It took twice as long as usual because my fingers kept slipping on my zippers and buttons, the tremor in them like a barrier.

Eventually, I made my way to the doors that led outside. I slipped out into the cool night air stumbling slightly, just missing the pool's edge.

I slowly turned to look at my surroundings.

Music from the party floated through the air, a melody dancing on the breeze. The shriek of drunken laughter mocked me as it drifted from the party, still going strong in the main house.

I pulled the sleeves of my cardigan down over my hands and huddled into its warmth, wrapping it around me like a comfort blanket.

The moon faded as it hid behind a cloud, casting the patio into darkness.

My skin suddenly prickled with awareness. Was someone there in the dark, watching me? I lifted my head and quickly turned, but nobody was there.

I remembered watching a movie where a girl was in a coma. All the time she was asleep, she screamed inside her head.

That's how I felt. On the outside, I was normal, but inside I was in pain, broken, and bewildered.

Bowie

The moon came out from behind the clouds again, paving my way as I began to stumble home.

"Baby." Bowie's voice was a croak that made me startle.

I blinked and looked up. My heart sank as I looked up at my man's stricken face. But still, a tiny sliver of relief swept through me.

At least he knew now.

Tears flooded my eyes again as a noise escaped his throat. "Jesus, Layla." Bowie's features twisted into a frown. "How many drinks did you have?"

"No more than three beers. It probably amounted to, maybe, two bottles."

"Two bottles of beer wouldn't get you in that state."

My eyes met his. I stared into their golden-brown depths. "I know."

I could see the cogs turning in his head as he began to work it out. "When was this?" he demanded.

"Six years ago. It was the only time I had sex until the night you took me home from the *Haven*. I saw the similarities when I spoke to Cara last week after she'd been drugged. It all came rushing back, and I knew I'd been drugged too. That's why I was distant. I was thinking it through in my head."

I watched his face turn from quizzical to angry, then a thread of shock flashed behind his eyes. He muttered one word. "Sunny."

Gentle hands pushed me away, and Bowie jumped up and began to pace the room. "That son of a bitch is Sunny's biological father?"

I felt my face crumble. "My girl can't ever know," I begged. "Promise me, Bowie. Not ever."

He returned to the bed, kneeling on the mattress and pulling me into his safe arms. "It's okay, baby," he crooned softly in my ear.

My chest tightened, and I began to sniffle. Bowie rubbed his hand up and down my back soothingly. "Baby. She'll never know," he assured me.

Devastation at the stigma she'd feel if she ever discovered the truth was already spreading through me.

"I-I'm sorry I didn't tell you before," I hiccoughed. "Maybe if I'd opened up about everything and hadn't been such a bitch to you that week, you wouldn't have been patrolling that night."

"Doe, it would've been someone else if it wasn't me. I survived it." He paused, then tipped my chin up with his finger. "Babe. Please don't tell me you've been feelin' guilty all this time?"

"Maybe if I'd told you all this sooner, things would've played out differently—"

"—Sshh, Layla, it's okay," he said softly. "It all worked out. I'm fine." He tilted my chin further to see straight into my eyes. "We're gonna sort this, baby."

I lowered my gaze. "It's all such a mess. I'm still coming to terms with it all myself."

Bowie dipped his head, catching my eyes. "No, Layla, it's not. Think about it, baby. You just gave us the breakthrough we've been lookin' for. We've got more to go on. We can stop him from doin' it to anyone else."

He shook his head and let out a self-deprecating snort. "All this time, and we never knew."

I pulled back a little so that I could take in his face. "What are you talking about?

He took my hand in his. "Layla, if Sunny's his kid, we've got his DNA."

Chapter Twenty-Eight

Bowie

After Layla told me everything, she fell asleep. Talking about her trauma put her through an emotional wringer because she zonked out as soon as I settled her down.

I prowled all over the house, unable to get her words out of my noggin.

All the while she was talkin', I could almost feel her confusion, the utter fear in her voice. I wanted to fuckin' strangle someone.

Sickness churned through my gut.

She was all alone. The father that doted on her was dead, leaving her a mean waste of space for a mother.

I dunno how Layla was still so sweet, considering all the reasons she had to rage at the world, but my girl was strong, and I loved her all the more for it.

She'd never be alone again. Even if somethin' happened to me, she'd have the club at her back, and so would Sunny.

I made my way into the backyard, worried that if I stayed in the house, I'd disturb her while I called Pop.

"Bowie. You, okay?" he barked down the phone.

"Send someone to get me, now, Pop. Call church."

Thirty minutes later, I sat in Abe's passenger seat as he pulled through the gates and into the club parking lot.

I was still thinkin' about my woman when I walked into the clubhouse.

The second I stepped inside, a loud roar went up.

My eyes shot up to see thirty-odd brothers all gathered in the bar. Shouts rang out through the din they were makin'.

"Good to see you, Bowie."

"Lemme see your bullet hole."

"You're a sight for sore eyes."

I looked around at the faces of my brothers and grinned. "Thanks, boys, I appreciate ya!" I called out. "Gimme a week, and I'll see you all in the ring."

A laugh went up. Shotgun stepped forward and clapped me on the back. "Welcome back, Bowie," he muttered, his eyes hardened. "Was worried about you there for a minute. Never wanna see that shit again."

I bumped his fist. "Thanks, Shot. Dad said you got the ambulance there, pronto."

"No problem, Bo," he said, shruggin' a shoulder.

Footsteps came from the corridor. I turned to see Atlas stompin' toward us. "Alright, alright, motherfuckers. You can all kiss Bowie better another time. We need him in Church."

Hoots of laughter rang through the bar.

The crowd began to thin out, the men goin' back to their games of pool or makin' their way to the tables.

We began to move down the corridor. Atlas glanced over his shoulder, lookin' me up and down. "What the fuck are you wearin'?" he barked.

Had he lost it? I was wearin' the grey sweatpants that Layla liked with a white tee. I'd just been goddamned shot. "I apologize, Atlas, left my monkey suit at the dry cleaners. Sorry if I don't meet your high fuckin' standards."

"You can wear what the fuck you want, asshole," he replied.

Bowie

He grabbed the handle and swung the door open. I strolled past him and into Church. "It's just that I can see the outline of ya shlong."

I rubbed the back of my neck in amazement as I looked at Dad, who sat in the big chair. "Can you believe this shit?" I asked.

The sound of stifled laughter made me look around. Abe was starin' up at the ceilin', lips twitchin'. Ice's hand was coverin' his mouth while he looked at his feet.

I turned back to Atlas. He was peerin' down at my dick, face twisted in a grimace.

Hell. I'd been away a week, and the brothers had lost their fuckin' minds.

Colt put his tablet on the table. "Did Layla tell you to wear them?"

I looked at him like he was touched in the head. "No."

He shrugged. "It's a thing. Women like men in grey sweatpants 'cause they're revealing," His voice was matter-of-fact.

Heads whipped around to stare at him, everyone's eyes bugging out.

Dad looked at Colt and winced. "What the fuck?" he said simultaneously as Hendrix muttered. "Jesus Christ."

Colt shrugged. "Yeah. It was all over social media a year ago. It's their catnip."

"So. What you're sayin' is, bitches like men wearin' grey sweatpants 'cause they can see their shlongs?" Atlas asked, eyes still huge.

Colt shrugged again. "Yep."

Atlas looked dazed. "Un—fuckin'—believable." He cursed under his breath.

Ice's throat let out a whimper. Abe looked up at the ceiling again, his shoulders shaking with mirth.

Dad glanced around the room, then crossed his arms in front of his chest. "Tellin' ya now, if you assholes talked about sweatpants and dicks durin' Church when

Bandit was prez, he would've shot you all in your goddamned heads. Now shut the fuck up. We got business to discuss."

"Blame, Atlas," Ice chuckled.

The SAA's eyes turned to slits. "How 'bout you blame, Bowie? He's the one wavin' his goddamned cock in our faces."

"You're a fuckin' asshole," I gritted out.

Abe tried to cover his laugh as Dad bellowed, "Enough!"

The room fell silent.

Pop pulled out a chair. "Sit your asses down, and let's get this fuckin' meetin' started." His voice turned to a mutter. "It's like dealin' with a bunch of fuckin' five-year-olds. His mumblings were drowned out by chairs scrapin' across the wooden planked floor as the men began to take their seats.

We all looked at each other in silence for a minute.

Dad cleared his throat and turned to me. "Just wanna say that we're glad you're okay, Bo. It was touch and go there for a minute, but there's no keepin' a Demon down, right, Son?"

"Thanks, Pa," I said quietly.

My dad was the shit. He wasn't always loved, but he was always respected by all who knew him. He was a hard man but wasn't scared to show his emotions.

"We got the bullet, Bo," Dad continued, voice low. "If we find the gun, we may be able to match it—"

"—*If* we find the gun," Ice interrupted.

Dad stroked his beard, somethin' he always did when tryin' to think through a problem. "Yeah, and it's still a long shot, even if we do."

He sounded dejected. Pop had been at the hospital every night I was there. He kept it together, and I'd heard he kept everyone else together too. His eyes were dull with fatigue. I was shocked that he wasn't reeling more.

Bowie

I rested my hands on the table. What I had to tell 'em was delicate, to say the least. I cleared my throat. "There's been a recent development. Had a powwow with Layla earlier today."

"Bet she's beside herself," Pop said in a dark tone. "It's fuckin' killin' me that we've got no leads on the shooter."

"That's just it, Dad. We may be able to find him through DNA testin'." I turned back to Atlas. "Have you still got those old DNA kits?"

He grinned. "Yeah, a few. No bitch has tried to hang me on the hook lately. I've been double baggin' it, like a good little Atlas."

Hendrix's eyes danced. "I'd double bag it if I were you too. I've seen the bitches you run with."

Atlas shot him a glare. I tapped on his arm to bring his attention back to me. "We need more. Can you get them?"

Dad leaned forward. "Son. What the fuck do you want DNA tests for?"

I blew out a breath and looked at each man individually. I'd asked Layla earlier if I could share what happened to her with the officers. She agreed as long as it went no further. These men may be fuckin' assholes at times, but they were trustworthy assholes.

Time to put it out there.

"I got a story to tell ya, but it ain't pretty."

Over the next few minutes, I told 'em everythin'. Anger rose through my chest again as the words rolled off my tongue.

I'd kept my shit together earlier when Layla told me, or I acted like I did. But now, there was no need to hide. These men would understand my reaction.

When I finished, the room went quiet again. Every face around the table was full of anger and fury.

Dad flew out of his chair, fists clenched tight against his sides. He stalked across the room to look through the window. "When I find him, he's dead," he snarled.

"No," I said quietly. "The fucker's mine. I'm gonna kill him with my bare hands."

Atlas's face was twisted. "I want in too."

Hendrix rapped the table to get everyone's attention. "We'll all get a hit. Bowie can finish the job. While we're workin' out how to use this info, I want all the men out patrollin'."

Colt looked up from his tablet. "Veep. He must know the heat's on. There've been no more assaults over the past week. The fucker's layin' low for sure."

"Don't care," Drix replied. "We're gonna be ready when he starts his sick shit again. We'll have men on every street corner. He won't be able to take a piss without us knowing about it first."

"What if he lies low for good?" Ice asked.

Colt turned to him. "He won't. He's been doing this shit for so long. It's gotta be some kind of compulsion with him."

"How d'ya work that out?" Drix asked as he leaned forward. "You been gettin' in his head? Watchin' that FBI show about the serial killers?"

Colt rolled his eyes. "It's not fuckin' rocket science Veep. We thought he'd been doin' this for three years, but from what Bowie's told us, it's longer. Right?"

Drix nodded his agreement.

"Nobody reported anythin' back when it happened to Layla. He couldn't have been doin' it frequently then 'cause nobody saw a pattern."

Atlas rubbed his beard. "So what?"

"He did four assaults three years ago. That's around the time when the five-o started lookin' into it more. The year after that, there were six that we know of. We're into another year, and he's already drugged five women. Okay, not all raped, but we're only in July."

Dad had a lightbulb moment. "Of course," he exclaimed.

"Can someone please tell me what the fuck the whizz kid's talkin' about?" Atlas asked.

Dad sat back in his seat. "It's been getting more frequent every year. What Colt's sayin' is that the sick fuck can't help himself. The more he does it, the more he needs it."

Colt nodded. "And now it's getting' to the point where we're onto him, and he doesn't give a fuck." He gestured to me. "He's even getting confident enough to shoot Bowie."

Hendrix slapped his hand on the table. "Fuck. He's spirallin', ain't he?"

"Seems that way," Colt agreed.

That feeling of impending doom hit me again.

I'd always thought the fucker who assaulted those women was a sick pervert. Now, it was beginning to get more sinister 'cause he wasn't only attacking women but also making sure to take out the people who threatened to stop him.

In short, he was fuckin' obsessed.

Colt rubbed the back of his head. "What bothers me is that, at some point, the assaults may not be enough for him. The high he's been gettin' out of what he does is obviously wearing off quicker every time. That's why it's happening more. At some point, it's gonna escalate."

Ice began to trickle through my blood.

It made perfect sense. There was no hesitation when the sick fuck shot me. The shooter was cool, calm, and collected. Robotic almost, like he was on a mission.

I'd thought about it a lot over the last week and weighed everything up. I reckoned that I was lured down that alley. He knew I'd come for him, and he was ready. He targeted me specifically.

The ramifications of it all chilled me to the fuckin' bone. Perhaps he planned it all along, wanted it even.

"We need to catch him before he offs someone," Atlas grunted. "If he's losing control, all of this'll just get a whole lot messier."

Dad looked up and blew out a frustrated breath. "Okay. So, we'll put the pressure on. Let's get out there in force. Spread the word that they shoot to kill. No fuckin' around."

"That won't be a problem," Ice said. "The brothers I've talked to are losin' their shit about Bowie. They're out for revenge."

Dad smiled proudly. "We got a good club, loyal men."

"In the meantime," I said, looking at Atlas. "We need a fuck load more of those DNA tests."

Dad raised an eyebrow. "What the hell are you up to?"

Anger stirred through me. The thought of what my woman went through that night made my blood boil. He wasn't gonna get away with it. When I caught him, he was a dead man.

I wanted justice for Layla, and I was gonna make sure she damned well got it.

A plan began to form in my head. I thought of all the different ways we could put those test kits to use. We could get samples of saliva, blood, whatever.

Where in town could we get that shit without anyone knowing? And more to the point, who could help us do it?

We needed someone loyal. Someone who understood the club and wanted to catch this pervert as much as we did.

For the first time that day, things were beginnin' to look up.

I knew exactly where we could go.

The Lucky Shamrock.

Chapter Twenty-Nine

Layla

Sunny danced around the house again, excited for the day ahead. We were going to a club cookout, and much like the barbeque, she couldn't wait.

Bowie was putting the food I'd made in the back of his truck when she nearly twirled into him.

"Whoa, Princess. Your mom'll kill me if I drop this cake," I heard from the hallway.

"Yes, I will," I called out.

"Sorry," Sunny yelled.

After a minute, Bowie came through to the kitchen.

I was washing dishes when he walked up behind me and grabbed my hip.

"What the fuck do you put in that kid's water?" He deadpanned. "'Cause I could do with a dose of that."

I turned my head to him and laughed. "She's high on life."

He pulled a face. "Dunno how she doesn't get dizzy, fall over, and crack her noggin open. Never seen a kid spin so fuckin' much." Bowie's hand snaked over to my belly. "Wonder if the next one'll be as fuckin' loopy?"

My stomach swirled with warmth. He was convinced I was pregnant.

The other day, when we had sex, he held me down onto him as he came. We'd done it again since, and he did exactly the same thing.

When I questioned him, he said he wanted to 'knock me up.' Then told me he'd do it again when I had the baby. I reiterated that we'd only been together five minutes, but he said he didn't care.

It was so confusing, loving him for as long as I had and initially getting rejected, then coming together, and him getting shot. I was dealing with being drugged and assaulted, and now this.

It had been an emotional rollercoaster.

Sunny came dancing into the kitchen. "Can we go now, Bowie?" Her face was a picture of excitement. We'd gone to the stores yesterday, and she was wearing a new cute frilly yellow swimsuit with matching shorts.

Cara persuaded me to get a few new things, too, and seeing as chunks of money kept appearing in my bank account, I splurged a little. I was wearing a new bikini, with new shorts and a pretty camisole top.

I must have looked okay because Bowie's eyes lit up when he saw me, then they darkened a little, and I shivered. Now he kept touching me, my back, my belly, my ass, everything.

And I loved it.

Bowie got down on his haunches and took Sunny's little hand. "It's a bit early, Baby Doe, but how about we go now, and I'll get in the pool with ya until the other kids show?"

My heart squeezed. Scenes like this made me melt for my man.

He was amazing with Sunny. He had watched her a couple of times while I went to work for a few hours. They made forts and read. He took her down the creek and told her the names of the bugs and plants.

Bowie

He'd been in our lives mere weeks, and I couldn't remember what it was like before, except things used to be duller somehow.

Now, I was living in technicolor.

Sunny squealed with delight. She loved his nickname for her, Baby Doe. She'd bloomed before my eyes, responding beautifully to his care and attention. It was exquisite to watch.

I think, like me, she recognized the safety that Bowie represented, and also, like me, she was grateful. She had her moments, I mean, she was five, but life was much better than it used to be, and my girl sensed it.

Sunny squealed in delight as he scooped her up in his arms.

"Gonna get Baby Doe contained in her car seat," he teased as her arms slid around his neck.

"Watch your wound," I called out as he disappeared down the hallway with her.

"Stop fussin', woman," he called back. "I'm good as gold."

I rolled my eyes, dried my hands, and went to find my purse.

It was time for a cookout.

―――

Iris, as usual, was in the kitchen when we arrived.

Sunny ran off when she saw that Rosie's kids were already out at the pool, torturing Sparky, the prospect.

Bowie bustled into the kitchen after me, carrying in the last of the food containers. He looked around. "Where the fuck did Baby Doe run off to?" he asked.

Iris grinned. "She saw the kids, said, 'later,' and ran."

"She's turning into a mini biker," I grumbled. "She called me dude the other day, and when I got home from work on Friday, I walked into the kitchen, and she greeted me with, 'yo'."

Rosie put her hand to her mouth and giggled.

Iris hooted out a laugh. "Happens to the best of us."

"What's wrong wi' that?" Bowie asked, looking quizzical.

Rosie walked over and patted him on the cheek. "Wait until she starts calling you a fucknut. Then you'll be sorry."

Bowie's face turned a weird shade of green. "Gonna go find Pop," he muttered. Then he bent down, kissed my cheek, and disappeared through the door.

Iris burst out laughing. "Think you scared him, Ro."

"He's going to have a shock when she turns into him. He won't be so sure of himself then," I said tightly.

Iris' eyes turned to me; all trace of humor was gone. "Sit down, girl," she ordered. "Wanna talk to ya."

My stomach dropped slightly at her serious tone. "Is everything okay?"

She pulled a couple of stools from under the counter for Rosie and me, then walked around to sit on the side opposite me.

Rosie went to the massive industrial-sized fridge, grabbed a bottle of white wine, and three glasses, then sat beside me.

"Now, don't get all snippy," Iris began. "But your man told the officers what happened to you, and Abe told me."

My chest twisted while humiliation heated my cheeks. "Oh," I said.

Bowie came home the other day, woke me up, and told me about the Church meeting. I was okay with it then, but honestly, I was beginning to worry that it would filter back to Sunny. Everybody knowing made it more real somehow.

Iris reached out and took my hand in hers. "Have you spoken to anyone about it?"

"About what?" I frowned.

Rosie put her hand on my arm. "Layla, you were raped."

Tears welled up in my eyes. I knew what they were trying to do, but I didn't want to discuss it. "I'm okay," I whispered.

Iris leveled me with a look. "I thought I was okay too, but I was as far away from okay as I could get."

My insides clenched, and another rush of tears came. "What?"

"I was raped by a rival club 'bout thirty years ago. Bandit, Bowie's grandpa, was the prez back then. The club was different, into all sorts of bad stuff."

I took a sip of the wine that Rosie had poured. When I was growing up, there were rumors that the club dealt in guns and drugs. "Go on."

"The Burning Sinners were bad news. The Demons, although rough, still had a semblance of honor. Ol' ladies and kids were off limits, but that didn't extend to the Sinners. One day, they grabbed me from a supermarket car park in the next town."

Horror swirled in my chest. "Oh, my God."

"They took me to an old factory they owned. Three of 'em took turns with me."

A tear rolled down my cheek. "I'm so sorry, Iris."

Iris smiled sadly at me. "It's okay. Abe, Bandit, and a few of the brothers came for me. They made sure those bastards never hurt anyone again." She squeezed my fingers. "My point is, I was able to make peace with what happened to me because Abe made me go and speak to someone."

"But Iris, what happened to me was different," I mumbled.

She lifted an eyebrow. "The circumstances were different, Layla, but not the outcome."

I swiped at my cheek. Maybe she was right. I felt better than I did a couple of weeks ago, but I still had bad dreams. Melancholy struck me at the oddest moments, and I'd find myself bursting into tears for no reason.

Rosie rubbed my arm. "We're here for you, Layla. You're part of the ol' lady tribe now. You're one of us. Anything you need, holler."

I looked at Rosie, then Iris, and my stomach began to warm. I'd only ever had Cara before. Now she was marrying Robbie, I knew our friendship would alter. I was thankful I had these women.

"Okay, I'll think about it," I promised.

"Good." Iris grinned. "Ro, fill me up. I'm hella thirsty all of a sudden."

"Drink up, Layla," Rosie ordered. "Got another three bottles in the fridge. Bowie can't drink because of his meds, so you can let loose."

I got off my stool, walked around the counter, and moved to Iris. My arms slipped around her neck, and I pulled her into me. "If you need anything. I'm here." I whispered in her ear.

"I'm okay, Layla, but I'm not sure if I'd even be here now if it wasn't for the rape crisis center. They saved my life. Just think about what I said. Okay?"

I pulled back and looked at her face. "You're so strong, Iris. You would have made it, regardless."

"Maybe, but back then, I wasn't coping. I thought I was, but inside I was broken. I may have survived, but I wouldn't be who I am now without the Demon's help." Iris patted my cheek. "I know someone you can talk to when you're ready."

At that moment, a small piece of my soul knitted back together. This woman had been through so much, and she survived.

Bowie had been amazing, but he didn't understand, not entirely. Men didn't have to think about the dangers that women faced.

Deep down, women felt uncomfortable even just walking down the street. We could be snatched in broad daylight; it happened all the time.

How could a man understand that kind of fear?

Walking alone, especially at night. Going on a date with someone you met online and even drinking in a bar with all your friends around you. Women had to factor in their safety at every turn. Much more so than men.

It was the way of the world, and it wouldn't get better anytime soon.

I looked at Rosie. "There's a gym in town. I wonder if they offer women's self-defense lessons?"

Her face lit up. "Yeah, they do. Sophie Green goes there, and she kicks ass."

I knew that name, but I couldn't place it. "Green?"

"You know. Bowie's doctor."

"Right!" I exclaimed. "I only ever knew her last name."

Iris let out a chuckle. "I'd be in on that. Sounds like a good time if you ask me." She gave me an evil smile. "I could test my moves out on Abe. It'd make a change for me to throw *him* around the bedroom."

Rosie began to laugh, and Iris joined in. A bubble of mirth rose through my throat, and I giggled.

Atlas walked past the door from the garden and popped his head in. "Jesus, fuckin, Christ. It's like a bunch'a witches cackling in 'ere." He made a face. "What's so goddamned funny?"

We began to laugh harder.

"We're gonna go to self-defense classes, boy, and then we'll kick your ass."

Atlas put his hands on his hips and looked up. "Fuck me, here we go," he muttered. Then, as he stalked away into the garden, I heard him bellow. "Abe, Bowie, you need to get your women in hand!"

Tears were rolling down my cheeks. I looked at Iris' and Rosie's happy faces and suddenly felt lighter than I had for weeks.

Iris was right. We were gonna kick ass.

Chapter Thirty

Bowie

Callum was just about to dig the key into the lock of his bar when I pulled up on my bike. I'd called him last night to arrange a meet. Now, I had everything crossed in the hope that he'd back me up.

Colt had been lookin' into how we could gather DNA.

Dad called a quick meet at the cookout yesterday, and we hatched a plan. Everything was riding on Callum.

"Yo. Motherfucker," he yelled as I cut my engine. "How you diddling?"

I took my helmet off and grinned. "Asshole. Don't need to diddle these days. Got me a woman, now." I put my kickstand on and dismounted.

Callum turned back to the door, twisted the key, and pushed the door open. "Heard a rumor you got yourself wifed up." He looked back and me and shook his head. "That 'she's mine' speech you did at Giovanni's, was all over town the next day. How the mighty have fallen, eh?" He flattened his lips, gesturing his head toward the door. "C'mon."

A huge grin spread across my face. Since I'd made my intentions known, nobody had bothered my girl. In fact, people were goin' outta their way to be nice to her.

A determination made my spine straighten. All I needed now was to catch the bastard that hurt her.

I followed Cal through the door. He switched on some lights, then pointed to a set of wooden swingin' saloon doors. "Follow me."

The scent of coffee filled the air. I trailed after him into a big kitchen containing a double grill and two deep fryers.

Cal pulled open the door to a huge fridge and took out some cream. "Coffee?"

"What the fuck, Cal. We just walked in the door. How have you got a big pot of coffee waitin' for ya already?"

Cal grinned. "Cleaner sets it up for me before she leaves."

"Jesus. You got 'em eatin' outta your hand."

"Yup," he agreed. "Got a girl for all seasons."

I quirked an eyebrow. "What you gonna do when you wanna settle down, huh? You'll still have 'em knockin' at your door when you're tryin'a feed the baby, the number of women you've got on tap."

Callum winced. "Don't talk to me about settling down, asshole. You'll give me hives."

"Your ma still on your back about getting a Mrs?"

He curled his lip. "The woman won't shut up about it."

"You'll fall, Cal, and when you do, I'll remind you of this little powwow."

Cal gave me a pointed look. "The day it happens, we'll sit in that bar with a bottle'a Midleton, and you can say, 'I told ya so.'"

I let out a laugh. "A thousand-dollar bottle'a whisky? You're on."

Cal poured two cups of java and handed one to me. He loaded his with cream, leaning his ass against the countertop. "So, you gonna tell me what the fuck's goin' on, Bowie?"

I took a chug of coffee, then put my cup down. I had to choose my words carefully to keep Layla and Sunny out of the equation. I'd promised her there'd be no comeback, and I wouldn't let her down.

"The Demons have gotten hold of the sick fuck's DNA," I began. "Turns out that a previous victim of his, a few towns over, had his kid."

Callum looked shocked. "Jesus."

"Yeah, it happened a few years before the pigs caught onto him."

"Right, well, it's a lead, at least. It's good to know things are lookin' up, but where do I come into it?"

My face turned serious. "We need the sicko's DNA to match it to the kid through a paternity test."

"How you gonna get that?"

"The best way is through saliva."

Callum's brow furrowed as he took everything in. The second he caught on to what I was implyin', his eyes went bugged out. "Jeez, Bo, that's gonna be a big job. Do you know how many men come in here?"

"Yeah, but we can narrow it down. If you give Colt your security tapes from the nights you got hit, he'll pinpoint the men who were here both times."

"Surely, it can't be that easy?"

I held my hands out. "Why not? Just keep the glasses or bottles back that those dudes drink from. Colt will be behind the scenes doin' the rest."

"What the fuck's he gonna do?" Cal asked.

"He'll swab the glass or bottle, then send the sample to a lab."

Bewilderment spread over Cal's face. "It's that easy?"

"I hope so. No guarantee it'll work. It depends on how much saliva we can collect. Also, you gotta understand Cal. It's illegal, a violation of rights."

Cal made a noise in the back of his throat. "Druggin' women, then assaulting 'em is a fuck of a lot worse. What about the victim's rights?" His head jerked in a nod. "Count me in."

Satisfaction crawled through me. It was the best outcome I could've wished for, but Cal needed to know the risks.

"Are you sure?" I asked. "If this backfires, it's your livelihood at risk."

He let out an annoyed snort. "Bowie, you think my livelihood's not already at risk? 'Cause you'd be wrong. Numbers have been declining for weeks. Girls are getting worried. They're stayin' home and inviting their girlfriends over instead of goin' out, and who can blame 'em?"

"It's a fuckin' nightmare, Cal. Even the *Haven*'s been affected, and he wouldn't fuckin' dare do it there, so I get what it's doing to your business." I stepped forward and clapped him on the shoulder. "We appreciate ya, Cal. Anythin' you need, the Demons are there."

"When do we do this?"

"We start this weekend. We got fifty testin' kits bein' delivered today. Colt will come by Friday and Saturday and get started."

Callum rubbed his jaw thoughtfully. "Got another idea. Saskia, one of my bartenders. Her sister got assaulted last year. I reckon I could get her to flirt with the ones we're targetin', maybe get some extra DNA, just in case the saliva thing falls flat."

"How?"

Cal shot me a cocky wink. "Hair follicles. We'll get 'em drunk as skunks, then send her in to get handsy, all touchy-feely, running her fingers through their hair. Believe me. She'll have 'em eating out of her hand."

I nodded. "That would work. I'll get the club to put some scratch behind the bar. Whenever any of 'em come in, give everyone shots on the house. You collect the glasses. Colt will be in here doin' the swabs. He'll bag 'em, add in a follicle. Job done."

He hooted out a laugh. "Bowie Stone, you are one sneaky fucker." His eyes narrowed. "But tell me. If this is illegal, the cops won't be able to use the evidence in court. What then?"

"Don't worry 'bout that, Cal. As my dear ol' grandpa, Bandit, used to say, 'there's more than one way to skin a cat.'"

He smirked. "I know a good clean-up crew if you need help takin' out the trash."

"What the fuck?" I muttered.

Cal's smirk widened. "Come on. You know Da's connected."

"Maybe, but he's not fuckin' Al Capone."

Callum shot me a hard glare. "Too fuckin' right, 'cause he's Irish."

I held my hands up. "Just sayin', your dad ain't Mob."

"He ain't exactly pure as the driven snow, either."

A thought struck me. "You gonna bring your pa in on this?"

"No choice. If Pa found out, and I hadn't clued him in, there'd be hell to pay."

Callum had a point. His Pop owned the bar. He had a right to know what we were up to. I just worried that details were in danger of gettin' out if too many people were in on it. "Just Lorcan and Saskia, Cal. We need to keep this on the low down."

"Yeah, I know." Cal clasped hold of my shoulder and looked at me. "It's a good plan, Bowie. Got no doubt that we'll catch the fucker."

Conviction burned in my chest. My eyes swung to my bud, and I leveled him with a stare. "Believe me, Cal. I'll catch the sick bastard if it's the last thing I do."

Chapter Thirty-One

Layla

"I'm home," I called out as I walked through the front door.

"In here, Doe," Bowie's deep voice replied.

I walked through the hallway toward the kitchen, noticing how quiet the house was. "Where's Sunny?" I asked.

Bowie was sitting at the kitchen table, tapping on his phone. He looked up at me as I walked in and grinned. "Rosie took all of 'em out for burgers, then to the flicks."

I approached him, dropped a kiss on his cheek, and pulled out the chair next to him. "Poor Rosie, having to wrangle all those kids," I said as I dropped onto the seat.

He gave me a wink. "I gave Ro some cash. She ain't hurtin'."

"I'll have to return the favor."

"No, you don't. Ro's got three hellions. We've only got one," he added under his breath, "so far."

A chuckle escaped me. "You're so convinced that I'm pregnant."

"I got bionic jizz, Doe. I'll be shocked if you're not."

I let out a sigh. "I'm worried you'll be disappointed."

He reached down and scraped my chair closer toward him, then took my hand. "Doe, if you're not, then I'll just have to work harder at it," he raised his thumb to his lip in that sexy way, "and that ain't no hardship."

"I love it when you do that," I murmured.

"I know, babe." He leaned forward so our lips were nearly touching. "Your eyes go soft and dreamy every time. Why do you think I fuckin' do it?"

He brushed his lips over mine, then kissed me so hard and deep that I felt it all the way down between my legs.

His hand slid to the bottom of my shirt. He began to roam underneath, then pushed it up until my bra was exposed. "I love you in white." He mumbled against my mouth. "It makes you look so fuckin' innocent. Makes me wanna dirty you up."

"I'm not," I breathed.

"You are," he rasped. "You're my innocent, good girl."

My pussy clenched at his words. Moisture flooded between my thighs, and I groaned out loud.

"You like being my good girl?"

I nodded eagerly.

"Then be good for me, and get on your knees."

Heat burned through my chest. "Here?"

He nodded. "Yeah, here. Gonna spread you out over that table and fuck you hard, get me?"

My pussy clenched at his filthy words.

I slid down on my knees and stared up at him.

He shook his head. "I want you naked." Then he stood, pulled me up by my arms, and slid my top over my head. Strong hands went down to my jeans. He flicked the buttons open, then pulled down the zipper.

My hands shook as I slowly slid the denim down my hips and off, ensuring I took my panties with them. My hands went to my back. I unclipped my bra, shrugging it down and off my arms.

As I stood under Bowie's heated scrutiny, my pulse began to thrum, every nerve ending sizzling with need.

Bowie

His gaze went from my breasts, over the curve of my waist, then down to my pussy, leaving fire in its wake. "Fuckin' perfect," he said.

I slid down to my knees, holding onto his thighs for balance, then drew eye level to the considerable bulge in his jeans.

My trembling fingers went to his buttons. I snapped them open one by one and pushed the bottom of his tee up. I trailed my finger down the thin trail of hair that ran down the middle of his flat stomach.

Bowie let out a long moan. I felt the kick of his thick length against my face, and my pussy clenched with need.

There was something so erotic about me being completely naked and him dressed. I was his to use in any way he deemed fit. The thought of being at his mercy made desire coil in my belly.

"Take it out, Doe," he quietly demanded. The hint of authority in his voice just added to the fantasy.

I reached inside his jeans and carefully pulled out his hard cock. My pussy gushed again when I realized he was commando, with no barrier.

As I released the throbbing length, it sprang up, hard and thick, then bobbed gently against my cheek.

Bowie's cock was a revelation. It was smooth but steely, with a perfect curve. Sublime.

He reached down and gently tapped my face. "Open your mouth, Baby."

I obeyed. My mouth fell open, waiting, then I looked into Bowie's eyes for confirmation that he was pleased with me.

His eyes blazed with triumph, and I relaxed.

My hand moved to grip the base of his cock, the same way he showed me last time. "Tighter, Doe," he demanded. "Harder."

I gripped him tighter, and again he groaned. "That's it, baby, just like that."

I blossomed under his praise.

With his hand still on my cheek, I leaned forward and covered the head of his cock with my mouth. Then I sucked him deep into the back of my throat.

My gag reflex kicked in. I tried to pull back, but Bowie held me firmly in place. "It's okay, Doe, just breathe through your nose and relax."

After a few seconds of getting used to the feel of him so deep, I began to move my mouth up, then down, sucking hard as I went. "That's it, baby. Take it like my good girl."

The ache between my legs was unbearable. I moaned around his cock.

"Yeah," he rasped. "Do that again." So, I did. The vibrations made his cock twitch. I looked up again, and a single tear fell down my cheek.

"Fuck, Layla. Look at you cryin' all pretty for me," he rasped. He began to thrust gently into my mouth.

His hand went from my cheek to my hair. He took a handful in his fist, thrusting harder. My hips began to rock forward of their own accord, seeking friction.

My free hand snaked up his jean-clad legs. I gripped his ass, pulling him into me harder with every thrust. Pine and leather filled my nose. I moaned again at his scent.

"Fuck," he gritted, rearing back, leaving my mouth empty, bereft.

I looked up into swirling, liquid gold eyes.

"Don't wanna cum yet, Doe. Wanna take my time with ya." Need caused his voice to thicken.

He gripped me under my armpits and hauled me up, turning me so my ass rested on the table.

"Spread your legs," he rasped. Another command. "Let me see what's mine." He pulled a chair toward him and sat, his face inches from my core. A tingle of alarm made me freeze. Nobody had ever been this close to me, never looked at me in this way.

Bowie

"I said open your legs." He tapped three times on the top of the bare triangle between my thighs. "This pussy's mine, Doe. Now be my good girl and do as I say."

Bowie's hands went to my knees and then pulled them apart. His eyes rested on my open core, and he grinned. "Prettiest cunt I've ever fuckin' seen, and it's all mine." He bent forward and nuzzled me right there.

I nearly shot off the table with the unfamiliar sensations he aroused. Nobody had ever put their mouth down there before.

He pressed on my stomach gently. "Lay back, Baby. Let me eat you." The force of his hand made me comply.

The scratch of wood against my naked back was strange at first. Legs open, completely exposed. Bowie nipped at the inside of my thigh, then worked his way up, every soft bite making me moan.

Suddenly his face was right there. Warm breath skated over my clit, and he latched on, sucking hard.

"Oh, my God." My voice was a shout, back bowing off the table.

"You taste like fuckin' strawberries." He breathed the words against my clit, His long, thick finger slipping into my core, and he sucked on me again. Hard.

That time, he didn't stop.

I couldn't think straight with his mouth on my clit, fingers stretching me out. I let out a loud mewl and rocked my hips into his mouth.

"Love this pussy, Doe." He rumbled the words against me, the vibrations making me groan.

"Don't stop, please," I begged.

"That's my good girl," he rasped. "Fuck my mouth."

My hips began to circle and grind against Bowie's face. Pressure began to build, a flicker of heat burning its way outwards.

"I can feel you clenching my fingers," he growled, voice thick with need.

My pussy gushed again, flooding his mouth. He groaned hard against my clit; the vibration sent me hurtling over the edge, and the orgasm ripped through me, its intensity making me wail.

My pussy was still clenching when Bowie grabbed hold of my hips. I let out a surprised squeal as he dragged me down the table and flipped me over, his hand pressing down onto my back.

With one hand buried in my hair, he slid his cock inside me in one hard thrust.

His long groan mingled with mine. I was so full of him, so stretched out that I felt a bite of pain.

"You're so fuckin tight, Doe," he said, then he began to thrust again.

Fingers dug into my hip, holding me in place while the other pulled my head back. His hips snapped against my ass, his cock going deeper with every hard stroke.

"I can't take it," I cried out.

"You can, baby," he gritted out. "Just relax and feel."

I closed my eyes, focusing on the intrusion. Bowie was right. After a minute, the pinch of pain receded, and need took over.

A few more thrusts and the pressure began to build again. I began to push up and back onto him in silent encouragement.

"Yeah, you like that, doncha, Doe? You want more?"

"Yes, don't stop," I cried as Bowie began to thrust harder. The table shuffled an inch across the floor with every hard pound of his hips.

Fingers left my hip, skating around to my front, then he pressed hard onto my clit. Little sparks of pleasure made me gasp.

"You gotta get there, baby." He groaned. "Your cunt's grippin' me so hard. I ain't gonna last."

His fingertips began to stroke across the sensitive bundle of nerves.

"Jesus, Doe," he grunted. "Your pussy's soakin' my cock. You should see how beautiful it looks, all shiny with your cum."

The words floated through my mind, his fingers working my clit faster. The table scraped further every time he pounded into me, and I began the climb again.

"Fuck, Doe. Gonna cum". His voice was a croak.

My orgasm pulsed through me. It started from my core, spreading to the top of my head, the tips of my fingers, and toes.

I went flying, higher and higher, until I yelled a keening cry of pleasure.

Bowie's moans filled the air. Then he let out a bellow as the warmth of his seed filled me up while he thrust hard inside me.

The flooding sensation set off another mini orgasm that made my sensitive clit throb. I groaned again, the little sparks bursting behind my eyes. I floated back to earth, quietening as Bowie's thrusts became slower, gentler.

"Jesus, Doe. I saw stars." A whisper against my nape.

We both moaned together. Bowie pulled out, and I was empty.

He turned me to face him, then his hand slipped back down to my pussy, scooping up the cum dripping from me and pushing it back inside.

"What are you doing?" I asked softly, mind still reeling.

"Want it to take," he replied. "It needs to go back where it belongs and do its job. If you're not knocked up yet, you soon will be."

I shouldn't have liked it, but the vow in his words wrapped around me like a warm blanket.

Bowie Stone wanted a baby with me. Beautiful.

He leaned down, grabbed the back of my knees, and hauled me up into his arms, bridal style. "Close your legs,

Doe. Don't want my cum escapin'. It belongs to you now."

I pulled my knees together.

"That's my good girl," he crooned into my hair as he carried me into our bedroom.

He laid me down on the cool sheets.

I smiled as the bed dipped with his weight. He wrapped me up tight in his arms. "Rest, baby," he ordered softly.

My bones were weightless in the aftermath of my orgasms. The warmth of Bowie's golden skin made my eyes droop, lulling me into a state of completion.

A satisfied smile washed across my lips. "Love you, Bowie," I whispered.

Then, I drifted away contentedly, with my man's heart beating hard against my cheek.

Chapter Thirty-Two

Bowie

"It's takin' too long," I snapped.

All the officers were in Dad's office. He'd called an impromptu meet. Shit hit the fan last night, making the air thick with angry tension.

Colt reared back slightly, shootin' me a glare. "It's not even been a fuckin' week, Bo. Calm your tits."

I looked at him like he was crazy. "What the fuck are you talkin' about? What tits?"

"It's just a saying," he explained under his breath. "It means chill the fuck out."

My hand went to grip the back of my neck. "Then say chill the fuck out. Jesus, I can't understand you half the time."

Dad scraped his hand down his face. "For fuck's sake. Here's me, with my ass puckerin', waiting to hear if Xan's gettin' out, and you two are scrappin' about tits." He shot a glare toward me, then turned to Colt. "Have the tests been held up?"

"No, Prez. They usually take around a week, but remember, we're sending in swabs containing less saliva than they're used to testin'. I know each bag also contained a follicle, but that means he has to carry out two tests, then compare the results."

"Mine only took about five days to return," Atlas declared. "I remember, 'cause my asshole was nippin' the whole time I was waitin'."

"I can't just send 'em to any old lab, Atlas. Jesus. The way we're gathering this DNA is illegal. You think I can just send 'em anywhere? You think they won't suspect anything when fourteen fuckin' tests turn up together, all for the same kid?"

"Can't you put a fire under his ass, Colt?" Hendrix asked.

"No. My contact is one man doing all the work by himself. Leave him be." Colt's face softened. "I'm sorry 'bout that girl, but we need to get this done right."

My gut twisted.

"Have the cops got a lead yet?" Ice asked.

Guilt made a lump form in my throat. "No, the cops searched the woods for clues, nothin'." My hand clasped the back of my neck. "She's seventeen," I said quietly. "Just a kid."

Atlas leaned forward, elbows resting on the desk. "Can't believe the parents are lettin' their kids go partyin' in the woods with all'a this shit goin' on."

"Try keepin' 'em in at that age. I wish you luck," Dad said. "And you gotta remember, until now, it's been contained to druggin' women in bars, brother. It's the first time he's snatched a girl off the streets."

"Like I said, he's craving more," Colt muttered. "It's only gonna escalate."

Frustration snapped through my chest while angry mutters went up around the room.

This mornin' when I told Layla, she started cryin', sayin' it's all her fault.

I told her to hush and that she wasn't to know, but it didn't help. My girl was feelin' guilty, and I was strugglin' to help. It had gone beyond me now. She had to go and speak to somebody trained.

I could talk to her all night if it would make her feel better, but apart from when she initially told me about that night, she refused to speak about it.

I put my head in my hands. "Layla's a mess. Keeps sayin' if she spoke up sooner, the girl wouldn't have got snatched."

"Jesus, Son!" Dad said. "It's not Layla's fault."

I tried to swallow past the lump that was stranglin' me. "Tell *her* that. She's startin' to break, Dad. I dunno what to do."

"Bo," Abe said. "Iris gave her the number of a counselor she knows. Did your woman call her?"

"Dunno, Abe, she won't talk about it."

"Want me to get Iris on it?"

I shrugged. "It can't do any harm. I dunno what to say to her."

Abe patted me on the back. "It's okay. Iris'll sort it."

"Son, your woman'll be okay," Dad added.

I nodded, but a feelin' of dread still gripped my insides.

A jolt went through me as the high pitch of a ringtone clapped through the air.

Dad froze solid for a second, looked down, and grabbed his phone. His face was stoic as he stabbed a button and put it to his ear. "Stone, speakin'."

The room went quiet. Dad listened, face intent, shoulders stiff.

Drix nudged me gently, then looked pointedly at Pop. "Xander." We all stared at Dad, listening, on tenterhooks.

Pop's lips twitched. "That soon?" A wide smile began to spread across his face. He looked at me, grinnin' big. "Got it," he said. "We'll be there."

He stabbed at his phone again and rested it gently on the table.

My heart began to go crazy, almost beatin' outta my chest. "Dad?" I croaked.

"Bowie, it's your brother."

My throat went thick. "Tell me."

He looked up at the heavens. "Thank you," he muttered. His stare swung slowly back down to me. "It's Xander." Dad's eyes danced with joy. "He's gettin' out tomorrow."

Chapter Thirty-Three

Layla

Sweat dripped down my face. My arms dropped to the sides, and I heaved out a breath.

I was startled as a voice from behind me said. "You did well, Layla. I find the punchbag really wearing."

I turned to see who it was. Doctor Green sipped from a bottle of water. She was dressed in workout gear, and her dark hair was scraped into a ponytail.

I gave her a low wave. "Hi, Doctor."

She smiled. "How's Bowie?"

"He's okay. Thanks." My voice came out distant.

She looked at me quizzically. "Are you okay?"

I nodded, only half hearing her, my head full of something else.

"Layla?"

I glanced up at her worried face, and my shoulders slumped. "I'm sorry, Doctor Green. I've just got a lot on my mind."

"I'm off duty. Call me Sophie." She smiled.

"Yeah."

"I hear Cara's getting married tomorrow. How exciting."

I rubbed at the stress headache pounding through my temples. "Yeah, she is."

"I've never seen you here before. Do you train?"

I nodded absentmindedly. "No, well, yeah, I guess. Me, Iris, and Rosie did our first self-defense class. I stayed behind to work on my strength."

"Hence the punchbag?" she asked.

Another nod.

"Did you enjoy it?"

"It was hard, but I already feel like I learned something."

My eyes prickled.

Since I'd heard about that girl getting attacked, my mind was all over the place. She was only seventeen. She'd been found wandering naked in the woods, drugged, scared, and had clearly been sexually assaulted.

I called Iris, devastated. She came over and insisted that we join the class today. I'm glad she did. I felt a little more in control already.

It was a shame that it couldn't take away the guilt gripping me.

Tears stung my eyes. I tried to blink them away. "I'm sorry," I whispered. "I can't seem to stop crying."

"Come on. Let's get you somewhere—" her eyes fixated behind me—"a little more private."

I glanced around. Brett and Robbie were laughing with Sydney Barrington over by the treadmills. She looked over her shoulder at me, smirked, then turned back to the guys. Robbie said something, and they all laughed.

Brett's eyes narrowed on me, and a cold shiver ran down my spine.

I looked back at the doctor as more tears welled up. "Okay."

She took my elbow, steering me toward the changing rooms. We went inside and around a corner to a small seating area.

She pulled out two chairs beside each other and plonked down in one. I sat next to her and folded my hands in my lap.

"Talk to me," she said softly.

Every muscle was wired.

My mind swirled with 'what ifs.' What if I hadn't been so naïve? What if I'd gone to the police when it happened? What if he did it again? My hands went clammy as dread gripped my chest.

"Layla? What is it?"

"That girl who was hurt last night."

Doctor Green's eyes flickered with anger. "Do you know her?"

"No," I murmured. "But-" my voice caught.

"Layla?"

My eyes swung to hers, shining with tears. "Maybe I could've stopped it."

The doctor's mouth fell open in shock. She recovered quickly and leaned forward. "Do you know something?"

"Not exactly."

Then she said something that shocked me. "I know the MC is investigating. I put Colt in touch with a friend at a DNA testing lab. He told me about the child and the poor woman he hurt years ago." She shook her head and continued. "I've treated some of the victims in the ER. He's been careful, never leaving any trace of DNA behind. This is a major breakthrough."

A squeak escaped the back of my throat.

Her caramel-brown eyes flickered slowly and began to widen. It was almost comical how big they got. I could practically see the cogs turning in her head.

"It was you?" She asked, her voice shocked.

I nodded jerkily.

"He's Sunshine's father?"

Another head jerk.

"Oh, Layla."

The tears began to leak down my cheeks. "I didn't even know that I'd been drugged. At the time, I thought I'd had too much to drink and made a stupid decision to have sex with some stranger at a party."

"How did you work it out?"

"Cara. I recognized her symptoms. It took me back to that night. It was the same way for me back when it happened."

The doctor nodded thoughtfully. "So, you worked it out, told Bowie, and now he's gathering DNA evidence to do a paternity test? How?"

"Callum O'Shea's helping him. They've narrowed down the suspects. Colt swabs the glasses and bottles, bags them, then sends them for testing. They're also, somehow, collecting hair follicles."

A huge smile spread over the doctor's features. "That's genius."

I let out a small laugh. The only burst of humor I'd felt all day. "I wouldn't call Bowie a genius exactly, but he has his moments."

She nodded like she was deep in thought, and her eyes widened again. "Oh my God, Layla. The club will know who it is any day no—" As the doctor spoke, a door banged shut, cutting her off.

We stared at each other in horror.

Fear flickered down my spine. "Oh my God, was someone just in here, listening?"

The doctor stood and stalked around the corner into the changing area. "There's nobody here now," she called out. "Maybe it was just someone poking their head around the door to see who was in here."

I relaxed slightly. "Surely we would have heard if someone came in?"

She walked back around. "Yes, definitely," she said worriedly as she sat.

"You can't tell anyone, Doctor Gre—"

"—Sophie," she gently chastised.

My lips quirked up. "Sorry. You can't tell anyone…. Sophie."

She looked me dead in the eye. "Never. If this got out, there would be an uproar."

"I know."

Sophie leaned back in her chair. "It's all going to work out, Layla. You'll see."

Unease washed over me. "I hope so, Sophie." I bit my lip as I tamped down the turbulence swirling through my stomach. "I really hope so."

Chapter Thirty-Four

Bowie

"Baby. I told ya, I'm not goin' to that fuckin' shit show," I said, tone determined.

"Bowie, who am I supposed to dance with if you're not there?" Layla's voice held a hint of sadness. I rubbed the back of my neck, cursin' the horrible fuckin' timing of this wedding.

Here I was, sittin' outside the penitentiary, minding my own business, waiting for Xander. He was due to walk out any second now.

Then my phone rang. Layla was callin', beggin' me to change my mind and go to Cara's wedding with her.

I banged the back'a my skull gently against the headrest. "Doe, baby. I can't betray my brother like that."

A disappointed sigh came through the speakers. "I know. I'm sorry, Bowie. I shouldn't have asked. Forget it."

My fingers rubbed the nape of my neck, guilt slashing through my chest. I felt terrible for Doe, but we'd already talked about this.

My brother's ol' lady was about to marry the asshole who put him in the slammer. How was I supposed to go to his wedding? I couldn't support that.

I closed my eyes, head shakin' in disbelief. Sweet fuckin' Jesus. At what point did my life morph into a Jeremy Springer show?

I blew out a resigned breath. "How 'bout I pick you up an hour early from the reception? I'll come in and give you that dance."

"Really?"

My gut swirled with acid. "Yeah."

Movement caught my eye. I looked up and saw the gates begin to slide open. Nerves moved through me. This was it.

"Layla, I gotta go. He's here."

"Good luck," she sang. "Give Cash my love."

I growled softly. "Don't fuckin' think so. That's just for me."

Apprehension began to swirl as I watched the silhouette of a man appear in the bright mornin' sun.

"Later. Love you, Doe," I muttered, ringing off.

There were a few vehicles parked outside the prison. It looked like a busy release day. The sun shone from behind the bodies that streamed outta the gates, makin' 'em silhouettes.

My eyes went from one to the next, not seein' him.

My heart stuttered, and panic rose through my gut as my eyes darted from one man to another.

After another minute, a guy with a familiar swagger walked out. The gates began to slowly close behind him.

There he was. My shoulders relaxed with relief as I took in the sight of my brother.

Xander had always been full of muscle, but now he was even bigger. I didn't get to visit him often because the auto shop was busy, so I noticed the physical changes immediately.

He stared toward my truck, and his steps faltered.

I whirred the window down, stuck my neck out, and yelled. "Yo. Motherfucker. Long time no see."

Bowie

A grin fell over his face, and he started toward me again.

Xander wore the same thing he'd worn on the day he went in. Jeans, a wife-beater, and boots. His dark brown hair was a bit longer on top than it used to be, but it looked good on him.

He swaggered to the truck, went to the passenger side, and opened the door. "Bo," he rumbled. "You haven't changed a bit." He climbed up and plonked down in the seat.

"It's not even been three years, Xander. I ain't gone grey yet."

Xan's arms and chest were more bulked up, highlighting the myriad of black tattoos. Cool tribal marks snaked up his nape, and his left bicep was covered with a steampunk wheel and cogs down under his shirt.

Seein' him after all this time made my throat thick. "Brother," I croaked.

He turned to face me, gripped me into a manly hug, and clapped me hard on the back. "It's okay, Gage. I'm back. It's all good." His tone thickened.

I cleared my throat, tryin' to cough away the burn.

He barked out a laugh. "You're a whiny cunt."

"Missed ya, bro," I said, tone low.

His head twisted to me. "You too. Now get me the fuck away from this hole. There's some POs I wanna beat to death. The faster you get me outta here, the better."

I laughed, then switched on the engine. "Fuck the prison officers. You ready for a beer?"

"Don't drink anymore, brother. It ain't good for me. Gonna get back to the club, check the bank accounts, grab my bike, and go get my woman."

My heart stopped. Anxiety clenched my gut. How was I gonna tell Xan that Cara was gettin' wed today?

"Xan—" I started.

"—I know my Cara's been runnin' with that slimy fuck, Bowie. Nothin' I can do about that. I screwed up.

She dumped me, then ran off. Then, I got locked up. She got her revenge. Now, she needs to wake the hell up. That fucker's bad news." His jaw clenched so tight that a muscle ticked. "She's my ol' lady."

I cleared my throat again. "Xan. It's today."

"Huh?"

"The wedding. It's today."

He let out a growl. The air turned thick around him as anger leeched from every pore. His fists clenched. "What time?" he demanded.

"One pm."

He glanced at the clock. "Thank fuck. We got a two-hour drive. We'll make it with thirty minutes to spare."

My eyes bugged out at him. "What the fuck, Xan? You're gonna turn up at the church? Congratulate the happy couple? Tell you what, we'll stop off on the way there and pick out a gift for 'em too."

Xan grunted out a laugh. "Don't be a stupid prick, Bo." His hand went to his chin, and he rubbed it in thought. My chest tightened. At that moment, he could've been my dad.

I froze as he spoke his following words.

"Put your foot on the gas, brother, and get me back to Hambleton." A grin spread across his face. "I got a wedding to stop."

Chapter Thirty-Five

Layla

"Bowie's not coming," I murmured sadly.

Cara took my hand in hers. "I'm sorry."

Disappointment tugged at my stomach. "It's not your fault. It's just that he feels like he's betraying Xander."

Cara chewed at her lip, then lowered her head.

I'd arrived at her mom and dads an hour ago. She was getting ready here for the wedding, but she was quiet and pale. She'd thrown up with nerves twice already, and it was only ten-thirty.

I squeezed her fingers. "You, okay?" I asked gently.

"It's silly, really. When you just said that Bowie feels like he's betraying Xan, I realized that's what I'm feeling too. Like I'm betraying him."

"Oh, Cara," I murmured. "Why are you doing this? Let's run. Now. We'll go, grab Sunny from Iris, then we can lie low until it all dies down."

Cara's eyes turned thoughtful but then hardened with determination. "It's just pre-wedding jitters. I'll be fine once it's all over." She began to chew on her lip. "God," she whined. "I need a drink."

A soft tap sounded came from the door. It cracked open, and Deb poked her head around. "Cara, *Blooms* just called. Their delivery truck won't start. The flowers are all at the venue, but they can't get your bouquet or men's buttonholes here."

Cara rolled her eyes. "Typical. Is Dad around?"

"No. There was a broken window reported at the high school. He's gone there to meet the police and get it replaced. I've got to go and check the caterers are all set up."

I sat up straight. "I'll go."

Deb smiled. "I was going to ask you, would you mind?"

"It's no problem." I gave Cara's hand a squeeze. "I won't be long."

"Thanks, Layla," Cara said. "We'll break the champagne out when you get back."

Deb raised an eyebrow. "I don't think you should be getting drunk before the wedding, Cara," she warned as she left the room.

Cara grimaced and looked at me. "Actually." She grimaced. "I'm starting to think getting drunk is the only way to go."

Lucy, the owner of Blooms, was mortified. "Tell Cara that I'm sorry, Layla. I don't know what happened. The delivery truck was fine yesterday."

I picked up the crate containing Cara's wedding bouquet and the single white roses for the men's lapels. "It's not a big deal. I'm happy to collect them."

Lucy came from behind the counter and walked me to the door. "I hope she has a fantastic day. I'll see you later at the reception."

I smiled goodbye to Lucy as she pulled the door open for me.

Bowie

The town wasn't busy; there were a few people outside Magnolia's in the distance, but it was quiet apart from that.

Many townsfolk had been invited to the wedding, even more to the reception. I guessed that most people were getting organized.

Disbelief crawled through my mind. I couldn't believe Cara was actually gonna go through with it. I thought she would have done a 'runaway bride' by now, but no. Cara was the most stubborn person I knew and always stuck to her word.

No way did I agree with what she was about to do, but she'd stuck by me through thick and thin, and I would do the same for her.

I turned away from the coffee house and began to make my way to my car. As I walked past the alley between Blooms and the bookstore, I heard a groan.

I pulled to a halt and listened.

Then I heard it again, a groan and a muttered. "Help!"

My heart began to speed up. Was somebody hurt? I quickly put the crate of flowers down on the sidewalk and walked into the mouth of the alley.

"Hello, are you okay down there?" I called.

I could mostly see. The light was dim, but there was definite movement.

"Help. Somebody shot me," a deep voice called.

My heart stuttered, then began to race. Somebody was hurt. What if the guy who shot Bowie in the alley had done it again?

Panic rose through my throat. I began to hurry toward the voice. The tap of my footsteps echoed up the looming brick walls on either side of me.

I spotted a broad figure wearing black, lying in a heap on the ground with their back to me.

Another quiet. "Help!" floated in my ears.

As I drew closer, I saw that the person was wearing a black hat covering the back of his head.

"Are you okay?" I asked nervously.

"Layla, help." The voice was familiar.

Trepidation crept through me simultaneously as a cold shiver ran down my spine. Something wasn't right. Every nerve ending fizzed, and my senses screamed to get out of there.

"I—I—I'll go get help," I stuttered. I stepped back, but then I froze as a quiet laugh floated through the air.

The figure began to move. He slowly stood, then turned. I let out a shocked gasp when I saw what was covering his head and face.

A black balaclava.

Horror swarmed through me. I stepped back again, turning so I could start to run. Pain ripped through the back of my head as he grabbed my hair and pulled me. I let out a cry. My back hit his front. Bile rose up my throat as his erection dug into my ass.

"Not so fast, Layla," he rasped in my ear. "Me and you have got unfinished business."

Fingers sunk into my windpipe, and my body began to tremble with fear. I opened my mouth to scream, but as my desperate wail rose, I felt a sharp pinprick in my neck.

Shock hit me, then the edges of the world began to darken.

"Wh—What did you do?" I cried, but my voice faded as the ground rushed to meet me.

A loud bump thudded through the air. A stab of pain rattled through my head. The world began to fade before my eyes. I groaned in pain.

My stomach turned when a sinister voice rasped. "Good night, Layla."

Then, everything turned black.

Chapter Thirty-Six

Bowie

We were twenty minutes out of Hambleton.

I'd been fillin' Xander in on everything that'd been goin' on in his absence. The drink spikin', the assaults, and Doe's involvement.

My brother's body stiffened as I went on. A grin spread over his features when I told him about the DNA testing. "Got a feelin' I know who's doing it, Bo. I got to know some people in prison who know about some weird assed shit."

My eyes bugged out. "Who?"

He rubbed the stubble on his chin. "We'll call Church, and I'll go over everythin' at once. It's a fuck of a story. You won't believe it."

"Xan, tell me."

"I will. Promise. But I want everyone together when I go over everything." He looked across at me and out a low chuckle. "Still can't believe you wifed up, Layla Hardin."

A frustrated breath left me. I could tell Xan was tryin' to change the subject, but he was stubborn. If he said he didn't want to talk about it yet, he wouldn't.

"Gonna put a ring on it and keep knockin' her up." I shrugged. "Though, not necessarily in that order."

Xan twisted his head to look at me. "So, you're over the Samantha thing?"

My lips quirked at the thought of the first girl I ever loved. Sam died in a car accident about seven years ago. A drunk driver careened into her driver's door and killed her outright.

She was eight months pregnant with our daughter.

"Yeah," I reassured him. "I admit now. It held me back for a while. It spooked me to the point where I nearly lost Layla. I felt like I was betrayin' Sam somehow, but my woman gave me another chance."

"Have you told Layla about her and your baby girl?"

I shook my head. "No, with all the drugs, the patrols, and the shooting, I never got the chance to explain. I'll sit her down soon." A smile tugged at my mouth. "I got the sweetest woman alive, Xan. She'll understand."

He shrugged. "I always liked Layla, Bowie. She was a good friend to Cara, especially after I—" He cleared his throat and started again. "When Cara needed someone, Layla was there."

We drove silently for a couple of miles, and a question formed in my head. "Xan. Cara's not like my woman. She's full of piss 'n' vinegar. You know you've got a long road ahead. And that's even if she forgives you, which I doubt."

Xan grinned. "You may like 'em sweet, Bo. But I like 'em sassy. I know how to handle my woman."

"Fuck that," I muttered.

Xan barked out a laugh. "Ya dunno what you're missin'. There's no feelin' like the one you get when a wildcat cums over all your dick, spitting, 'n' snarling." His hands reached down to adjust his crotch. "Sorry, Brother." He chuckled. "It's been a long time."

I winced. "I'll stick to my Doe. But good luck with that."

Xander threw his head back and began to laugh, then stopped as my phone began to buzz on the dashboard.

"Who's that?" Xander asked as he made a grab for it. "I already spoke to Dad." He held the screen up and stabbed the green button. "Good fuckin' day to ya, Colt. Hope you ain't got too comfortable in my chair."

Colt's voice snapped through the Bluetooth connection. "Bowie. We've got a positive result. A ninety-nine point nine-eight percent paternal match."

My gut turned. I glanced at Xander, whose face was turning to a snarl. My brother's temper was legendary.

Gotcha fucker. I thought. *It's time to pay the piper.*

Shouts began to rise in the background. Dad was bellowing at someone. Footsteps pounded on wood as the men ran to follow the prez's orders. Pop shouted again, voice deathly. "Tell Bowie to get back here. Now!"

Ice crept through my gut. All emotions drained out of me. Dad sounded like he was gonna blow. That feeling of doom crept through my stomach again.

My jaw clenched. "Out with it, Colt. Who's the dead man?"

Colt let out a breath, and in a dead tone, he gave me a name that turned the ice in my gut into a burning fire.

"It's Robbie Henderson, Junior."

Chapter Thirty-Seven

Layla

A voice was shouting, but it seemed far away, like it was coming from another room. I wished they would tone it down. I was trying to sleep.

I attempted to move, but a dull ache gripped me. A groan of pain escaped me. Jesus, my back was in agony.

My arms seemed weighted down by something. I tried to lift them, to see, but they were too heavy. Why was I so weak?

I tried to open my eyes, but my lids were heavy like they were made of lead.

Why was everything so hard and cold?

A jolt went through my entire body as I forced my eyes open.

It took a few seconds to understand what was in front of me. The world seemed tilted. Then I realized I was lying on my side, on hard concrete.

A big pillar loomed up in the middle of the room. I saw a flash of a red brick wall, but it was dark. My brain felt like mush, so I wasn't sure.

Confusion whirled through my brain.

I desperately tried to remember what happened, how I got here. I remembered going to Blooms, leaving, going to my car, and... My teeth began to chatter, shock ripping through me.

Oh my God.

My mind cleared, and images flashed behind my eyes.

The man wearing the balaclava. The pain from the tiny prick of a needle.

I'd been drugged.

My heart began to thud as panic rose through my chest. Shallow breaths sawed in and out. I tried calming down, but the fear took over, and my vision weakened.

The shouting started up again. The thudding of my heart seemed to beat inside my ears, partially drowning the words out.

My body stilled.

They got my DNA…. matched it to the brat… I don't fucking know… you need to come now. I'm supposed to be getting married in an hour.

The words were distorted to my ears, like when you talk through one of those creepy voice machines. Disorientation muddled my brain. The drugs doing the same job as they did six years ago.

I tried to think through the conversation and make sense of it. "C'mon, Layla," I whispered. "Think."

I'm getting married in an hour, floated through my head.

He was still talking. I concentrated on his voice and speech patterns. It was familiar. My teeth chattered with fear. I knew him.

Then he began to bellow.

I heard them in the gym. Cunt was talking to that do-gooder doctor… yeah… that O'Shea prick's in on it, too… yeah.

For some reason, it didn't click. I just kept trying to remember. Who was getting married on the same day as Cara? My brain refused to accept the truth that, deep down, I already knew.

Something pinged in my memory.

Bowie

Recognition smashed into me full force, stripping away the confusion. Utter dismay clawed at every organ. Fear prickled through me like a disease.

I stilled as a name floated through the muddy waters of my mind.

Robbie.

Chapter Thirty-Eight

Bowie

Dad, Hendrix, and Atlas were waitin' outside when we sped into the clubhouse parkin' lot. The second my truck stopped, I swung open the door and leaped down.

I'd called Layla, the second Colt, and I hung up. Her fuckin' phone was switched off, and I immediately knew something was wrong.

Layla's phone was charged and ready to go at all times. Especially when someone else watched Sunny, in case anything happened. She was a mama bear about it.

My woman was supposed to be helpin' Cara get ready, so I called her and asked for Layla. Cara told me that Doe had gone to pick up some flowers ages ago but hadn't returned.

Fear spiked through me. What the fuck was goin' on?

Next call was to *Blooms*. The number was still on my favorites list from all the times I'd sent my Doe flowers over the last few weeks.

Lucy said that Layla had left there over an hour before. She ran outside to look around for me. That's when she found the crate containing the bouquet Layla had collected earlier.

It was on the ground, by an alleyway. Layla's car was still parked on the side of the street.

Dread crept through my gut. Henderson had her. I just knew it.

"Dad. Have you found her?" I demanded.

He shook his head. "No, Son."

"What about Henderson?"

"Kit, Reno, and Shotgun went by his apartment. Nothing. Nobody's at his folk's house. He's disappeared."

"Brett Stafford?"

"Him too."

I heard my truck door thud shut. Pop looked over my shoulder. One side of his mouth tipped up.

"Dad?" Xander's voice was thick with emotion.

Dad's eyes shone with happiness. He grabbed my brother and pulled him into a hug. "Good to have you home, Son."

Xan clapped his shoulder, then took a step back. "We've got a problem. If Henderson's snatched Bowie's ol' lady, we need to find 'em, fast."

Dad cocked his head, a quizzical look on his face. "What's goin' on?"

"You don't know half of the shit that Henderson's pulled," Xander gritted out. "I asked around in prison. He's been runnin' with some sketchy people. They're into some bad shit."

Dad rubbed his beard. "Why didn't you tell us this before?"

"Think Pop. How much privacy did we get on your visits?" Xan asked.

"Next to none."

"Right, and every letter that goes through the mail room's checked. If anyone had gotten a clue that I knew somethin', they would've slit my throat."

Shock moved over Dad's features. "Jesus, son. What the fuck are you involved in?"

Xan rubbed the back of his head. "One of my old cell mates was transferred in from another prison. He did time with a guy who got paid a lot of scratch by some organization. It was to take the fall for somethin' that I think Henderson was involved with."

Dread pricked at me. "Organization? Fuck, Xan."

Xan nodded slowly. "I'll go over everythin' in Church, but right now, we have to find Layla." He clasped my shoulder and turned me to face him. "Trust me, Bowie. If we don't, she'll disappear."

I rubbed at my chest, tryin' to ease my growing panic. "Pop, what about Cara?"

"Boner said she was already on her way to the venue when he went to Seth's place. Freya's been tryin'a get her on the phone." Dad grimaced. "Poor girl's s'posed to be getting wed in thirty minutes."

"I'll go sort it," Xan growled. "Where?"

"The Meadowlark."

"That fuckin' stuck-up place?" he griped. "Where's my bike?"

"Here," Dad replied. "Knew you'd wanna ride." He threw some keys underarm to Xander, who caught them midair.

"Prospect!" Dad bellowed.

Sparky jogged over from the direction of the auto shop. "Yeah, Boss?"

"Cash's bike's just inside the garage. The midnight bike."

Sparky's eyes got huge. "The cool dark blue custom, with the universe sprayed on it?"

Xander jerked a nod. "Yeah, that's it. Now chop fuckin' chop."

Sparky nodded, then jogged to the enormous garage where we stored our rides.

Dad's eyes darted back to me. "We'll find her. Cara may know somethin'."

"Cara doesn't know shit," I muttered. "If she did, she wouldn't've agreed to marry that sick fuckin' pervert in the first place."

Atlas clasped my shoulder firmly. "She may know of somewhere he could'a holed up. We've searched all over, but no luck. We even looked in that old warehouse. Ya know, the one just outside town?"

"Cash. She's ready." I turned to see Sparky walkin' Xan's bike toward us. "I charged her battery yesterday when Prez said to get it ready. Welcome back."

Xan jogged to meet him. He grabbed the brain bucket hanging from the ape bars and put it on, pulling the chin strap tight. "Let me know if he turns up, Dad. I got a score to settle with that fuckstick."

Dad growled. "I want you away from it. You're on parole. If it all turns to shit, you'll be the first one they arrest. Especially with your history."

Xan's swung one leg over the saddle and flicked a switch. The engine roared to life. He gave us a loose one-finger salute, then pulled out the gates and down the street.

Misery ebbed through me, a tide of fear washing away every spark of hope. My guts twisted. "What if he kills her? I can't fuckin' do it again. It was bad when Sam— Fuck. If anythin' happens to Doe, it's gonna destroy me."

Dad's strong arm slid across my shoulder, pulling me into his chest.

"We'll find her son," he vowed. "We'll get to Layla, even if we have to burn the whole fuckin' world down to do it."

My chest clenched with terror.

I closed my eyes, attempting to block out the pain streaking through my heart. My gut churned as my inner voice whispered the words that I'd been too damned terrified to say out loud.

What if we're too late?

Chapter Thirty-Nine

Layla

Robbie had been talking on the phone for what seemed like hours, then suddenly, everything was quiet.

Footsteps echoed all around me. Eerie taps pitter-pattered over the ground all around me. I didn't know if it was the drugs in my system or I was going crazy, but they seemed to ring in my ears.

Then they stopped, and a quiet voice sang, "Laylaaaa."

I froze.

Fear slithered under my skin. I tried to regulate my breathing. Maybe if I pretended to be asleep, he wouldn't hurt me. I was no threat if I was still drugged and sleeping.

My eyes closed. I focused on breathing softly and rhythmically, ignoring the fear that sliced through me. I just breathed.

Awareness prickled at me. Someone was walking around me. I could feel eyes boring down at my body. I kept my lids closed and breathed.

More eerie footsteps tapped on the hard ground, sending tiny vibrations through me, and I breathed.

I felt a presence close to my face, then puffs of air skated across my cheek. I pushed down the urge to shudder, and instead, I breathed.

"I know your awake, Layla," he spat out, close to my ear. His voice was odd. It sounded like Robbie but also different. The tone was slightly higher pitched.

Then a laugh pealed through the air. It bounced off every concrete wall, rattling through me like an alien force. I wanted to scratch at my skin, get it out of me.

Everything was distorted, almost other-worldly. Fear clenched at my chest so hard that I thought my heart would beat out of me, leaving a hollow recess behind.

A thundering shout hollered close to my ear. "Boo!"

Pain shot through my skull, like scissors snipping at my skin. I groaned out loud as my eardrum thumped with a pulsating ache.

Robbie laughed again. A hyena's chatter cackled all over the room. The acoustics made it seem like a herd of wild animals surrounded me.

Whack.

A burst of pain burst through my back.

Whack.

More blazing pain radiated through me, forcing a reaction, and I groaned out loud.

"I fuckin' knew it," Robbie bellowed. "I knew you were awake."

Another high-pitched laugh cut through the room.

I tried to roll on my back, but the blazing ache that burned my skin stopped me in my tracks. My gut roiled at the thought of anything touching it, even the cold ground.

My stomach clenched with a wave of sickness. Water dripped from my face. Shock went through me as I realized that tears were trickling from my eyes.

Whack.

Oof. My stomach this time. A dull ache spread through my torso.

My body turned inwards, and as I doubled over on the ground, a shriek filled the air. An awful dying animal noise.

Bowie

Oh my God, was that me?

My body began feeling weightless, like floating on a vast ocean. Was I dying? I began to choke out a cough. The thought of leaving Sunny, and Bowie, splintered me into pieces. I had to hold on, had to stay awake.

Then my vision began to fade again. "No, no, no," I whispered.

I tried to cling to the cold ground, clutch onto the hard concrete, and welcome the stabbing ache. I knew where there was pain, there was life. I did everything to hold on.

Whack.

More searing pain across the back of my head caused my body to jolt, and I felt myself being pulled into a deep, dark abyss. A place of no pain, no coldness, and no regret.

A place of sweet relief.

Chapter Forty

Cara

Robbie wasn't here.

Robert Senior had been raging over the phone for the last hour. I could hear him shout. "Find him!" "He's got to be somewhere!" "I don't care!" "You're fired!"

Mom and I were waiting in a small room attached to the back of the main hall, where my fiancé was supposed to be waiting for me.

The guests were already inside.

My wedding dress swirled around my hips, flowing down to the floor. It was gorgeous. I felt like a princess.

Shame the groom wasn't here to see it.

My gut twisted and turned, but it wasn't because my fiancé had disappeared. Layla had gone out to run an errand for me earlier and hadn't returned.

My mind was wracked with uncertainty. Even if Robbie did show up, I couldn't go through with it without Layla.

"He'll be here, Cara. I'm sure there's a perfectly reasonable explanation," Mom said reassuringly from the chair by my side.

Panic rose through my throat. "It's Layla I'm worried about."

Mom took my hand in hers and looked at me. She began to laugh. Her blue eyes twinkled like sapphires.

"Mom?"

Her laughter began to fade then she patted my arm. I swallowed at the concern shining in her eyes. She quirked an eyebrow and then said the words that blew my mind. "Shall we go home now, Darling?"

A small choke escaped me. "What?"

"You're not going to marry him, Cara. Robbie's not for you. He dims your fire. Your man. Your husband, he'll want you to burn for him."

The well of tears blinded me.

Mom stood, then pulled me up gently. "Robbie's ice, you're fire. If you go through with this ridiculous charade, he'll extinguish everything you are." Her eyes softened. "Cara. Fire needs fire to burn."

Relief prickled through me.

She was right. My brain screamed that being here, waiting for Robbie in this dress, was all wrong.

When Robbie asked me to marry him, I was so broken and lost that I didn't know what I was doing. I just wanted the ache to go away. And if I was honest with myself, I tried to make Xander hurt the same way he'd hurt me.

My eyes widened at Mom. "What about all the money Dad spent?"

She started to chuckle. "Honey, I'll tell you a secret. Robert Senior wanted all of this pretentious crap, so Robert Senior paid for it."

For the first time in months, the rocks in my chest loosened. It was like the clouds parted inside my mind, allowing a beam of clarity to stream through. Finally, I was thinking clearly. I knew what I had to do.

"Well then," I said to Mom, picking up my skirts. "I better tell everyone to go home."

Mum's eyes danced. "That's my girl."

I picked up the bouquet retrieved earlier from the sidewalk outside *Blooms*. My skirts swished as I turned and walked up to the big, wooden double doors.

I held my back straight, then, with both hands, I threw the doors open wide.

Ninety-eight pairs of eyes all turned to me. Forty-four to my left, forty-four to my right.

I didn't even know ninety-eight people. They were mainly business associates of Robbie's father.

With a huge, fake smile plastered across my face, I began to walk. Slowly at first, then as I neared the registrar, my steps became more sure.

I got to the end of the aisle and turned to face everyone.

All of the curious eyes didn't faze me one bit. It was nothing compared to staring down a classroom full of teenagers.

My dad was talking furiously with Robert Senior. The anger secreted from his pores before it rose and crackled through the air.

I cleared my throat. "Ladies and Gentlemen. I'd like to thank you all for coming today, but—"

—Bang. A door slammed in the distance.

I frowned as footsteps thudded across the marble floor. I panicked. *No, please, not Robbie. Not now.*

"Where's my woman?" a deep, familiar voice demanded.

A soft laugh. My mom?

Butterflies began to dance through my belly. Anxiousness crawled through my chest.

No, no, no. Not him. No, no, no.

My emotions pinged like they were on high alert. I let out a humorless laugh. *He wouldn't dare.*

Footsteps, getting closer and closer, caused shivers to run up and down my arms.

A tall figure loomed in the open doors.

Recognition made my heart stop, then thud back to life, like it did the first time he ever smiled at me. My mouth dropped open.

Xander 'Cash' Stone.

My beautiful betrayer.

A golden-brown gaze met mine. It tugged at my chest the same way it always had since I was eighteen. It was tangible, like a giant magnet thrust between us, dragging us together.

My heart raced. Burning fire trailed up my gullet, followed by a rush of tears.

Then the pain came. Still as brutal as it was, on the night that I caught the love of my life grinding the dick - that was supposed to belong to me- inside another woman.

The same night that I became somebody else.

The bastard's muscles rippled across his arms. Thick thighs drove him towards me. He was a powerhouse. Even more dazzling than before.

His scent swirled through my nostrils, amber and bergamot. I inhaled deeply because how could I not? I'd starved myself of it.

Brown eyes burned into mine, full of fury, but I wasn't scared. I'd seen him lose his shit many times, and it was magnificent.

It was such a shame that I abhorred every inch of him, inside and out.

Such a shame that he broke me into tiny shards.

Such a shame that I hadn't been able to breathe properly since that night because every time I did, the ache pulsed through me again.

Shallow breaths only.

"Wildcat," he murmured.

A frustrated tear rolled down my face. "Fuck off."

A smile spread across his features, lighting him up. "The only way you're gettin' wed today is if I'm the fuckin' groom. Wanna say I do, baby?"

My belly twisted with anger. "Get out!"

His smile fell. "Look, Cara. Layla's in trouble, your," he grimaced, "fiancé's snatched her. We need your help."

Bowie

My heart dropped into my stomach at the exact second as the crowd collectively gasped. Shock snapped through the air. Ninety-eight people began to mutter in disbelief.

My throat closed up. "What?" I croaked.

I was startled as another voice boomed. "What?" Robert Senior.

Xander's face twisted. He spun to face the older man, then pointed his finger. "Your pervert son is the one doin' all the spikin'. We got proof. DNA from one of his victims."

Nausea rose through my throat. I covered my mouth with my hand, stunned.

Senior pulled out his phone, stalked the aisle, then disappeared through the doors. His wife, Elise, stood, then swayed on her feet. Shock moved across her face. Then she quickly followed her husband.

Whispers began to rise, and suspicious eyes bored into me.

My hands began to tremor violently. Quiet mumblings stabbed into me like little needles piercing my skin.

Bile burned my throat. Had I been sleeping with a rapist?

Horror crept through my chest. Layla had told me about Sunny, the DNA. Everything began to slot together.

My fiancé was Sunny's biological father.

He raped my best friend.

Guilt began to creep through my insides. How did I not see it? My stomach turned over again. I let out a low moan, willing away the wave of sickness that rolled through my belly.

Xander held his hand out. "C'mon."

I stared up at him, bewildered.

Robert's voice began to float from the room I'd just been sitting in with Mom. "He's lying. My son would never—" he paused before continuing. "He's a liar!"

Strong hands gripped underneath my ass. Suddenly, I was airborne. Xander hauled me up. My gut connected with his shoulder, causing a huff of air to escape my lungs. My world was upside down.

"Time to go, Wildcat."

Hurt clawed at me. "Let. Me. Down!" I shrieked. I began to beat the bastard's back with my wedding bouquet. "How fucking dare you?"

I watched as petals from my bouquet floated to the floor as he carried me back down the aisle, leaving a trail of delicate white in our wake.

"I hate you." My throat was thick with humiliation.

He responded with a stinging slap to my ass and a growl. "Well, I fuckin' love you, Cara. Always will."

Chapter Forty-One

Layla

Robbie's voice was low as he spoke down the phone in a hushed tone.

God knows why he was quiet. He was in the same room as me. I could hear every word.

The drugs were beginning to wear off. I was still dopey but not as bad as before. The only problem was, with lucidity came waves of heart-stopping pain.

Robbie's voice floated over. "I wanna kill her. It's too dangerous to wait for your men to collect her."

A pause. "How much will you get for her?"

Another pause, then a quiet laugh. "Okay, I'll let you sell her, but I want someone from your catalog instead. I need a fix."

Catalog? What was he talking about? Sell her? Did he mean me? Dread clutched at my stomach, making me nauseous.

Sell me to who?

No, no, no.

I needed to get out of here, now. My eyes darted around the room, looking for something, a weapon, a way out, but my heart began to race again as footsteps tapped against the concrete floor. I squeezed my eyes closed.

A shoe scuffled across the ground. "Don't bother pretending. I can hear the change in your breathing."

Robbie's voice carried that creepy high-pitched whine again.

I felt him close, and suddenly, my scalp began to burn. He pulled me up to a sitting position by the hair, dragging me across the floor. My already sore back scraped across the hard ground, and I yelped.

"Sit and stay," he bellowed. "You never do as you're told. Even when we fucked, you were trying to get away. Why can't you ever just sit still?"

His bellowing voice rang in my ears, inspiring more terror.

I scrambled on my ass, back to the wall. "W-why are you d-doing this?" I asked shakily.

Robbie began to pace. "Why couldn't you just leave it alone?" he whined, hands pulling at his hair. "Cara won't marry me when she finds out about your brat."

I looked at him in disbelief. "Oh my God, Robbie. How about the fact that you raped me? Raped others? How about the fact that you kidnapped me, brought me here, and beat me? Sunny's the least of your problems."

The tap of shoes pacing sounded across the room, then back again. Robbie was so caught up in his head that he didn't even hear me.

"All that work," he spat. "All that time it took me to get her away from that biker cunt. It's all been for nothing." He stopped suddenly and lifted his stare to me. "You!"

My eyes widened as he stomped toward me. I scrambled backward until my spine hit the wall. Pure fear made a gargled noise escape from deep inside my throat.

One hand grabbed my hair, scalp burning as Robbie forced me to look up at him, towering over me.

Slowly, he pulled his arm, clenching his hand into a fist.

My head rattled back as it smashed against my temple. White lights danced behind my eyes, and my back crashed onto the floor again.

"Cunt," he snarled. The voice of a devil.

I let out a moan as the force of his punch began to radiate through my head in waves, pain ebbing and flowing through my skull.

Love you, Doe. Bowie? His voice seemed so far away. I opened my eyes to see him standing before me, his beautiful golden eyes shining.

"You're here," I mumbled joyfully.

I reached out to touch him and sobbed as he faded away before my eyes.

"Love you, Bowie," I whispered before everything went dark again.

Chapter Forty-Two

John

Two P.M. and nothin'.

Bowie was goin' outta his mind, snarlin' at everyone who came close, jumpin' every time the phone rang.

My boy was distraught.

Cara didn't know anything, though I think she was in shock. Henderson Senior wouldn't even talk to us. Brett Stafford was missin'.

We were truly fucked, up the ass, with a cactus.

The thing was, I knew someone who may be able to help us. I hadn't seen her in a while. I stayed out of town these days just to avoid her.

Resignation washed over me. I didn't have any other choice.

I stabbed at my phone and scrolled down to the very bottom, to the number represented by one letter. 'Z'

My heart leaped three feet high as I stabbed the call button, put the cell to my ear, and waited.

"John," she breathed. "I was just about to call you but was stuck at the wedding venue. If I had left, it would've looked suspicious."

"Is *he* there?"

"No. He drove away just as you called."

"Can we meet?"

"Yes. Our place. Twenty minutes."

I let out a grunt of agreement. "Be careful.

The sounds from the creek were familiar, but at the same time, not. It'd been a while since I'd come down here. The memories were too painful.

I stood still, lookin' at the clear water swirlin' over the stones, and my mind flew back in time.

We used to be down here all summer, me and her. This place was where I noticed that she grew up and was beautiful, and mine.

Me and the other club brats used to hang here, causing trouble, just bein' kids. She and her friends used to sunbathe on the shore, dangling their legs in the water when it got too hot.

It's where I took her virginity, where we fell in love.

"John?"

Her voice still affected me, even after all these years. I spun around, and my heart clenched at the sight of her. She still looked like she did back then. Just a bit older and even more beautiful.

My pulse thudded. The adrenaline that'd gripped me all day made my heart thump hard again. "I need your help," I rasped.

Her face twisted. "I knew *he* was a monster. I've always known, but I didn't know about this, John. I swear."

"You think I blame you for what he did, Leesy?" I asked as I took a step toward her. "I'm desperate. We need to find Layla. Can you help?"

One delicate shoulder lifted. "The only place I can think Robbie could take Layla is a new building development they've just invested in. It's about thirty minutes from here. There are still some old houses they haven't got around to leveling yet."

She pulled her phone out, and her fingers began to tap. The ping of my phone in my pocket made me jump.

"Directions." She stared up at me with yearnin'. My heart tugged at her bright blue eyes.

"I hope you find her, John."

I jerked a nod, meaning to walk away, but somethin' made me stop. "Are you okay, Leesy?" I asked quietly. "D'ya need my help?"

Her brow crinkled as she shook her head. "I'll take him down. I'll make him pay for everything."

Worry nagged at me. "Be careful."

She nodded and smiled sadly. "You too, John."

I watched her turn, my eyes following her as she walked to her car and drove away. Takin' my soul with her.

Chapter Forty-Three

Bowie

"Let's fuckin' move," I demanded, looking across the massive field at Robbie's black Porsche. "We haven't got time for this."

My guts were swirling all over the place. I was chompin' at the bit to get to Doe.

Dad clasped me on the shoulder. "Stick to the plan, Son. If you go in half-cocked, it's Layla that'll suffer the consequences."

My blood cooled. "Okay. Got it." I nodded. "Let's just get movin'."

Earlier, when Dad got back to the clubhouse with the anonymous tip, we jumped straight on our bikes and headed out.

Mapletree was an area west of Hambleton. It had been earmarked for development by some big corporations.

It was about a thirty-minute ride. We made the journey in eighteen.

When we got closer to our destination, we switched off our bikes and walked them to the edge of a cluster of trees bordering a few small cottages.

That's when I spied Robbie's car.

For the first time in hours, hope had sparked in my chest. While Dad, Atlas, Drix, and Ice were making plans. All I could do was stare at that buildin'."

"Just get your woman, Bo," Dad ordered. "We'll do the rest." His hand slipped into his pocket, and he pulled his phone out.

He tapped on it, then put it to his ear. "Freya. Gonna send you some directions. Get here, stat, and bring your medical bag with you."

My Dad was a tactician. When he left the military, every government agency in the Western World tried to recruit him. He was that good.

I trusted him more than anyone. He had knowledge, experience, and a determined streak, making him stand out as one of the best.

If anyone was gonna get Layla back, it was him.

"I want him dead," I gritted out.

Dad and Atlas looked at each other, then back at me, and nodded.

"He won't survive this, Bowie," Atlas rumbled. "It's gone too far, but we need to be careful. Just follow my lead. Got it?"

"It looks clear. Can't see him at the front of the house. All the windows are missin', so at least we don't have to break the glass." Drix's voice was emotionless as he looked through the binoculars.

Our VP was another military man, the best scout out there, and a scary accurate shot.

My gut jerked in fear for Layla. "Can we go now?" I demanded.

Dad nodded, then turned and slowly began to stalk toward the house. Drix fell into line behind him, then Ice, then Atlas. My jaw tightened with stone-cold focus, and I began to follow.

All the buildings were abandoned. There were only three, but we knew which house he'd holed up in because Henderson was a stupid prick and parked his car outside.

Bowie

I rubbed my clammy palms down the side of my jeans. Adrenaline began to pump through my blood, giving my fingers a slight tremor.

As we got closer, I reached shakily into my pocket for my Glock, then slowly pulled it from my cut.

All I could hear was the rushin' of blood in my ears. My heart was thumping so hard that I worried it'd give us away.

The closer we got, the lower Dad bent forward at the waist. We all followed suit, then ran behind him as he sprinted for the buildin'.

By the time I arrived, Dad had his back tight against the wall.

We all lined up beside him. He over at us and brought a finger to his lips, demanding silence.

He ducked down and crawled under a window. Slowly, he raised up, took a peek inside then quickly lowered again.

My heart was in my throat as he gave us the thumbs up. Suddenly, catlike, he leaped up, grabbed the empty windowpane, and jumped through.

Drix craned his neck at us, grinned, and followed him.

Ice did the same.

Atlas looked at me and gestured to the window. "You're quicker than me. Go."

I skated past him and then rested my hand on the wooden ledge. I pulled myself up and through the opening in the wall, then jumped down to the other side, my Glock in the other hand.

The room was dim, with no light outlets or a switch, just sunlight streaming through the window. I heard a grunt and a thud behind me as Atlas jumped down into the room.

Dad was already at the door, the other men creepin' silently behind him. I joined the end of the line and watched Dad poke his head around the open doorway.

He looked back at us, gave us the thumbs-up sign, then moved.

The passageway was dark and narrow. It led toward another open doorway at the back of the house. One by one, we entered a kitchen that contained a big old cast iron sink attached to a wall and an old wooden, built-in pantry.

The hole where the back door was meant to be, was bricked up. My eyes took in the walls that looked like they were about to cave in on us, and I shuddered. This place was a dump.

A whisper floated on the breeze, a sound coming from somewhere in the distance. Was that a groan?

Adrenaline pumped through me. I immediately turned to Dad. His eyes had shot down to the floor. He slowly moved his foot toward the edge of the old rug he was standin' on and gently toed it to one side. I realized that he was looking for some kind of hatch that led down.

Nothing.

He looked up again, and his eyes flew to the pantry door.

Pop gestured to it with his head. "The Underground Railroad used to build stairs leading to secret basements where slaves could hide out. They made 'em look like cupboards or pantries," he whispered.

He moved silently across the room and cracked open the pantry door.

"Dunno why he bothered tryin'a hide," Atlas muttered. "His car's outside, clear as day."

Ice put his index fingers to his temple, then circled it. "He's a crazy fuck, Atlas," he said quietly. "He's losin' his goddamned mind."

Dad opened the door wider, poked his head through, then pulled back and closed it again.

He beckoned us over and pointed. "Wooden stairs. He's gonna hear us coming. Nothin' else for it. We need to be fast and hope we catch him off guard."

He looked at us all in turn, eyes steely. "Are you ready?"

He waited for our nods, then turned back and flung open the door. He let out a loud bellow, then began to race down the rickety steps.

We all followed, sprintin' through the door, then down the dark narrow wooden stairs. Our boots clattered on the wood, causing a hell of a din.

My breath sawed in and out, heart poundin'. All I could think was to get my girl out, then end this shit.

As I neared the bottom, I could see into a dark room. An old oil lamp hung on one wall, casting a dim glow.

My heart lurched when I saw a small body stretched out on the floor in a heap. It stuttered when I saw long, chestnut hair flowing across the grey concrete.

It was Layla.

Shouts came from one end of the room, but I was so hellbent on gettin' to my girl that I blocked it out and didn't even look.

The bellows from the men got louder. I fell on my knees behind her; deep-rooted fear shivered through me when I saw her eyes were closed.

I leaned down to her ear. "Doe?"

Nothing.

My throat got tight. My hand went to Layla's shoulder and shook it gently.

She was still.

My chest felt like it was cavin' in. I couldn't breathe through the hard rock that blocked my throat. In my head, I began to pray.

Jesus Christ, please. Let her wake up.

My hand pulled at her shoulder, and I gently got her onto her back.

My chest burned. Layla's face was a mess. Blood streamed from a cut on her temple, and she was covered in bruises. I gently pulled her tee up to see her abdomen was purple and blue.

Horror washed through me. I shook Doe again, panic rising through my chest. "Layla," I shouted. "Wake up, baby."

Her eyelashes flickered. "Go away," she murmured. "You're just a dream."

Relief flooded my veins. Some of the dread began to free up my chest, allowing me to suck in a breath.

"Come on, baby," I pleaded. "Open your eyes. It's me."

One hand snaked under her back, the other behind her knees. "Gonna get you outta here, Doe." I pulled her into my arms and slowly stood, careful not to jolt my girl.

She released a low wail into the room. "It hurts, Bowie," she cried, then she began to moan softly.

"I'm sorry, baby. I'm so sorry." My gut clenched, thinking that I could be hurting her more.

Loud scuffling sounds came from the far wall.

Thwack, thwack. Flesh hitting flesh.

"Get her upstairs," Dad bellowed.

My eyes narrowed at the sight of Atlas holdin' Robbie up from behind. Dad's big meaty hands were punchin' Henderson's gut so hard that his entire body jerked in shock with every hard *thwack* that connected.

I headed for the steps leading up to the kitchen, taking care to twist my body so I didn't bang Layla's head on the walls. I ran up the narrow staircase and back out into the main house.

Worry swirled in my gut. Layla was cryin' in pain. I needed to get her outta here, away from that sick fuck.

At least she was awake. Henderson didn't kill her, and that was all that mattered to me. As long as she was alive, everything else could be fixed.

I staggered back through the hallway toward the old front door. I had to get Layla away from this house of horrors. As I approached the rotting wood, I raised my leg with the sole of my boot facin' out and kicked hard. Then again.

Bowie

The door fell through with a big crash.

I moved outside and over to the soft grass. A curse escaped me when Layla moaned in pain as I gently laid her down. "Freya's on her way, Doe," I crooned softly. "Hold on."

"Bowie," Layla whispered.

My heart twisted with relief as her eyelashes fluttered open, and she asked. "Where's Sunny?"

A thick laugh escaped me. If she was askin' about our girl, then at least her brain was still intact. "She's with Iris, Doe. Right where you left her this mornin'. Abe's got eyes on her. She's safe."

Her shoulder's slumped with relief. "It was him, Bowie. It was Robbie." Layla's eyes drooped and closed. Her head lolled to one side, making my heart plummet.

My hands went to her hair and swept it gently away from her face. "Keep your eyes open. Please, baby," I begged.

My hand shot to her neck, feelin' for a pulse, for any sign of life. My throat tightened with fear, then loosened when I felt a tiny beat against my fingertips.

"Jesus," I muttered as I fell onto my ass, relief pouring outta me. "Thank fuck."

My ears pricked up at the sound of a car approachin'. My eyes flew up to see Freya speeding down the gravel path toward us.

I leaped up, waving my hands, guiding my sister toward us. "Freya," I yelled. She tooted her horn and bombed straight for me.

I had my head in my hands, tuggin' on my hair. All sense flew outta my head; I couldn't think straight.

The car ground to a halt.

Freya flung open the door and flew out, medical bag in hand. Her face went white when she saw my girl lying on the grass, and she ran toward her. "What happened?" she demanded.

I felt like I was gonna puke. "Henderson beat her," I snapped. My tone softened as I pleaded to my sister. "Help her. Please, Frey."

Freya got closer, falling on her knees next to Layla, feeling her pulse, and looked up at me. "Jesus, Bowie. He's beaten her to a pulp." She pushed Layla's shirt up, shakin' her head. "I gotta get her to hospital. This is too big for me. She needs X-rays."

"Freya?" Layla's voice was small and frightened.

She was awake again. Thank fuck.

I dropped back to my knees, gripping her hand. "You're gonna be okay, Doe. Freya's here."

My other hand went up and clasped the back of my neck. Unease began to creep through me.

My head flew up as voices rose through the air.

Dad barreled through the front door, dragging Robbie across the floor by his wrists. A painful scrape sounded as Henderson's back slid across the gravel.

I got to my feet slowly, rising up, furious, vengeful.

Pure hatred for the sick excuse for a man on the ground raged through my bloodstream. As I stared down at him, my mind began to clear into a single-minded focus.

Let justice prevail.

I cracked my neck from side to side, the way I always did before a fight, but then my mind flew back to Layla as she let out another low moan.

"We need to get her to the hospital, Frey," I said urgently.

"Bowie?" Layla called, her usual sweet voice thick with distress. "Can you help me get up? Please, Bowie."

My head slowly swiveled back to Layla. My heart gave a shocked jolt at the sight of her sitting up. I'd been so fixated on Henderson that I hadn't noticed.

"Take it easy, Doe. Go slow," I warned, steppin' toward her.

Bowie

Freya smiled. "It's a good sign, Bowie. If she can move and walk, her back's not broken."

"I think it's just bruised," Layla mumbled. She slowly held her arms up to me. "Help me. Please."

My knees bent so I could lean down to support her back. I gently pulled her to her feet. She was so light in my arms, so small and delicate. I was sick to my stomach that Henderson did this to her. Fuckin' coward.

"Help me to the car, Bowie," my girl demanded softly. She took my hand in hers, then looked up at me. A huge lump formed in my throat when I saw all the marks on her face.

"Come on," Freya called, already at the car.

I stroked Layla's cheek and shuffled her toward the vehicle. "Let's go, baby."

Grey doe eyes drooped to half-mast before widening again. "Bowie. What are you gonna do to him?" she asked, her sweet voice a whisper.

My jaw clenched again. "You don't wanna know."

Her perfect bruised jaw went tight. "Make sure it hurts."

A surprised laugh flew up and out my throat. My kind girl contained a little streak of bloodthirsty.

"Stay. Deal with *him*. Then come," Layla said gently.

"Doe, you couldn't keep your eyes open ten minutes ago. I ain't leaving ya."

Her hand tightened on my arm. "It was the drugs. They're wearing off now. Please deal with Robbie. I can't rest easy until you do."

I was torn. Layla needed me, but I got where she was comin' from. She couldn't relax until he was wiped off the earth. It was the only way she could get any peace of mind.

We got to the car, and I pulled open the door. "I'll follow soon," I promised, helping her into the car. My hands pulled at her gently, arranging her beautiful body on the passenger seat.

I clicked on her seatbelt then my eyes lifted to Freya. "Look after her, Sis."

Freya nodded. "Always."

"Don't be long," Layla said, leaning on the rest.

I pecked a light kiss on her mouth, then stood to my full height and slammed the car door shut with an ominous thud.

The engine started. My eyes followed them down the road as Freya slowly drove away.

Conviction flowed from my head to my toes. My body turned slowly toward Dad. My eyes lowered to the ground, relishin' the sight of Robert Henderson, Junior, sprawled out, hurt and bleeding.

Dad's big boot was pressed down on the fucker's windpipe. My lip's quirked. Good enough for the scumbag.

My boots thumped toward him, feet movin' of their own accord. I was so caught up in my head that I didn't realize I was moving until I stood over him and looked down at his evil, sick face.

Dad, Atlas, Hendrix, and Ice looked like gods of vengeance. Straight backs. Stern, blank faces. Arms folded across their chests.

Judge and fuckin' jury.

Anger pulsed through me. I reached down with both hands and grabbed Henderson's collar, haulin' him to his feet.

A high-pitched whine pierced the air as I grabbed him by the throat. I ignored it, pulled his face close, and stared straight into his eyes.

"You're a fuckin' dead man," I spat, squeezin' his windpipe. "You had it all. A charmed life. Money. Everything you could'a wanted, and now you're gonna be nothing."

Anger boiled my insides.

My head pulled back and cracked forward again, smashing hard into his face. Blood exploded from

Henderson's nose. He stumbled back, then fell onto his ass.

His pained howl curled through my ears.

He yelped as the first boot connected with his kidneys. Atlas. The next one to the back of his skull, Dad.

Hendrix stalked forward. He drew level, pulled his boot back, then smashed it into Henderson's sick, perverted dick. I swear I heard his nuts crack.

Henderson rolled around on the floor, groaning with agony. His eyes were round with shock.

I made my way to him and hauled him up again.

"Kill me." He gasped. "And you'll go to jail. My dad will make sure you disappear. You'll never be found."

Pop laughed. "Big words, Henderson. But your dad can't help you slither back under your rock this time. We've got DNA evidence. Layla'll testify that you took her, then beat her. Even if they can't prove you raped those girls, they'll still get ya' for kidnap and battery. Everyone'll know how sick you are—even Daddy."

The other men muttered their agreement.

My hand loosened its grip from around his throat. "You got me all wrong, Henderson. I ain't gonna kill ya."

His eyes flashed with victory, but it slowly morphed into fear as I continued. "You're gonna kill yourself," I told him, my voice a promise of death.

Robbie gulped. "No. I'm not."

"Poor little Robbie knew he'd been caught. Couldn't deal with goin' to jail. He had no choice. He had to turn the gun on himself." Humor laced Atlas's voice.

"Put these on," Ice said from behind me, then held up a pair of leather gloves.

Dad stepped forward and slowly extended his arm. "Look what I found down in his sick little den." Silver metal glinted in the sun, a gun wrapped in cloth.

"I'll bet that it's the same piece that did you, Bowie." Atlas' deep laughter rose through the air. "Was it

Robbie? Blink once for yes, twice for no. I love me some fuckin' karma."

Chuckles filled the warm air.

Henderson looked around wildly. His eyes were panicked at first, but then viciousness glinted behind them. He was a sight, with blood drippin' down his face, down over his teeth. I could see the insanity that leaked out of him. Pure Evil. A monster's true nature slithering out.

Loony fuckin' tunes.

Slowly, Atlas stepped toward Robbie's back and gripped his arms tightly, holding him in place from behind. "It's time," he said with a shrug. "Got things to do. People to see."

More chortles flittered through the ether.

The satisfaction swirling through my insides made me smirk. I pushed the gun into Robbie's hand, then curled my gloved fingers over his.

He let out a pained grunt as Atlas forced his arm up, takin' the gun higher, toward his head.

"Time to pay the piper, Robbie," I sang.

The sun's rays glinted off metal as the gun jabbed into Robbie's temple.

"Angle it out slightly, Bo. Let's make sure the fucker shoots his own face off."

"No. No. No," Henderson shrieked, slumping back into Atlas, resignation spreading over his features. "Please don't," he pleaded.

Atlas let out a chuckle. "That's it, Henderson. Beg nice 'n' loud. Just like that young girl begged you to stop." His eyes glinted with anger. "You're a waste of fuckin' oxygen."

Retribution coursed through me. This sick fuck had drugged and assaulted endless women and an underage girl. He'd gone after Layla, then targeted her, treated her like she somethin' to play with. His toy.

Never again.

"I won't do it," he screamed.

"Oh, you will," I snarled. "And I'm gonna help." My finger slipped over his, forcing it down and squeezing the trigger.

My eyes stared into his. I slowly pressed his finger down, harder and harder. "The Demons'll see you in hell, asshole."

"Please. No," Henderson begged. "I'll never do it again."

"I know you fuckin' won't," I replied. Content in the knowledge that my face was the last thing he'd ever see.

"Nooo," he wailed. I'm sorr—"

Bang.

Chapter Forty-Four

Layla

Freya called Sophie Green on the way to the hospital.

She was waiting outside with a gurney when we pulled up, ready to rush me into X-ray.

After she took countless pictures and examined me, Sophie determined there were no breaks in my back. Though, I did have two cracked ribs.

As the day went on, the pain subsided into a dull ache. Freya said it was because the bruises were beginning to form. Though I was sure the painkillers helped too.

The worst part was when they scraped my nails and wounds for DNA.

It was six years too late, and that was on me.

The minute I caught my reflection, I burst into tears. I begged Freya to make Iris keep Sunny for a couple more days. My girl's heart would hurt if she saw me like this.

My face was swollen. I had a massive cut on my head where he'd punched me so hard that he's broken my skin, a black eye, and a badly bruised cheek.

I couldn't even begin to process my emotions.

Sophie said I was still in shock, and to make the most of it, because as soon as it wore off, I'd be a babbling mess. She called it like it was, which made me laugh. In a way, I kind of appreciated it.

They took me up to a room. Doctor Sophie wanted to keep me overnight for observation because I had a concussion. That wouldn't usually be a problem, but because I'd been drugged again, there was more of a risk.

She'd gone to see if my blood test results were ready. I'd also asked her to check for signs of a baby, though, at that point, I dreaded it. A pregnancy would be tainted by what happened with Robbie, with what he did to me.

I was lying back in bed, trying not to cry, when I heard a soft tap on the door. I looked up as it slowly swung open. "Cara," I breathed.

She closed the door behind her and looked at me on the bed. Her eyes caught on my face, and she winced. "This is all my fault," she whispered. "I should have seen it. I should have known."

"Nobody knew. It's not your fault-"

"-He's Sunny's father," she croaked.

"No," I said firmly. "He's nothing. She's mine, not his."

Cara walked toward me. Pain flashed in her eyes as they swept over my face. "What did he do to you?"

"I'm okay," I reassured her, trying to swallow past the burn in my throat. "It's done, Cara. We just need to stick together, like we always do. Like we always have."

Her eyes welled up. "I can't."

I looked on in shock as a tear streaked down her face. The only time I'd ever seen Cara upset like that was over Xander. I was the crier, not her.

Then her words hit me. "What do you mean you can't?" My chest tightened; did she blame me?

"I need to get away, clear my head." Another tear. "I feel so guilty, Layla."

"Why? He did it, not you."

"I slept with him. I had sex with a man that raped countless women, including a teenage girl and my best friend. I need to get my head straight."

Bowie

"Where will you go? When will you be back?"

"I'm going back to Kansas, just for a while. I'll keep in touch. So much has happened, Layla, ever since Xan-" She dug the heels of her palms in her eyes. "I can't deal with it anymore. I need help and can't get it while he's around."

"I love you, Caca." I used Sunny's baby name for my friend when my girl couldn't pronounce her Rs.

We had so many good memories. Cara was the only person who'd been with me through everything. A small sob stuttered from my throat.

Cara gave me a sad smile. "Love you too, Layla. I promise I'll call when I'm settled." She squeezed my hand, then she turned slowly and left.

My eyes burned with tears. Cara hadn't been herself for years. On the outside, she was the same bubbly, fiery woman. But underneath, she was lost. I understood, but I would still miss my friend so much.

I was still crying thirty minutes later when I told Bowie.

He held my hand and stroked his thumb over mine. "Xan's gonna tear Kansas apart lookin' for her," he said quietly.

"No, Bowie. He needs to leave her alone. She needs time, and he has to give it to her. He's part of the problem. Ever since his betrayal, she's been looking for affirmation in the wrong places. I think Robbie played on that."

Bowie frowned, then gestured toward me. "Move up."

I shuffled across the bed to give him room. As he climbed next to me, the scent of his soap wafted up.

I inhaled his scent. "Did you shower?"

His arm snaked around my back, pulling me into his chest. "Had to, Doe. I was covered in Asshole's blood."

Disbelief flashed through me. The rumors about Robbie were already all over town. I'd heard two nurses discussing it, then Bowie confirmed everything when he came to my room.

"I can't believe he killed himself," I said, my voice shocked.

Bowie froze for a second, his body stiffening. "Yeah. He had a gun on him. I went to stop him, even got my hand to his, but I was too late. He did it before I could stop him." His voice was tight.

Strong fingers stroked my back. "Cops were called. There'll be an investigation, but the guy Dad knows said that the blood splatter pattern and gun residue on his hands indicated that he did it. They'll rule it as suicide." He rested his chin on my head. "It's over, Baby. After you have a powwow with the cops, we can all move on. Up to you if you wanna tell 'em 'bout Sunny. The fact he nabbed you earlier today is evidence enough. They'll know when they compare the DNA they scraped off you to his."

"Yeah," I murmured.

My thoughts raced. If I told the police about what happened at Brett's party, I risked everything coming out. Everybody would eventually find out about Sunny. I wondered if knowing who her father was and what he did would affect her as she got older.

My job as a mother was to protect her. I wouldn't risk it.

"I've asked Sophie to recommend a good counselor for you." Bowie's tone held a thread of wariness.

"Okay."

He tipped my chin up to face him. "What do ya mean, okay? I thought you'd lose your shit, Doe."

I rested my face back onto his chest. "No, Bowie. I want to move on and learn to deal with everything. I need to do this." A shudder ran down my spine. "I can't believe how he set me up like that."

"Yeah," he agreed. "Fender worked on *Bloom's* truck at the auto shop. Someone definitely tampered with it. And those two kids swore they saw Henderson break that window at the school. He knew it would take Seth outta the equation, leaving you to collect the flowers."

A memory from earlier pinged.

"Bowie," I said apprehensively. "I heard him talking. I think he was involved in some kind of human slavery. He was going to sell me."

Bowie's whole body went taught. He tipped my chin up again. "What?"

"Robbie said he'd get a good price for me, though it's all pretty sketchy because of the drugs in my system." A shudder ran through me. "I feel like I'm trying to recall a horrible nightmare. I know what happened. I just can't quite grasp the details."

Bowie shuffled further down the bed until we were face to face. His eyes swirled liquid gold as he grasped my hand in his.

His other hand cupped my cheek. "Listen, baby. Nobody's gonna hurt ya. I'll protect you and Sunny until the day I die. Don't worry. I'll sort it out. Got me?"

My shoulders relaxed. The feeling of safety that Robbie had stolen away began to penetrate my insides again, washing away the fear and anxiety.

I didn't know what the future was going to bring. Nobody did, but whatever happened, I knew I'd have Bowie by my side.

My lips tipped up. "Yeah, Bowie. I got you."

I brought his fingers up to my lips and kissed them.

Love you, Bowie," I whispered.

His eyes danced. "Love you, Doe."

Liquid gold swirled with adoration as he took me in. He grinned that sexy grin that took my breath away, even as a girl.

"Remember, Layla," he said as he gently kissed my forehead. "Me and you against the world. Forever."

Epilogue

Bowie

It was January, and snow blanketed the ground. It was one of the worst winters on record, but I didn't notice. All I could see, and feel, was my Doe.

We'd just gotten wed.

We fucked off down to the Town Hall and just did it.

Xander stood at my side. Dad and Kit at my back.

Abe gave Layla away while Iris blew her nose. Sunny was a bridesmaid, as was Freya. Cara came home after six long months away in Kansas to be Maid of Honor.

She said she was back to stay.

I guess we'd see.

My Doe didn't want a fuss. She was shy. The thought of all eyes on her as she stood at an altar gave her a panic attack. So, we just did it quietly.

But we still had to have a reception, right?

The second we walked back into the clubhouse, the party began. There was booze, food, cake, and music.

Kids were runnin' around, screechin', being pains in our asses. Abe was bein' that embarrassing uncle trying to dance all funky and failin'. Then a fight nearly broke out over a woman.

All in all, it was perfect.

I pulled back slightly and gazed down into my wife's beautiful face. "Told ya I'd give you a wedding dance."

She rolled her eyes. "Only took you six months."

My sweet Doe was beginnin' to get a bit more confident, and shock horror, I found I liked a little bit of sass after all.

I traced my hands down her body, then gently over the swell of her stomach. "Sorry, babe, was busy knockin' you up."

Layla hadn't been pregnant when Henderson took her, which in hindsight, was a blessin'.

However, as soon as she'd healed properly, I started trying again, and my bionic jizz hit the jackpot on the first try.

Grey, doe eyes met mine, dark with desire. Layla was a horny pregnant woman. She couldn't get enough, not that I minded.

No siree.

I grinned down at her. "Your doe eyes are beggin' for me to fuck you, Layla."

"At last." She sighed. "Where are we going to do it this time?"

I thought a minute, then a lightbulb went off in my noggin. "Come on." I tugged her off the makeshift dance floor and toward a door. As we stepped up, it opened, and Freya came through.

"Where are you two going?" she asked.

Layla looked down at her toes at the same time as I smirked.

My sister's eyes narrowed. "You two don't stop. Don't you get tired?"

Layla's shoulders began to shake. My lips twitched.

"Guess I'll keep an eye on Sunny. It is your wedding da—" she began, then her voice trailed off as her eyes fixated on somethin' over my shoulder.

I craned my neck. "What's up?" I demanded, scannin' the room.

It was just the usual suspects, plus a few new ones. Layla had invited Magnolia, Lucy, Emmie, and Mrs. Fenton. Anna and Tris, of course.

Lucy was smilin' up at Colt. He was runnin' his hands down her back, flirtin' up a storm.

My stare swiveled back to Freya. Her eyes flashed with hurt. "Go, enjoy yourselves," she mumbled quietly, then walked away.

My fist clenched when I saw the shine in her eyes. Confusion made my brow furrow.

I glanced at my wife. "What the fuck was that about?"

She winced. "Well, it seems Freya likes Colt, and Colt's either being a dick or he's not interested."

My gut froze with trepidation. "That can't ever happen, babe. She's off-limits. No brother can touch her. Dad doesn't want her involved with the club in any form. It's why he's payin' her way through med school. He'd blow a fuckin' gasket if Colt went there."

Layla shrugged. "You can't help who you love, Bowie."

My heart flipped. "Guess not, Doe," I tightened my hold on her hand, "but if Colt decides he loves Freya, I guarantee Dad'll slit his throat."

Layla shook her head and laughed. "You're so dramatic sometimes."

My hands pushed against the door, and it swung open. My fingers entwined with my wife's, and I tugged her toward the rooms. "Baby. Dad shows you his nice side, but believe me. He can be fuckin' ruthless."

Layla pulled me to a stop and tugged her hand from mine, punchin' her fists to her hips. "Wait, one minute. Are you taking me to the rooms?" Her voice tightened. "I don't want to catch an STD. I'm carrying precious cargo."

"C'mon, Doe," I crooned. "Live a little. We'll go muss up Xan's sheets. He's anal as fuck, changes 'em every day."

I grabbed her hand again and started to walk again. She began to giggle, then pulled me to a stop for the second time. "Wait!"

My eyes swung upward as I muttered a curse. "Thought you wanted to fuck, Doe? I'll need to pop a blue pill by the time I get your inside your pussy 'cause by then I'll be goddamned ninety."

Her eyes went big. "I do, but tell me something. You said Xander hasn't had sex with anyone since he came home from prison?"

"Right?"

Her brow furrowed. "So why does he change his sheets every day?"

"Jesus, fuck, Doe. He's just a clean freak. Now, come on." My hand tightened around my wife's, and I dragged her down the corridor toward Xan's room. As we got closer, a faint moan sounded.

My feet slowed, eyes dartin' to Layla. I put my finger to my lips, a sign for her to be quiet, and I listened.

Noises were definitely coming from Xander's room. My feet took a step closer, curiosity tuggin' inside my chest.

Layla's eyes went huge. Her mouth fell open as another low moan floated through the corridor.

"Perfect," I griped frustratedly. "There goes my tumble."

Her cheeks went bright red. "Oh, my God. Is he having sex?" Her eyes turned to slits. "His little hiatus didn't last very long. So much for saving himself for Cara."

I shushed her, tryin' to listen. My gut roiled as her words pinged through my noggin. Xander wouldn't…. would he?

April had been tryin' to get with him since he got outta prison.

He told her no, constantly. He wasn't interested in the slightest. She didn't have a chance in hell, seein' as she was the woman who came between him and Cara in the first place.

My heart sank. What if he'd finally given in? He hadn't fucked anyone for at least three years. His dick must've been close to exploding.

I shuddered at the thought. My previous eight-month celibacy gig was bad—e'fuckin'—nough.

Grunts and moans floated from the room.

Yeah, take it good. This is my pussy. Fuck yeah.

Then a woman's voice.

I fuckin' hate you. Cash.

A growl. *You call me Xander.*

Less talking, more fucking... Cash.

Layla tagged on my sleeve, looking at me with shocked eyes. "Oh, my God."

I shushed her again just as Xander spoke.

Gonna stretch you out good, baby. Did Needle Dick not fuck you right? You need my big, fat cock, doncha, Wildcat?

Another high-pitched moan.

Shut the hell up, and fuck me.

Layla dragged on my sleeve again. I glanced down to see that her eyes were bugging outta her skull. "Oh, my God. That's Cara." Her shock was almost visceral.

My thumb went to my lip in thought. "Well, fuck me," I murmured under my breath. "How the hell did he bring her around? Cocky bastard."

Layla slapped my chest. "I thought Cara hated him?" she whisper-shouted.

I rubbed at the spot where she hit. "Don't sound like that to me, babe. But then they always were kinky fuckers. They loved all the hate sex. I'm sure it's why they argued so fuckin' much."

Layla's face dropped. "She only got back today, and she's given into him already." She began to wring her hands. "Bowie. This is going to end in tears."

A wave of laughter ebbed up my throat. I grabbed my wife's fingers and tugged her into me, gently stroking my finger down her cheek.

My heart flipped as I gazed into grey doe eyes, full of all the love in the world. "C'mon." I laughed. My feet retraced our steps, and we began to head back the way we came.

Looking down at my woman's face again, I grinned. "Better saddle up, baby," I said, smiling at my wife. "'Cause we're gonna be in for one hell of a ride."

THE END

Cash and Cara's story is coming in late 2022

**Thank you for reading
I would be grateful if you could take the time to leave a review on Amazon.
Many Thanks**

Stalk Jules

Jules loves chatting with readers
Email her
julesfordauthor@gmail.com

Join her Facebook Group
Jules Ford's Tribe | Facebook

Instagram
Jules Ford (@julesfordauthor) • Instagram photos and videos